"Why do you always go out of your way to point out how different we are?" Lily asked.

Ash was looking right at her, one arm dangling over his bent knee. His eyes were clear, sober. Suddenly he didn't look drunk at all. Maybe he never had been. "I just don't want you to forget, that's all," he said. "It's easy to get mixed up when you're in the jungle. I don't want you to forget that you're who you are, and I'm who I am."

"And you think you might corrupt me?"

"That's what's driving me crazy, Lily." His mouth twisted into a lazy, seductive smile. "I'd *love* to corrupt you."

AMAZON LILY

amazon
lily

———

THERESA WEIR

BANTAM BOOKS
New York   London   Toronto   Sydney   Auckland

This edition contains the complete text
of the original hardcover edition.
NOT ONE WORD HAS BEEN OMITTED.

AMAZON LILY

A Bantam Fanfare Book / published by arrangement with the author

PUBLISHING HISTORY
Doubleday Loveswept edition / January 1994
Bantam edition / July 1994

Special thanks to David Laflamme and Davlin Music for permission to reprint
lyrics from the song "Hot Summer Day" from the album *It's A Beautiful Day*,
copyright © 1968 by Davlin Music Publishing Co. / ASCAP

ISBN 0-553-56463-3

Published simultaneously in the United States and Canada

Bantam Books are published by Bantam Books, a division of Bantam Doubleday
Dell Publishing Group, Inc. Its trademark, consisting of the words "Bantam
Books" and the portrayal of a rooster, is Registered in U.S. Patent and Trademark
Office and in other countries. Marca Registrada. Bantam Books, 1540 Broadway,
New York, New York 10036.

PRINTED IN THE UNITED STATES OF AMERICA

RAD   0 9 8 7 6 5 4 3 2

This book is dedicated to all of the people who crusaded on behalf of Amazon Lily—people I've met and now call friends, people I have yet to meet, and people I will never meet. You made an amazing amount of noise, and I thank you for it. This book is as much yours as it is mine.

amazon
lily

chapter one

The bush pilot was already an hour late.

Corey McKinney numbly regarded the tattered Amazon map taped to the wall in front of her. The word UN-CHARTED was slashed across it in several places, the letters bold and taunting. She wondered if she'd lost her mind. It wasn't like her to be daring. It wasn't like her to be so far from home.

With a sigh she slouched even farther down in the green vinyl chair, her travel-weary gaze drawn once again to the yellow cellophane fly strip dangling above her. For some reason she found it fascinating. It wasn't just the fact that she hadn't seen one since she was five, not since the days when she'd hung around Red Sisna's gas station drinking strawberry cream soda with her dad. No, it had to do with the way the strip clung to the center of the unbalanced ceiling fan while the grimy blades hypnotically shifted the hot, stale air. The fly strip, loaded with what had to be at least a hundred flies, fluttered and twisted. It seemed to be making a statement of some sort.

She ran pale, slim fingers through the tangled waves of her fair shoulder-length hair, lifting it away from her damp neck. There was nothing left of the subdued style she'd tortured her hair into this morning. The humidity and heat had seen to that.

She let go of her hair and leaned her head against the sticky vinyl chairback, trying to ignore her nagging thirst. She couldn't remember when she had ever been so hot and miserable. It wouldn't have been so bad if she hadn't still been wearing the clothes in which she'd left zero-degree Chicago. But now the long-sleeved yellow blouse and white corduroys clung to her sweating skin like devices of torture.

The doubts that had been plaguing her for the last several hours grew stronger. Had she made a mistake in coming here? A month ago, in the comfort of Reverend Michael's office, a trip to Brazil sounded exciting, and she had never really done anything very exciting before.

The congregation of Corey's church was considering funding a reserve called San Reys which was located deep in the Amazon jungle. But before the funding could be approved, the church elders had insisted upon sending a representative to South America to personally meet with the reserve's owner, George Dupree, and bring back a thorough report. Corey's degree in social work, her year of practical nursing, and some fast talking was all it had taken to convince Reverend Michael that she would make an ideal emissary. But now she wondered.

Come on, Corey, she told herself. *You're just hot and tired.* What could be so hard about it? She could take notes; she could take pictures; and she could surely take the Amazon jungle for a week.

What she needed was sleep, she decided, closing her burning eyes. She would just try to sleep until the bush pilot arrived.

"You must be the Lily-Libber who's going to San Reys."

The deep voice that came slicing through Corey's sleep-fogged brain was gravelly and rough-edged.

She dragged open heavy-lidded eyes to find herself contemplating a ragged pair of grubby blue tennis shoes. She allowed her gaze to pan slowly northward, leaving freeze-framed images etched in her mind's eye: long jeans faded to almost white except along the stitching; a copper waistband button with moldy lettering; a large expanse of chest-filled, sweat-soaked T-shirt; a stubbly field of several days' growth of whiskers; dark aviator sunglasses that met the dusty, sweaty brim of a New York Yankees baseball cap.

Corey's head was bent back at an uncomfortable angle. Of course, Santarém, Brazil, wasn't Illinois, and this person certainly wasn't like any case she'd ever handled in her job as a social worker.

The squalid air-taxi building was really little more than a shed, and it had been crowded before, with just Corey and the flies. But now, with this man in front of her giving off his angry aura . . . She couldn't see his eyes, but she could read enough of his expression to know that she was being regarded as a lower form of life or something he might have scraped off the bottom of his shoe.

She knew she wasn't an American beauty. Her skin was too pale, her brown eyes too large for her small face, giving her a fragile, old-world appearance that was a burden in these modern times. People had a tendency to either overlook her completely or coddle her. But his reaction was something totally new.

The man's attention shifted from her to the smashed red packet in his hand. He pulled out a flattened nonfilter cigarette, smoothed it until it was somewhat round, then stuck it in the corner of his mouth. One hand moved across the front of the faded green T-shirt that clung damply to his corded muscles. He slapped at the breast pocket. Not finding what he was searching for, both of his hands moved to the front pockets of the ancient jeans that covered those long, athletic legs. There was a frayed white horizontal rip across his right knee, tan skin and sun-bleached hair showing through. Change jingled as he rummaged around to finally pull out a damp, wadded-up book of matches.

"Damn," he muttered after the third match failed to light. "Gotta quit sweating so much." He tossed the bedraggled matchbook to the floor. Cigarette still in his mouth, his hands began a repeat search of his pockets.

Corey reached over to where her twill shoulder bag was lying on a stack of tattered *Mad* magazines. She unzipped a side pocket and pulled out the glossy black and gold matches she'd been saving to add to her matchbook collection.

He grabbed them without so much as a thank-you. "That's right—" he said, striking a match, "you girl scouts are always prepared." He shook out the match and tossed it to the floor.

"Are you Mike Jones?" She hoped to God he wasn't the pilot she was waiting for.

"No." He inhaled deeply, then exhaled, blowing a thick cloud of smoke her direction.

"Do you know when Mr. Jones will be here?" she asked, willing her eyes not to bat against the smoke.

"*Mister* Jones had a slight setback. He was unconscious last time I saw him." The man read the ornate advertisement for the Black Tie restaurant on the match cover, then tucked the matches into the breast pocket of his T-shirt. The knuckles of his hand were red and swollen, one finger joint cracked and covered with dried blood.

"I found Jones in a local cantina, drunk out of his mind and just itching to fly. Had a little trouble convincing him it would be in his best interest if he stayed on the ground. My name's Ash—Asher Adams, and it looks like I'll be flying you to the reserve. If you still want to go."

Corey pushed her earlier thoughts to the back of her mind. "Of course I still want to go." She hadn't come this far to back out now.

"You want my advice?" He pulled off the navy-blue cap and swiped at his sweating forehead before slapping the cap back over shaggy brown hair. "Go back home. Get married. Have babies. Why is it you women have to prove you're men? You come here thrill-seeking so you can go home and be some kind of small-town hero. So your whole puny story can be printed up in a little four-page county paper and you can travel around to all the local clubs and organizations with your slide presentation, and all your friends can ooh and aah over you."

Corey felt heated anger flushing her face. She pressed her lips together in a firm, stubborn line. What an obnoxious boor! In her years as a social worker, she'd never, *never* come across anyone like him. And thank God for that, she fumed.

Asher Adams took another drag off his cigarette, then flopped down in the chair across from her, legs sticking out in front of him, crossed at the ankles. "Go back home," he said in a weary voice. "This is real. It isn't some Humphrey Bogart movie. This isn't Sleepyville, Iowa, or wherever the hell you're from—"

"Pleasant Grove, Illinois," she flatly informed him. "And I don't need your advice. I don't want it." Who did this overbearing man think he was? She hadn't taken vacation time to come here and be insulted by an ill-tempered woman-hater. And he talked as if she planned to settle in the jungles of Brazil. There was nothing further from her mind.

She zipped her bag and grabbed up her cream-colored wool jacket. "I'd like to leave now."

He made a slow process of removing his dark sunglasses, hanging them on the frayed neck of his T-shirt, and rubbing his eyes. Then he looked at her. "Haven't you heard a thing I've said?"

"Are the supplies I brought in the plane? I'm ready to go." Her voice was cool. One thing she'd learned in dealing with wayward boys was to let them have their little outbursts, then proceed as if nothing had happened. She knew how to deal with him. He was a hired bush pilot, nothing more.

"Ah, hell!" he snapped, struggling to his feet. He probably wasn't used to being defied, especially by a woman. "Listen, I just logged some twenty hours of flying time in the last three days. I'm beat. I landed an hour ago, my only thoughts being a shower and bed—"

She softened somewhat. She was tired herself and knew how it could shorten one's temper.

"So if you're going, let's go and get this farce over with."

The man had absolutely no concept of good manners. She stood up and flung her jacket over her arm. She wasn't going to let his attitude affect her own.

"My name is Corey McKinney. If we're going to be traveling together . . ." Her words trailed off. He obviously didn't care what her name was.

He just stood appraising her, eyes squinted against the smoke of his cigarette. "Oh, I know who you are. George Dupree told me you were coming. I'm just surprised they sent such an infant, right off her mother's—" He paused, apparently deciding to not be so crude. Then he gathered new thoughts, new ammunition. "The Amazon's hard on a person. It makes old ladies out of pretty little girls—if they live that long. Because the natives, and the jungle, aren't always friendly, and nobody here plays by the rules. You wanna know why? Because there aren't any rules."

Corey wasn't going to let this hulking bully intimidate her. She was an adult. She gave blood, paid her taxes, and had voted for two presidents. "This is all very interesting and dramatic, Mr. Adams. But I'll be here only a week at the most. Hardly enough time to shrivel away," she stated in her best social worker's voice.

"Take it from me. A week can seem like a lifetime when you're cut off from the rest of the world, living in a musty, moldy hellhole."

"Well, I'm ready to see this hellhole," she announced. "And I'm probably just as eager, more so maybe, to get this 'farce' over with as you are."

He reached out and opened the screen door, a mocking smile seeming to tug reluctantly at the corners of his mouth. Corey half expected to have to catch the door before he let it slam in her face, but surprisingly, he stood aside, and with an elaborate sweep of one arm motioned for her to pass.

Before she could step out, the small, dingy room began to tilt and turn black, shafts of light darting across the back of her eyes.

Good Lord! Surely she wasn't going to faint. This was too ridiculous! She'd never fainted in her life.

Taking deep, stabilizing breaths, she desperately fought the light-headedness. Slowly the darting lights faded and she became aware of two things: of being steadied by strong hands, and of being studied by the most unusual pair of eyes Corey had ever seen. They had dark lines running through the smoky-gray, giving them a strange multifaceted, starlike pattern. Profound, deep, vulnerable eyes . . . and they belonged to Asher Adams. Now she thought she detected something that the dark sunglasses had previously hidden: sorrow reflecting from the depths of those gray pools. If eyes were truly the mirrors of the soul, then Asher Adams had a very sad soul.

Gradually she became disturbingly aware of something else: the masculine way he smelled—of damp skin, tobacco, and the cockpit of an airplane.

"You almost fainted," he mocked, the amusement in

his gravelly voice bringing her back to reality. "Sorry, but I left my smelling salts in the parlor."

She wrenched away, her knees strangely weak. "I did not almost faint."

"The hell you didn't."

"I've never fainted in my life."

"Come on. You're not as good a girl scout as you pretend to be," he chastised. "You're still dressed for Sleepyville, not the Tropics. Nobody wears clothes like those in the Amazon." His strange eyes, still uncomfortably close, broke away from hers to flicker briefly down her pale linen blouse and white corduroy pants to the toes of her soft leather walking boots, causing a strange, languid heat to follow the path of his gaze.

"I didn't see a sign marked Women's Dressing Room," she mumbled shakily.

He gave a harsh laugh. "And you won't. You passed the last outpost of civilization a long time ago, Lily."

The taunting name straightened her spine, steadied her legs. "Why do you keep calling me that?" she snapped.

"That's what you are, aren't you? All you social-worker types? Trying to be tough, like a man, while at the same time trying to make up for your empty nest by butting into other people's lives. Martyring yourself so you can pat your own back." He was holding the door open again. "What are you waiting for? Tighten your chastity belt and come on."

She could cuss at him, but that was against her nature. She could kick him, but she wasn't a violent person. So she would just have to turn the other cheek. Not looking up, she pushed past him. How could she have thought he was hiding a deeper sensitivity? A vulnerability? What a joke. Her radar had certainly been off. Way off.

The screen door slammed. His long strides quickly caught up with her shorter ones as he passed her. There were two planes near the air-taxi building. One was silver and in relatively good shape as far as Corey could tell. The other was a dull, dusty red and looked ready for the scrap heap. With a sinking feeling she watched him approach the junker, the soles of his tennis shoes leaving a trail on the mushy, bubbling asphalt. He gave two sharp whistles, and a short-haired, middle-size mutt of a dog appeared from around the corner of the building. It hopped on the plane wing and vanished through the open door.

chapter
two

After taking off, Ash directed the small fan so it blew in Corey's direction.

The cockpit reminded her of an old MG she'd once ridden in, with its black leather instrument panel full of glass-covered gauges, and the smell of hot oil burning off the roaring engine.

The breeze from the fan wasn't cool by any means, but at least it stirred the air. The only problem was that the pilot was now puffing on a cigar, and the fan was wafting the smoke right in her face.

"Are you supposed to smoke in a small aircraft like this?" she finally choked out when she couldn't stand the stench any longer.

He lazily shifted the cigar to the other side of his mouth. "Helps me concentrate on my flying," he said, the offending object held tightly between his teeth.

No wonder his voice was so gravelly, smoking those foul things. "Do you think that this one time you could concentrate without it?" she asked with a slightly affected cough.

"Jeez! Not one of them too," he muttered. "I suppose you've got a 'smoking stinks' T-shirt in that suitcase of yours."

The dog, which was sleeping on a box behind the pilot's seat, lifted its head at the sound of the raised voices. Then it closed its eyes and put its head back down on its front paws.

With an irritated motion Ash stubbed out the cigar, then stuck the dead butt back between his gleaming white teeth while Corey thought dismally of the pink, lily-covered T-shirt in her suitcase crammed and buried somewhere in the chaotic disorder directly behind them.

She looked out the side window. They were flying low, the Amazon River rushing under them, sprawling into the curved horizon like some huge tentacled lake rather than a river contained within banks. Triangular patterns of afternoon sunlight danced on the water's surface, sparkling like the diamonds of so many Amazon legends. Occasionally a fish would splash, leaving behind a rippling ring. At this particular stretch of river there was no shore. Solid jungle began where water left off, looking like a giant's well-tended garden of broccoli and vivid green cauliflower. From here it was hard to imagine that another world, another way of life, existed under that thick canopy of vegetation. An exhilaration that was part excitement, part apprehension ran through her.

Suddenly the plane dropped several feet, Corey's stomach dropping with it. She grabbed at the worn edges of the musty leather seat. "Is it always this rough?"

"It's the humidity rising off the river," Ash explained. He took a long drag off his cigar, then remembered it wasn't lit. "It'll get better pretty soon, but not much, because then we'll have the humidity rising off the jungle."

"Great," she mumbled nervously, letting go of the seat.

His laugh ricocheted off the sheet-metal walls of the aircraft. "We've got about three hours to go, so just sit back and enjoy the flight."

Corey dug her 35mm camera from her khaki bag and began taking pictures. The lens framed an expanse of vegetation and river, just catching the edge of the plane's fuselage. She pressed the shutter release.

"See this gauge?" Ash asked as she replaced the camera's lens cap. With an index finger he tapped on a glass dial of the instrument panel.

He did have nice hands, even with a split knuckle, she grudgingly allowed. His fingers were long and tan, sun-bleached hairs showing in the glaring sunlight.

"This is the turn and bank indicator. Shows us if we're flying level." He tilted his control wheel slightly and the horizontal, plane-shaped needle in the gauge dipped. Then he straightened it. "Want to fly her?"

She looked in horror at the black half-wheel in front of her. "I don't know how to fly."

"Come on. Try it. It's easy."

Not even wondering if he'd lost his mind, she put her camera away, then gingerly put her hands on the sun-baked control wheel.

"That's a good girl scout. Don't push or pull it. That controls the pitch."

She could feel the life of the plane in her hands; under her feet she could feel its pulsing heartbeat. This wasn't too bad.

"How's it feel?"

"Ah . . . okay . . ."

"Good. Now just Zen it till I get back."

"Get back? Where are you going?" Her voice came out a high-pitched squeak. Where *could* he go?

Bent almost double, he moved between the cramped seats to the small storage area behind them.

"Mr. Adams! Get back here. I don't know how to

fly!" He was crazy. He had to be. She was alone with a crazy man.

He cursed as the plane tilted and his head came in solid contact with the metal ceiling. "The gauge, Miz McKinney!" He wasn't being polite all of a sudden. The Ms. was a drawn-out sarcastic hiss.

She quickly focused on the dial he'd shown her earlier, leveling out the wings. "Mr.—Ash," she pleaded, this time not letting her eyes stray from the black and white gauge in front of her. "Hurry, please!"

She heard a click right behind her. "Just getting us some refreshments. I like to keep up with the big airlines." Then, thank goodness, he was heaving himself back into his seat. Out of the corner of her eye she could see him opening a blue thermos, then tipping it up to drink.

"You can let go now," he finally told her. Before she did, she looked to make sure he had at least one hand on the control wheel.

"Water?" he offered almost pleasantly, holding the jug toward her. "Sorry, I don't have any cups."

Unconsciously she ran the tip of her tongue over her dry lips. She was thirsty, she'd been thirsty for hours. She took a drink, then handed the thermos back to him.

"Here. Open this, will you?" he asked, tossing a small box at her.

She caught it. "Twinkies?" Somehow he didn't strike her as the kind of guy who ate Twinkies. He seemed more the type that would go for the worm in the last swallow of mescal.

"It's food of a sort, and I haven't eaten since this morning."

What had she gotten herself into? If she went five hours without food she got dizzy, and here this man was piloting a plane. "You're the one who was in such a hurry to leave Santarém," she reminded him, still resenting the fact that he'd called her trip here a farce.

"Don't like to keep the customers waiting."

Corey gave a snort of complete disbelief, then peeled the lid open on the small box. *"Chocolate* Twinkies?"

"Yeah. They're kind of hard to find. I bought them for George Dupree. He's got this Twinkie hangup."

She unwrapped one of the small packages, inhaling deeply as the sweet chocolate smell drifted up to her nose. Then she looked down at the box and swallowed. She hadn't eaten since Chicago, not unless she counted that package of M&M's she'd picked up in Tampa.

"They're not as good as the originals," he informed her after he finished one. "Unless you've got a thing about chocolate. Toss me another, will you?"

She opened another package. "Do you think Mr. Dupree will mind?" Guilt clutched her. *She* had a thing about chocolate. A sinful, constant craving she was always struggling to control.

"Go ahead. Have one. George doesn't even know I bought any. And give one to Bobbie."

She gave the dog a Twinkie, then opened a package for herself.

"Ever met George Dupree?" Ash asked.

"No . . ." Corey answered hesitantly. Ash didn't seem the type for small talk. "But I read his letter requesting funds for San Reys. He sounded very dedicated," she said, taking a bite of the sweet, cream-filled dessert.

Ash grunted and kept his eyes focused on the horizon. "For a do-gooder, he's okay. A little eccentric, but okay. You'll probably get along just fine; he has a soft spot for kids."

That was the second time he'd accused her of being a child. People sometimes mistook her for a teenager, but never a child. "I'm twenty-five. And I think I'm mature enough for this kind of trip," she informed him, unable to keep the irritation from her voice. She took the last bite of Twinkie, rolled up the cellophane, and stuffed it into the box.

"Twenty-five?" he asked incredulously. "You look

like you just graduated from the sandbox. Bet you have a helluva time buying beer." He glanced at her ringless fingers. "Not married?"

"No, but—"

"Wait. Let me guess. You're engaged to a guy you've known since grade school, a Dudley Do-right, and you're going to get hitched as soon as he gets his law degree. Then you'll raise your kids in the same sleepy little town you and Dudley grew up in."

Was she so easy to read? So staid, so dull? Then her defenses bristled. Todd loved her. And there was nothing wrong with the kind of life this man was ridiculing. What did he know? A semi-derelict pilot with probably no roots at all.

Corey was content with her life and proud of the rural community of Pleasant Grove. Since she was an only child, her parents had depended on her to help on the farm. After graduating from college, Corey had taken a small apartment in town but soon found that she missed doing morning chores; missed plowing with her dad's old green John Deere; missed being a part of the seasons; missed her folks and grandmother.

Farm families look after their own, so when Grandma McKinney became ill and bedfast, Corey moved back home to help take care of her. A year later, after her grandmother died, Corey decided to stay.

There was something reassuring and faithfully stable about Pleasant Grove. It was unchanging. People grew up, married, lived, and died, all within the radius of a few miles. Everyone knew one another, faults and all. And everyone expected Corey and Todd to eventually marry. It wasn't talked about, just expected. Like everyone in town expected Toad Farley to plant his potatoes on Good Friday.

"My boyfriend's not going to be a lawyer. He's working on his internship. He's going to be an anesthesiologist," she sniffed, slightly horrified by her lofty tone.

"Anesthesiologist, huh? I used to know a guy who was an anesthesiologist. He told me he got a real charge out of getting his patients doped up, then looking at them in their birthday suits. Sometimes he'd even get his camera and—"

"Stop it!" she shouted, somehow resisting the urge to clap her hands over her ears. "I have no desire to hear about some perverted friend of yours."

He shrugged. "Suit yourself. Just trying to make a little conversation."

She realized that her teeth and jaw hurt from clenching them so tightly. She'd never, never known anybody so abrasive, so irritating, so immature! She might look young, but she at least acted like an adult.

She shot him a sidelong glance. He had no excuse. He had to be thirty . . . maybe thirty-five. There were finely etched laugh lines at the corners of his eyes, but she couldn't detect any gray in the brown, slightly wavy hair that lay shaggily against the back of his neck and stuck out around the edges of his cap. Oh, she had him pegged. He was a loner and a drifter. One of those Peter Pan boys who had never grown up, who couldn't accept responsibility.

Five minutes later Ash took another drink of water, screwed the lid back on the thermos, and thrust it toward her. "Hang on to this, will you?"

Next thing she knew, they were making a sharp, banking turn. "What are you doing?" The wing on Corey's side pointed earthward toward plots of green divided by a network of narrow rivers.

"Landing."

Fighting the G force, she brought her arm up to look at her watch. They had been in the air for only an hour.

The plane leveled out, and she slowly set the thermos down by her feet, alarmed to find light shining through a jagged, rusty crack in the floor, but not as alarmed as she was about stopping here, in the middle of an uninhabited jungle. "I thought you said the trip would take three hours."

"It does. But we're gonna have a slight layover."

Her mind raced. He had told her there were no rules.

"Why are we landing here?" She couldn't keep the slight tremor from her voice. Maybe he was the kind of guy her mother had always warned her about.

He didn't answer. Instead, he shifted the fan so the air was blowing full in his face. She looked at him more closely. Perspiration was beaded on his forehead, and his hand, as he reached for the landing gear switch, trembled. Was he ill? Or was he a deviate, wrapped up in the throes of whatever sick plans he had for her?

Don't be ridiculous, she chided herself, trying to block out her mother's voice. Long ago she'd learned to take Grace McKinney's dire warnings with a grain of salt.

"Low on oil," Ash announced.

Corey's eyes scanned the array of gauges until she spotted the one marked oil. The needle was close to the red. Mentally she gave herself a good shaking for her immature reaction, for letting herself fall victim to situational neurosis, if there was such a thing.

"I'm going to set her down on that *playa*—the floodplain." He indicated the bare strip of ground that ran parallel to the tributary of water.

The landing was rough and erratic. Corey half expected the plane to break apart any second as it bounced over the cracked, curled clay of the riverbed to finally come to a jarring stop.

Ash cut the engine, then half lying, half sitting, he stretched to reach behind Corey's seat, pulling out a narrow brown paper bag. Then, settling back in his seat, he slipped out a fifth of Jack Daniel's, tossed the crumpled paper sleeve behind him, and unscrewed the bottle cap.

"I thought you were going to put more oil in the engine." The dread was back in Corey's voice. She watched in hypnotic dismay as his head tilted and he took a long, deep swallow. He *was* the kind of guy her mother had warned her about. All the signs had been there, screaming at her. His appearance. His attitude. She should have never, never gotten into the plane with him.

"I don't care what you do with your free time," she said bravely. "But right now you're being paid to fly me to San Reys."

"Should've known you were a teetotaler too." He tipped his head back again, bottle to his mouth.

Slowly she unlatched her seat belt, then inched her fingers toward the door handle, her heart sounding like thunder in her ears. What a fool she'd been to put her life in the hands of someone like him, someone who hadn't even been part of the agenda so carefully thought out and orchestrated by Reverend Michael. A total stranger had told her to come along with him, and she had meekly followed.

Wasn't it just possible that Asher Adams had fabricated the story about the other pilot? She had a nightmarish vision of this poor Mike Jones, bound and gagged, blood dripping from his temple, running into his eyes. A lot of criminals settle in South America. She was sure she'd heard that somewhere. Or was that something else her mother had told her?

Corey's heart was pumping like a freight train, her breath coming quick and shallow. God, she didn't know when she'd ever been so scared! Horror stories about rape clicked into her mind in fast motion. Submit. That was the word of the hour, the word for this very type of situation, where the attacker might prove an actual physical threat. Submit, and you might escape injury.

But submitting was the last thing she had in mind.

From the corner of her eye she could see his profile, the victimizing wolf's profile, for that's how she thought of him now, eyes be damned. Luckily those eyes were closed, his head tipped back against the seat, the Yankees baseball cap off and tossed over a lever. For a moment she lost herself as her eyes perused him, from the nickel-size smallpox vaccination scar on one gleaming bicep, to the worn jeans. Her gaze traveled southward, briefly visiting the flat-planed stomach and hip, then moving to contemplate a hard thigh muscle.

She imagined how that tempered, virile-looking body might feel pressed against hers . . . bearing down . . . A pulsing shiver shot through her, settling somewhere in the region of her lower stomach. She swallowed convulsively.

She had to get out of there.

She wrapped her fingers around the hot metal of the latch. Watching the pilot, she pulled down on the handle, wincing at the loud, ominous click that reminded her of an empty gun chamber.

Ash opened his strange gray eyes and looked directly at her. She was the innocent lamb; he was the wolf in wolf's clothing.

chapter
three

"What the hell's your problem?" Ash demanded.

Corey froze, one foot out the airplane door.

"From the look on your face you'd think you hopped into a plane with Norman Bates. Haven't you ever seen anybody trying to fight off a malaria attack before?"

"Malaria?"

"Yeah. I've had a thing going with malaria for the last three years. I get too worn out, go without sleep for too many days, the malaria takes over. Forty winks and I'll be good as new." With that he closed his eyes, crossed his arms over his chest, and slumped even farther down in the seat.

Corey let out a deep breath. Malaria. Did she ever feel like an idiot. Obviously she'd inherited her mother's penchant for overreacting. Asher Adams might be rude and abrasive, but he probably wasn't the type to physically abuse somebody. His abuse was done verbally.

"You're going to sleep? In *here?*" she asked in disbelief. Now that the engine was off, so was the fan, and the small compartment was stifling.

"Sure not sleeping outside with all those damn bugs," he mumbled, eyes closed.

"You should at least have a shot of chloroquine. I brought some with the donated supplies."

His eyes flew open. "Chloroquine? You've got chloroquine? I had some malaria tablets, but I don't know what happened to them."

It was annoying to find herself being regarded with such tolerance all of a sudden—now that she had something he wanted. If she weren't so eager to put an end to this delay, she'd tell him to find the antimalaria drug himself.

Instead, she made her way between the cramped seats, stooping as she went. Really, the guy was a pig, she decided as outdated American newspapers crunched under her feet.

There had been no order to the pilot's packing of the small compartment. It reminded her of an impatient child's closet, the door quickly shut to stop an imminent avalanche. Boxes were stacked haphazardly, with no regard for their size. A pair of tattered jeans had been flung on the floor, and the stench of stale cigar smoke had settled in the small area.

"It's under the sleeping bag," he directed with a mutter.

She reached across the boxes to yank at the rumpled sleeping bag. A pillow minus the pillowcase tumbled to the littered floor. She finally found the cardboard box that contained the medical supplies, pulled it out, then waded back to the front.

Ash scooted up in the seat. "Better give me a double dose. I've kinda built up a resistance to the stuff."

"How much do you weigh?" She was looking at the instruction sheet that had been packed with the small vials of medicine.

"Just fill the syringe."

"I will not. What's your weight?"

"Little over two hundred."

"Three cc's. That's your limit," she announced in a professional tone. She filled the syringe.

"Give me the needle." Ash turned sideways in his seat, hand outstretched for the syringe. Most of the color had drained from his face, and he was sweating profusely. "Give me the damn needle," he repeated impatiently, a tremor running through his arm.

"You can't give yourself a shot."

"It won't be the first time."

"I can give it to you. I've had a year of nurse's training."

He let his hand drop to his knee. "Go for it."

She started to dab at his bicep with an alcohol-soaked cotton ball. He jerked away.

"Not in the arm," he griped.

"It should go in a muscle," she told him patiently.

"No. I've had 'em in the arm before. They don't work as fast."

She dreaded to find out just where they worked faster.

"Just give it to me in the thigh or rear end. Here." He impatiently slapped the front of his leg. "Come on. Just do it through my pants. We don't have all day—unless you want to spend the night here. It's gonna be dark in a few more hours."

"I can't give you a shot through your pants. It's not sanitary. Your arm should be fine."

"Oh, come on." He stood up, his arm brushing against her breast, his hair against her cheek, while the dog regarded them with faint interest. Bending at the waist, Ash unsnapped and unzipped his jeans, then quickly pulled them and his white shorts down far enough to expose one pale, flat-planed hip.

Corey felt the color rising in her cheeks, and silently

cursed the light complexion that mirrored her every emotion.

He leaned over the control panel. "Come on," he complained, forehead on his folded arms, "do it. You wanted skin, you got skin."

He had a definite tan line, his left buttock standing out starkly against the burnished teak of his muscle-ribbed back. "I never said I wanted skin," she protested. Her hand shook as she reached out and dabbed the cold alcohol on one firm hip. She took a deep breath. What was the matter with her? She'd seen a male body before. But she couldn't recall ever seeing one like this, or seeing one that had this effect on her. He made her think of those sinfully gorgeous hunks she'd seen on billboards in Chicago—the ones advertising men's underwear.

"Hurry up, would you, Nurse Ratched?" he drawled, startling her out of her ruminations. "I'm sure you're enjoying the view, but I can't stand here mooning you all day."

Corey had been called more names in the last two hours than she had been called in her entire life. She had also put up with two lifetimes' worth of verbal abuse. There was a limit to how many insults a person could take. Corey gave the needle a slight twist before removing it.

A string of curses a sailor might envy shot from Ash's mouth. "You should've told me you flunked nurse's training. That felt like a goddamn ice pick."

Corey made some appropriately sympathetic noises while wiping at the alcohol-diluted blood that was trickling down the firm flesh of his backside. "Sorry. The needle must've been dull."

"Yeah. Sure." He quickly snapped and zipped his jeans, then dropped into the seat, all the fight gone out of him. "Let Bobbie out, will you?" he asked in a weary voice, eyes closed. "And don't go into the jungle, not even to use the little girl's room." He scooted farther down in the seat. "If I'm not up in an hour, wake me." In less than a minute he appeared to be asleep.

"Looks like it's just you and me, Bobbie," Corey said as she turned the latch and opened the door. Bobbie's whole bottom wagged as he looked up at her, since he didn't have much of a tail to speak of. He was an ugly dog —all brown, an ear gone, scars on his head. But he had an air about him, a character. Gray hairs around his eyes and across his muzzle spoke of age, but he moved with the surefootedness of a much younger dog. Corey found herself wondering about him, curious to know if Ash had owned him all his life.

Bobbie bounded out and dashed toward the slowly moving river, stirring up a swirl of bright yellow butterflies. Corey stooped through the doorway and off the wing, the cracked ground giving slightly under her booted feet. A bird call sounded from the jungle behind her and was rapidly answered from across the water, the sound carrying clearly through the motionless air.

It felt good to inhale without breathing musty leather, fuel, and burnt oil, she thought, lifting her shoulder-length hair from her neck and wishing she had on some of her cooler clothes. But there was no way to get to them, buried as her suitcase was in the storage compartment. Instead, she loosened her collar and rolled up her sleeves.

Was it safe, she wondered, looking at the plane and the suspicious black streaks on its underbelly. There were circular areas where red paint and rust spots had been sanded down to bare metal, but the job had never been finished and now the bare metal was rusting. She didn't know anything about planes, but she knew she'd never seen one so squat and naked-looking, and oily.

A resigned sigh escaped her. The whole situation was a joke or a bad dream, she couldn't decide which. If she wasn't so hot, sticky, and tired, she might just laugh. What an inept operation this Adams fellow ran. Landing to take a nap, an associate too drunk to fly, and this plane, looking like it was ready for a major overhaul.

A cloud of tiny flies suddenly appeared and started buzzing around her. When one landed on her arm, biting viciously enough to draw blood, she grudgingly decided Ash was right. A musty cockpit was preferable to being eaten alive by a bunch of nasty bugs. She shook her arms and ran for the plane, leaving Bobbie outside to sniff around since the flies didn't seem to be attracted to him.

Ash was still asleep. And he didn't look very comfortable with his head against the door like that, but that was his problem. The fifth of whiskey was nestled between his legs. One hand was lying limp, his fingers curled around the thin neck of the bottle.

She reached over and slipped it from his lax grip, looked at it a moment, then brought it to her mouth and took a couple of exasperated swallows. Normally she didn't drink. The last time she had tasted whiskey, it had been mixed with lemon juice and administered by her grandmother for a sore throat. But the utter absurdity of the situation just seemed to call for some kind of drastic action on her part. And there was something satisfying about bringing that brown bottle with its fiery liquid to her lips. She replaced the cap, leaned back in her seat, and shut her eyes.

Ash woke up and stretched—as much as he could in the cramped quarters. Then he looked over at his traveling companion. She was asleep. He decided he liked her better that way, when her brown eyes weren't staring at him in reproach. She wasn't what he'd expected. She wasn't some broad-shouldered roller derby queen with a butch haircut and combat boots. No, she was damn fragile-looking, and whoever had allowed her to come here was nuts.

He took the opportunity to silently admire her. The

shirt buttons at her slim throat were undone, her sleeves rolled up. There was something about her pale, calm beauty that brought to mind the picture of the angel that had hung above his bed at the state home: the pink, parted lips and absurdly long eyelashes, their golden tips casting spiked shadows across her heat-flushed cheeks; the damp wisps of light baby-fine hair curling and clinging to her neck and face, the humidity making small frizzy curls where her hair parted.

His gaze dropped lower. He could just make out the swell of her breasts underneath the yellow shirt, her chest rising and falling with each soft breath. His eyes drifted down to boyishly narrow hips and long legs, then back to her face, her mouth.

He reached out and carefully withdrew the bottle of Jack Daniel's from her relaxed fingers, the clean smell of her damp, translucent skin drifting up to him.

He wondered how she would taste. He wondered what she would do if he leaned over and tasted her. Just in time he remembered that he liked her better asleep.

A banging sound woke Corey up.

The hood of the plane was open, or at least the thing she would call a hood. The pilot had his head inside, doing something.

And she had to go to the bathroom. Darn. Why hadn't she gone earlier, when he was sleeping? Well, while he was occupied with the engine, she would just slip into the jungle.

She was poised to duck between some thick fronds when Ash's voice stopped her.

"Where do you think you're going?"

She looked back to find him staring at her, an oil can in his hand. "I have to—" She waved her hand toward the jungle. "You know . . . go to the bathroom."

"Just go behind the plane." He dismissed her and turned back to the engine.

"Forget it." He might drop his pants whenever and in front of whomever he pleased, but she wasn't about to go to the bathroom a few feet from him. "I'm going into the jungle."

He looked at her again, impatience unhidden in his expression. At first Corey thought he was going to argue, but he finally shrugged, saying, "Just don't go in very far. And don't touch anything."

She gave him a mock salute before ducking away, finding herself suddenly plunged into semidarkness. The air was heavy, smelling like damp earth and sweet flowers, and a pungent scent that was like a mixture of vanilla and cinnamon.

Insects hummed, filling the air with an orchestrated drone that rose and fell in hypnotic waves. Some of the palms and ferns she brushed past as she followed what could almost be a faint trail looked remotely like plants she might have seen at home. But for the most part everything was new and unfamiliar. Trees ranged in size from scrawny saplings to creaking giants that made her dizzy when she looked up to where their branches touched the turquoise sky. Some trunks were dark purple with strange, twisted bark; others were smooth and the color of aged ivory. There were other trunks she couldn't see at all: they were covered with a blanket of compostlike material, playing host to an array of different types of ferns and smaller plants.

Corey did what she had come for, then turned to go back. It didn't take her long to discover that while she had been admiring the wonders of the jungle, she'd failed to take careful note of her directions. But she wasn't worried about being lost. She was sure Ash was still within shouting distance.

"Mr. Adams!" Her cry stirred up a flock of yellow birds from the huge tree branches overhead. They merely flew to the next tree, settling in a flutter of color and noise. Then a hideous-looking red and orange insect the size of a grasshopper landed on her arm. She could feel the small barbs of its feet clinging to her skin. Corey let out a small shriek, frantically shaking her arm until the bug flew away, disappearing into the darkness.

"Mr. Adams!" She didn't like being in this strange place all by herself. "Ash!"

Something moved. Leaves shifted and rustled, then Bobbie erupted from the underbrush and dashed up to her, looking quite proud, his bottom wagging furiously. Corey let out a relieved breath and bent to pet his scarred, coarse hair. "You're a regular Rin Tin Tin." The dog gave her hand a lick, then bounded back in the direction he'd come.

Ash was leisurely strolling toward them through the overgrown jungle. And it struck Corey that he looked at home in this wild place.

"I told you not to come this far." He stopped and tilted his cap back on his head, then put his hands on his hips. "Still looking for the door marked Ladies' Room?"

"Very funny." Corey edged her way around a leaf that was large enough to fan a sheik. "I couldn't find my way back. Everything looks the same."

Ash's annoyed expression suddenly changed to that of alert concentration. "Stop. Don't move!" He was staring at the ground near her feet, his whole body tense.

Corey stopped in confusion. "What's wrong?"

He began edging toward her in a half circle, talking as he moved. "You're standing right on the edge of a Xingu death pit."

Her chest constricted and her heart felt as if it had stopped beating. "Oh, God." The words were forced from a dry throat.

"Take a step backward, but do it real easy."

"I . . . I'm afraid to move," she whispered, unable

to draw her terror-filled eyes from his, her muscles frozen into immobility.

"I can't believe that. A girl scout like you?" he chided in what she half-consciously recognized as his method of coaxing her into action. "Come on. You can do it." He was only a few yards from her now.

Just as it seemed that her foot was finally receiving her brain's command to move, there was a loud crack, like a limb snapping, followed by the scuttling of earth as the ground under her shifted and gave way. A scream tore from her throat and echoed in her ears as she fell.

chapter
four

Desperately Corey raked her nails across the topsoil as she slid into the gaping hole that had opened under her feet. Ash lunged forward, his strong fingers locking around her small-boned wrist, the rescuing grip sending a shaft of pain ripping through her arm all the way to her shoulder.

"Ash!" Her voice came out a terrified croak. With her free hand she struggled to secure a hold on the crumbling wall of the pit. Dirt fell away under her flailing fingers, skittering into the darkness below.

Oh, God! She was going to die here, in this awful place!

A terrified sob escaped her. She squeezed her eyes shut and clamped her jaw together. She could smell damp soil against her cheek, taste it on her lips. She thought of all the gardens she'd helped her mother put in. It would break her parents' hearts if anything happened to her.

"Give me your other hand!"

Slowly she forced her eyes open, then looked up. Ash was lying on his stomach, his free hand reaching for her.

"Come on," he coaxed, his eyes locking with hers. "Let's have your other hand."

She felt reassured by his calmness. After drawing a trembling breath she struggled to bring her hand up to his, stretching until their fingertips touched. Then her hand was secure in his tight clasp. She cast a glance over her shoulder. "Hurry!" she whimpered in renewed terror, kicking her feet in a desperate attempt to find a foothold. "There are sharp things down here! Spears! They look like spears!"

"If you don't shut the hell up and hold still, you'll get us both killed!" Annoyance was back in his voice.

Her breath caught on a half sob. He was dragging her up, dirt falling in her face and down the front of her blouse. He let go of one of her wrists to grip the back of her pants, hauling her out of the darkness and into the light, into the firm security of his steel-banded arms.

She clung tightly to him, blood pounding in her brain as she pressed her face to the comforting softness of his cotton T-shirt. Her fear-racked body was sprawled across him, her breasts crushed against his rock-hard chest, thighs separated by his lean, solid hips, their panting breaths and bodies interwoven.

They stayed that way for a time before Ash spoke. "Somebody . . . must have moved the damn outhouse," he said, his chest rising and falling as his lungs gulped in the heavy air. She could hear and feel the thunder of his heart beneath her cheek.

Her own breath was still coming in gasps. Even in the aftermath of her fear she was conscious of a liquid flame spreading through her. She tried to quiet her pounding heart, while at the same time trying hard not to think of the intimacy of their positions, or his masculine scent, his solid hardness.

When she didn't say anything, his hands moved with

familiarity across her back to grasp her by the shoulders, the fingers of one hand somehow finding her aching muscles, kneading away the pain. "Hey, Lily. You okay?"

He stopped rubbing her shoulder and pulled himself into a half-sitting position, with Corey on top, embarrassingly intimate, his startling eyes boring into hers. Never in her life had she been in such a situation, so wrapped around a man she hardly knew. The left side of her face tingled, where his unshaven cheek had rubbed.

"Yes, I'm . . . I'm okay," she finally managed to say in a breathless voice, willing her mind to concentrate on the pain in her wrenched arm while she futilely struggled to draw her gaze from his.

A slow-dawning smile lit the gunmetal of his eyes, causing them to crinkle at the corners. "Is this the kind of thrill you were seeking?" he asked in a rough, sexy voice.

Corey's heartbeat echoed in her ears as she watched the humorous gleam in his eyes darken and begin to smolder. With supreme effort she gathered her scattered wits, heat rising in her cheeks. This was the same man who had taunted her, the very man who had said cruel, horrible things to her. There was absolutely no way she could be attracted to him. "A thrill is what you get when you ride a roller coaster, or hang glide," she protested.

"Maybe." He flashed his wicked-wolf smile. "Maybe not."

"Let me up!" She was beginning to panic.

"Hey, honey, you're on top," he drawled, not bothering to let go of her arms.

"Let go of me, you . . . you oaf!" she cried, pushing ineffectually at the solid wall that was his chest.

"Oaf?" He sounded amused.

She should have stopped with that, but she was scared. *He* was scaring her. "Oaf. Ill-mannered clod, whatever. I'm sure there are several names that would fit you."

Anger flared in his eyes, quickly replacing the amusement she'd seen seconds earlier. With a deft movement he rolled over, pinning her slight body beneath his hard, virile one.

"There. That's more like it. I should be the dominant partner, don't you think?" His gravel-throated voice was smooth, threatening.

He brought his elbows down to the ground on either side of her face, then forced her legs apart with his knees so he was nestled hard and compactly against her. She could feel every inch of his body pressing her to the ground.

"You might be trying to be a man, but you sure as hell feel like a woman." His crystal-gray eyes were only inches from hers. "And I think you're the one who needs a lesson in manners. Most damsels don't get ticked off when they're rescued. Most damsels, or in your case I guess I should say Lily-Libbers, demonstrate good breeding by thanking their rescuers." He moved suggestively against her, leaving no question in her mind as to what kind of thanks he referred to. "Don't you think that sounds like a good idea, Miss Manners?"

"You're disgusting," she hissed, fighting the fear that was mounting in her. She twisted and pushed under him, trying to get away, but it was useless. He had her where he wanted her.

"Mmm. That's nice," he sighed dramatically. "Just keep moving like that."

She stopped and held herself completely still, except for her chest, which rose and fell in short, quick movements.

"Say thank you and I'll let you up." His voice was smooth as syrup.

The hell she would. She closed her eyes tightly, but that was worse. With them shut she was even more aware of his body lying heavily upon hers.

"Say it," he insisted. One of his hands worked its way under her blouse, then moved to stroke her rib cage.

"Get off me, Adams." The words came out a panicky whisper. He was crushing the air from her lungs. She couldn't take a decent breath. And her every sense was riveted on the rough hand that was stroking her side, moving higher, leaving a trail of tingling flesh in its wake.

"Don't," she managed to gasp. "Please don't."

Her breath caught as she felt his mouth brush her cheek, then move down to the delicate skin of her throat. Kissing, tasting her with his tongue, making her feel weak, causing a tightening sensation in her abdomen.

She would have expected somebody like him to be rough, but he wasn't. Not at all.

His mouth left her body, and she sighed, eyes fluttering open. She could see him looming over her, see his lips moving closer again. He was going to kiss her on the mouth this time, and there was absolutely nothing she could do about it.

His lips pressed hotly against hers, tasting slightly of whiskey and salt, their very softness surprising her. How could a man's mouth be so soft? It moved over hers slowly, and very, very thoroughly.

Her muscles and bones turned to warm butter. There was a huge roaring in her ears, like a waterfall. The jungle faded, South America faded, the planet Earth faded. It was just the two of them and these wonderful new sensations.

Her mouth slackened to accommodate his deeper, more probing kiss. How could a mouth be so wet and erotic, she wondered dimly. One of her hands unwittingly lay against the back of his neck, urging him even closer. The other hand had found its way under his T-shirt, and was stroking the sweat-slicked steel of his back.

Involuntarily she tightened her knees, embracing him within her legs. Even through their layers of clothing she could feel his arousal, large and throbbing, pressing insistently against her. Then he was shifting her body to the side, slipping a hand inside her bra so that her aching breast, damp with perspiration, lay hot and full against his kneading palm. She let out a moan and arched against him while heat spread through her, making her feel weak and faint.

"Ash—" It was a plea for something, she didn't know what.

He heard her speak his name, felt her small hands gripping his back, pulling him closer, felt her legs wrapped tightly around him, her passion taking him totally by surprise.

God! A small part of his brain, the only part that could still think, couldn't believe this was happening. She had pissed him off with her name-calling, and her holier-than-thou attitude. But he'd been good enough to save her goddamn life, hadn't he?

He'd intended only to knock her down a few pegs, only intended to *kiss* her. But this. He'd never been turned on so fast in his life. He had to get a grip on the situation. Somebody here had to show some control. He knew he couldn't just take her like this. He didn't have her figured for the type to enjoy some casual sex, then go on about her business.

The best thing to do would be for him to get up and act as if it was no big deal. Treat it lightly, then forget about it. Best for her. Best for him.

She arched against him, her tongue stroking his, one hand moving to tug impatiently at his hip while she moved invitingly under him. He groaned and took a deep, self-controlled breath.

His lips broke away from hers, the smoldering light in his eyes hidden as he quickly rearranged her bra, then pulled her blouse down, all the while concentrating on steadying his ragged breathing. Her hands moved to his arms, her eyes glazed and dark as they watched him, her chest rising and falling rapidly.

"You're welcome," he finally said.

"What . . . ?" Confusion clouded her heavy-lidded eyes.

"I said, you're welcome." He couldn't stop his smile, wondering how long it was going to take her to come around, how long before she gave him hell. He moved back slightly, so they weren't fitted together like two puzzle pieces. "That was one of the best thank-yous I've ever gotten," he said lightly. He moved away from her and stood up. Then he reached down and pulled her to her feet.

Corey stood there for a minute, feeling dazed and shocked, aware that during the time Ash had held her, she'd been completely oblivious to her surroundings.

She ran a tongue over her swollen lips. She couldn't believe what had just happened. Not what Ash had done. That didn't surprise her. No, what shocked and scared her was what *she* had done. Nothing like this had ever happened to her before, not even with Todd. She and Todd had made love a few times, probably more than a few times, but it hadn't been exciting, just messy and inconvenient, leaving her with a feeling of emptiness. She had even worried that she might be what people termed frigid. Well, if she was, Asher Adams had thawed her out, to her dismay and self-disgust.

"The pit was made by local natives to catch animals, not people," Ash was saying as he slapped dirt from the backside of her pants with his cap.

She pushed ineffectually at him with a weak hand. Pit? She had forgotten about the pit. Somehow it didn't seem so important now. She had other things to worry about, like whether or not she was oversexed.

"It's about the only way for the natives to catch animals. Their weapons are still primitive."

He was acting as if the last few minutes—or had it been hours?—had never occurred. Corey kept her eyes averted. With a trembling hand she pushed the hair from her face, all the while aware of her hot, damp cheeks, all the while aware of the warm, salty taste of his skin still on her lips. Now she could finally understand how girls got into trouble. It was easy.

But it was different for men. She knew that. They do it, and it's over. No big deal. Like playing a round of golf or going to see a movie.

Ash bent down to retrieve his sunglasses, which had somehow come through the ordeal unharmed. He put them on, then slapped the Yankees cap on his head. "You should have listened to me. I warned you not to go into the jungle."

"Yes . . ." She was relieved that her voice sounded almost normal. "I can see that now."

"It was probably a good lesson."

No kidding, she thought, watching his wide shoulders as he led the way out of the jungle. Well, she decided, straightening her own shoulders, if he could put the whole incident behind him, so could she. After all, they would be at San Reys soon, and then she would never have to see him again. *Ever.*

Two hours later, as the small bush plane bounced through pockets of hot and cool air, Corey sat with her notebook balanced on one knee, trying to describe what she had seen of the Amazon so far, and trying to forget the existence of the person beside her. She was no journalist, and visually descriptive words eluded her. She found herself jotting down things like *beautiful* and *fascinating,* leaving her feeling inept and frustrated. In her mind she took herself back, recalling how the jungle had smelled like a hothouse full of flowering plants, how the heavy stillness of the air had reminded her of home right before a summer storm . . . and how Asher Adams's mouth had felt pressed to hers.

Corey slammed the notebook shut, stuck her pen in

the spiraled wire, and jammed the tablet back into her bag. Never glancing in the direction of the man next to her, she crossed her arms at her waist and stared out the passenger window, feigning interest in the distorted shadow of the plane as it scuttled over umbrella-shaped treetops. Surely they would reach George Dupree's soon. Her nerves couldn't take much more of this.

A few minutes later Ash cut back the engine power. "There's San Reys."

Corey looked in the direction he pointed and could see an area where the green of the jungle was split by a narrow strip of bare ground with a shallow river or tributary running parallel to it. At the end of the strip in a clearing stood a squat wooden structure with a thatched roof, looking like something out of *National Geographic*. She looked for more houses. There weren't any. *"That's San Reys?"*

"Yep."

"But, the name . . . I thought it would be a village."

"In the jungle every house has a name. San Reys was named after one of the lost cities of Eldorado."

She barely had time to digest this new information before Ash buzzed the area, sending a white clutter of hens scattering and flapping about the dirt yard.

"Just to let George know we're here," Ash explained, pulling the plane back up and guiding it into a wide, banking turn, the struggling engine protesting loudly.

Corey reached up and tried to tame her humidity-strewn hair, her fingers catching on a twig. She pulled it out, then leaned over and ruffled the tangled curls, odd pieces of broken leaves and dirt falling onto her lap.

Ash allowed her a quick, amused glance. "Don't get too spiffed up for George. He doesn't notice things like that. You'll see what I mean when you meet him."

Soon the wheels were touching the ground, the plane bouncing along at what she thought to be an alarming rate of speed considering the short length of the landing strip and the building at the far end. She gripped the edge of the seat, forcing herself to keep her eyes open until the plane rolled to a stop only yards from the house. The engine sputtered to silence, leaving her with ringing ears.

Now she could see that the building had been set several feet from the ground on stilts. And the porch windows, which ran the entire width of the front, were covered with green mosquito netting.

Ash flung open the door and jumped down, Bobbie bounding out after him. Corey stayed in her seat, struggling with the catch on the safety belt. She finally got it unlatched, opened the door, then stepped onto the rubber-protected area of the plane wing. Ash was there waiting, hand outstretched to help her down, and she hesitated.

She didn't want him to touch her. Let's face it, she chided herself, she was afraid to have him touch her. And why the sudden show of manners, she wondered as she cautiously placed her hand in his firm, sure grip. He was probably just making certain she didn't step through the fabric-covered area of the plane wing.

Just as soon as she felt the ground under her feet, she pulled her hand away, but could still feel where his fingers had pressed against the tender skin of her wrist.

"This is Elvira," Ash said, introducing the large white nanny goat that had come up to nudge his leg, her familiarity leading Corey to surmise that Ash must be a frequent visitor here. "Hope you like goat's milk. She gives almost a gallon a day. Ever milk a goat?" His question was a challenge, as if he knew she hadn't.

"A few times," she said, a smile tugging reluctantly at the corners of her mouth. She could tell by his expression that he didn't believe her.

"Just how rural is this burg you're from?" he asked as he scratched the goat on the head.

"*Very* rural. I can plant the straightest row of corn you've ever seen."

He tilted his cap back farther, gray eyes sparkling against the setting sun. "Row-hopper, huh?" He sounded almost interested. Then he turned and bounded up the steps, two at a time, shouting as he went.

"George! Hey, George! Your social worker's here! You know, the one with the butch haircut and hands that can crush stone!" He turned his head, giving Corey a quick wink and a blazing smile.

Her heart momentarily caught in her throat.

Then he was swinging the wooden screen door open. "Come on in," he coaxed.

Corey stood in the middle of the yard, arms crossed over her chest, purse strap dangling over one wrist. "I don't think we should just . . . go in."

Ash turned and did exactly that, the door slamming behind him.

Corey rubbed her gritty-feeling eyes, then tugged her purse away from Elvira's nibbling mouth. What if she had come all this way and George Dupree wasn't even here? She didn't want to consider it. Things just seemed to be going from bad to worse, and she was too tired to figure anything out right now.

Through a haze of fatigue and muddled emotions, she remembered her duty and pulled out her camera, centering the one-story building in the viewfinder. It fit perfectly, being almost square if the porch wasn't considered. The house was made of a dark red wood that was unfamiliar to Corey. On one side of the building, leaning against a stilt as thick as a railroad tie, was a beat-up fenderless motorcycle with knobby tires. She pressed the shutter release, fleetingly wondering how old George Dupree was. She hadn't pictured him as someone who would drive a motorcycle.

She turned around and centered the viewfinder on Ash's plane, hoping the shimmering heat waves rising from the fuselage would show up in the print. Beyond the plane was a trail leading downhill through a tangle of shrubs and trees, a few patches of sparkling water just discernible through some of the leaves. She clicked the shutter, then put her camera away.

A wet, musty breeze touched her hot face, followed by the gentle tinkling of chimes. Corey looked up at the wide wooden porch to see what had made such a delicate sound. Hanging from the rafters was a set of chimes. Not made of fairy bells or angel wings as the sweet tones had suggested, but fragile-looking gears, dozens of them, ranging in size from the smallest of the tiny pearl buttons that had adorned the dainty gloves she'd worn to church as a child, to the size of Queen Anne's lace, the frilly white flower that decorated the roadsides back home. And all the gears were hanging by threads too fine to be seen.

It was whimsical, and she loved it. Who had taken the time and care to fashion such a thing? George Dupree?

Her thoughts were interrupted by Ash, who came bounding down the steps, a piece of paper in his hand. "A note from George," he explained. "This should really tick you off. He's in Santarém. We probably just missed him."

"Santarém?" Her worst fears were realized. "Why would he do that? Didn't he know I was coming?"

"Oh, he knew. George is king of the scatterbrains, so he probably just forgot. Says he finally got an appointment with Carlos Santiago. He's the head of the Brazilian Indian Foundation. George is trying to get him interested in helping finance this place. Here—" He handed the note to her. "See for yourself."

The writing ran uphill, and was almost indecipherable, looking more like Egyptian hieroglyphics than English. But it was as Ash said. If George Dupree received a grant from this foundation, then that could mean her trip *was* on its way to becoming a full-fledged farce, just as Ash had predicted.

She resisted the urge to crumple the wrinkled, smudged paper into a ball and give it an angry toss. "This is ridiculous! I came all this way to see him and visit some of the native villages. Now what am I going to do? Stay here, in the middle of the jungle, by myself, and wait for him to come back?"

Ash glanced around the yard. "You won't be by yourself."

"No," she agreed in disgust. "Of course, I'll have Elvira. Whom I'm probably supposed to milk twice a day. And then there are the chickens. I'm surprised he didn't leave orders for me to cut the heads off a few while I'm here."

"I'm staying too," Ash mildly announced.

Corey made an impatient sound. Obviously Asher Adams wasn't as immune to her as she had thought. Now he wanted to play Tarzan and Jane. Well, she hadn't traveled miles in a plane that should be condemned, and suffered heat and verbal and sexual abuse, to spend a week alone in the middle of the jungle with the direct cause of her suffering.

"As soon as I pay you for flying me here, your job will be done."

"Hey, I don't want your money. I'm no freelance pilot."

"What are you talking about?"

"You obviously don't understand, Lily." He reached into his T-shirt pocket. With two fingers he pulled out the cigar butt, then lit it with a match, Corey's match. "I was on my way here anyway." He took the cigar from his mouth and casually surveyed the glowing tip. "You see, I live here."

chapter
five

A continuous drone filtered into the sleep-filled corners of Corey's mind like a million cicadas all singing the same note. Eyes closed, she groaned and rolled onto her back, a clammy sheet tangling around her bare legs. There was a smell to the heavy air, a damp mustiness, and in that limbo state between dreaming and waking she wondered why she was sleeping in her grandmother's stone cellar.

From a long way off came the high-pitched squawking of a bird, like sound effects from a jungle movie. Her eyes flew open and she found herself staring at a Three Stooges poster nailed to the wall of the small wood-planked cracker box of a room.

Asher Adams's room.

She didn't know where he'd spent the night, since she'd been dead on her feet by the time he propelled her there. She had managed to ask him why he hadn't told her he lived at the reserve. His answer had been simple and direct: He hadn't wanted her to come. The idea was George's. Ash hadn't had anything to do with it.

Corey's sleep had been uninterrupted, except for the disturbing times when Asher Adams's mouth moved over her eyelids, her lips, and her body. She'd never dreamed such erotic dreams about Todd, dreams that made her wake up blushing and breathless. Were dreams really unconscious desires? That unwelcome thought was quickly pushed to the back of her mind.

She kicked away the white sheet and sat on the edge of the bamboo-frame bed with its thin, sprawling mattress, her cotton nightgown settling around her thighs, the rough-planked floor gritty under her feet.

What was she going to do now? she wondered, leaning her elbows on her knees, chin in her hands. She wanted to be taken back to Santarém right away, this morning. But she couldn't allow Ash's presence to cloud her judgment. Her trip had been paid for with church money. She couldn't leave until her job was finished. She might not be a forceful person, but she wasn't a coward.

She ran fingers through her tangled curls. The humidity had already made the wavy strands twice as thick as usual, and she knew she probably looked like one of those fuzzy-haired girls in a Maxfield Parrish painting. But she had more serious things to worry about than her hair.

None of this had turned out as she had planned. She had been prepared to do without things like electricity and hot, running water. That hadn't bothered her. It was just that she had imagined it happening so differently.

In her mind she had pictured herself being greeted in Santarém by a smiling, dark-skinned little man who knew very little English; pictured him flying her to San Reys, respectfully pointing out interesting sights along the way; pictured being greeted enthusiastically by George Dupree, an elderly gentleman who would have the bearing of a monk, the only thing missing being a dark cassock and sandals.

And here she sat, staring at a Three Stooges poster. Beside it hung a motorcycle calendar, wrong month, wrong year. Beside that was a huge aeronautical map of the Amazon region. Several spots had been circled. Underneath was an ornate-handled dresser that would probably be pretty if not for the chipped white paint. None of the drawers were shut, socks and wrinkled T-shirts hanging out. The top was loaded with junk, some of it disgusting, like the moldy stuffed parrot with empty black holes for eyes. There was a dusty, half-finished whiskey bottle, two huge pink-and-white conch shells, a dried blowfish, necklaces made of nuts and feathers, boxes of rifle shells, and crumpled cigarette packs. A treasure trove. The Littlest Angel and his earthly delights, except that Asher Adams was no angel.

She got up, went over to the dresser, and lifted the practically weightless blowfish. A curled black and white photograph fell to the floor. Feeling guilty, she picked it up and started to set it back on the dresser, then stopped.

It was of two solemn boys, one dark-haired, the other fair. They were sitting on cement steps in front of a brick building. Both wore identical clothes: dark shorts, white shirts, and leather shoes. The older, blond-haired boy looked about twelve. But it was the younger boy who caught Corey's attention. It wasn't hard to recognize Ash. Not with those eyes. Both knees were skinned and he had a cut on his forehead.

There was something melancholy about the picture, making her think of photographs taken back when people didn't smile for them. She had often wondered if they didn't smile because it wasn't the fashion or if there was simply nothing to smile about.

For the first time she wondered how Ash had come to be in the Amazon. He certainly didn't seem the philanthropist type.

She was putting the picture back when she heard a plane flying low over the reserve.

George Dupree must be back.

Corey tossed her suitcase on the bed and quickly dug out a pair of jeans that felt limp and damp, having absorbed moisture from the air. She slipped them on, thinking that they weren't nearly as faded as Ash's, but they were old enough to be cool. She was closing the last button on her white sleeveless cotton blouse when the plane landed, taxiing to a stop not far from her window.

She tugged a brush through her blond hair, pulled it back, and fastened it with a rubber band, winding tendrils already escaping around her face and neck.

Doors slammed, chickens squawked, then a dog began barking.

"Get the hell out of here, Jones," came a gravelly voice she already recognized as Ash's. But today it was heavy with dislike.

"Not till I get the two hundred bucks you owe me for stealin' my fare yesterday."

"Nobody owes you a cent. You don't get money for being wasted."

Corey moved to the green-mosquito-netted window. If she stood to one side she could see Ash and the man who was obviously Mike Jones, the pilot who had been scheduled to fly her to the reserve. Ash, dressed in a white T-shirt and jeans, had his back to her. The other man, wearing a blue chambray workshirt with huge sweat rings at the armpits and neck, faced the window. He was almost as tall as Ash and probably outweighed him by about a hundred pounds.

"You're a helluva one to talk about being bombed," Jones said, glaring through black greasy hair that hung to his feverish eyes, making Corey think uncomfortably of wanted posters she'd seen in the post office. "You've spent half your life readin' the bottom of a table."

"At least I *can* read."

"Think you're so damn funny, don't you? Well, I'm not laughing."

Bobbie snarled, baring yellow teeth.

"Make that mutt of yours shut up." Mike kicked, and the dog jumped away from the swinging black engineer boot, a growl rumbling deep in his throat, head low. "I hate that damn dog."

"Looks like he harbors the same deep feelings for you," came Ash's dry comment. "He knows pond scum when he sees it. So why don't you just get the hell out of here."

"I'm not leavin' till I get my money."

Bobbie let out a series of threatening barks.

"If you don't make that dog shut up, I will." Mike's hand went to his waist, and the next thing Corey knew, he had a pistol pointed at Bobbie. "Call him off."

Corey could see Ash's shoulders and back muscles tense under the cotton of his T-shirt. "Bobbie, get back," Ash commanded.

The dog paused, then started barking again.

"Get back!"

A growl rumbling in his throat, Bobbie backed off to lie down near Ash. Corey let out her breath, not realizing she'd been holding it. But her relief was short-lived.

As soon as Jones lowered the gun, Ash lunged, propelling the big man to the ground, both expelling their breath in a loud *whoomp*. The gun went spinning across the dirt-packed ground. Mike Jones drew a fist and swung, the blow making a dull thud, like a baseball contacting solidly with a catcher's mitt. Ash let out an enraged bellow and struck back. There was a frenzied burst of high-pitched barking, followed by the sound of snapping teeth as Bobbie joined in, clamping on to Jones's pant leg.

Corey ran from her room, through the littered kitchen-living area to the narrow porch, almost tripping over a rusty generator. She jerked open the screen door and hurried down the bowed wooden steps.

"Call off your dog!" Jones screamed, trying to shake

the dog free of his pant leg. Ash pinned the man's shoulders to the ground with his knees.

"Call him off!"

"I'm sick of you and your damn guns," Ash panted, blood dripping from his nose, falling on Mike's face. "Don't ever pull one around me again." He glanced over his shoulder at the dog. "That's enough!"

Bobbie let go.

"You're crazy, you know that?" Mike said through gritted teeth, small eyes glaring hatefully beneath bushy eyebrows. "Who the hell but you would go so nuts over a damn dog."

Corey could see the tension in Ash's clenched hands, his taut muscles. "Ash, let him up," she begged, afraid it was going to start all over again.

With a quick, disgusted shove, he let go of Jones and struggled to his feet, then went over and scooped up the gun. He was looking in the cylinder when Mike let out a high-pitched, wheezing laugh.

"It ain't even loaded!" he said, hefting himself upright.

Ash slammed the cylinder back in place and tossed the gun at him. "Somebody should've locked you up a long time ago."

"They tried, but they couldn't catch me," Mike boasted, shoving the pistol into his thick belt. His gaze suddenly fell on Corey, his squinty eyes losing their hardness, becoming interested.

"So, this is the fare you cheated me out of." Blood and sweat ran down his face. "Don't look like yer typical social worker to me." He was staring, not at her face, but at her body, and from his expression, he must have liked what he saw.

Corey could feel the heat of the Amazon sun stealing through the clinging fabric of her blouse, falling warm on her damp skin. She drew her arms in front of her, suddenly feeling as if he could see right through her clothes.

"No wonder you were so anxious to pick her up," Mike said, sneering.

"Leave her out of this." Ash crossed straight arms in front of him to grip the hem of his blood-splattered white T-shirt. He peeled it over his head, tan muscles rippling and gleaming in the tropical sun.

"She's out of your league, Adams," Mike said, his beady eyes sidling from Corey to Ash. "Way out."

With the wadded-up shirt Ash casually wiped at the sweat across his smooth, tan chest, then just as casually dried his armpits. "You're not telling me anything I don't know." He tipped back his head and pressed the shirt to his bleeding nose.

Disgusted yet fascinated, Corey watched the play of sunlight and shadow on Ash's muscles. His bronze skin was amazingly smooth and clear, unmarred except for a thin white scar trailing from below the flat nipple of his left breast, to disappear into the waistband of his jeans. Where had he gotten a scar like that? If this morning's display was any indication of his habits, then she'd just bet he had picked it up in some barroom brawl.

She tried to forget how firm and satiny that skin had felt under her fingertips. Forget the way his hard, solid body had felt pressed so intimately to hers. She was forcing her gaze away when her focus froze.

On one bulging bicep was a tattoo. His shirt had previously covered it, but now the tacky thing was exposed in all its vulgar glory. She was even close enough to read the ornate blue lettering: BORN TO RAISE HELL.

She exhaled slowly. *A tattoo.* She couldn't believe it. He had a tattoo.

With her index finger she half-consciously touched her bottom lip. She, Corey Jane McKinney, had been kissed by a man who had permanently disfigured himself with a tattoo. And not any tattoo. It wasn't a couple of unobtrusive initials, or some small discreet design. No,

Asher Adams had to have a tattoo that said BORN TO RAISE HELL.

"You'll probably be needing a ride to Santarém," Mike told her. "Seeing as how George is gone, and knowing nobody'd want to be stuck here with a crazy bastard like Adams."

Corey was still studying the gaudy calligraphy on Ash's arm. She looked up at Mike, then took an unconscious step away.

"If she wants to go back, I'll take her," Ash said.

Mike ignored him. "If you're smart, you'll leave with me. Tell you what. You pay me the two hundred bucks you owe me for yesterday, and I'll fly you back to Santarém now, no charge. What do you say?"

"I don't owe you anything," Corey said. "And I'm going to stay here long enough to come up with a report that contains more than an account of a fistfight."

Ash laughed, the volume slightly muffled by the shirt still pressed to his nose.

"You'll be sorry," Mike Jones warned. "Adams is crazy. Only somebody who's crazy would spend years chasing after a ghost."

Hand and shirt dropped to Ash's side, and Mike turned to him. "An' you know what else I think?" he asked with a sharp, hate-filled laugh. "I think the wrong brother died. If you ask me, it should have been *you*."

Ash sucked in his breath, raw pain unguardedly exposed in the lusterless shadows of his eyes. In that instant, before he turned and walked away, it seemed as if Corey could see all the way to his soul.

Mike Jones watched as Ash and the dog disappeared into the jungle, then he looked back at Corey, a sneer on his face. "If we're lucky, maybe he'll get lost like his brother." When Corey didn't answer, he continued. "You've probably heard of Lucas Adams, the guy who started this place. He went for a walk in the jungle one day and never came back." Mike let out a loud snort. "A few days later Asher Adams shows up here, all set to find him. That was three years ago, and the crazy bastard's still lookin'."

The smirking smile made Corey feel sick, made her feel dirty.

His gaze moved downward to the front of her blouse. "I think you better come back with me. You don't want to get mixed up with a crazy man."

She took another step back.

His smile faded. "Don't tell me you're gonna join Adams on his ghost hunt. You saw how he is. How he goes nuts over nothing."

"Children can say terribly cruel things," Corey said in a thankfully level voice, "but I always chalked it up to ignorance and inexperience. What's your excuse?"

"Well, it ain't ignorance." He stepped closer and grabbed her by the arm. "An' it sure as hell ain't inexperience. I can do it all night long."

"Let go of me—" She tried to jerk out of his grasp. His breath was sour, and his sweat reeked of yesterday's whiskey. At first the damp grip on her arm only tightened, his thick fingers digging into her flesh. Then he released her and she stepped back.

"You'll get tired of babysitting," he said angrily, jerking his head the direction Ash had gone. "When the malaria's strong in him, an' he goes nuts on you. Then you'll be *prayin'* for Mike Jones to come back."

Nobody deserved to be left alone with a bastard like Jones, Ash told himself as he made his way through the jungle.

He stopped, then turned around. He was almost to the clearing when he heard the sound of an engine turning over, followed by the heavy chug of a winding propeller.

Then the porch door slammed, telling him everything he needed to know. Jones was leaving; Lily was staying.

Ash turned and made his way along the narrow path to the water's edge. He sat down, back braced against the trunk of a Brazil nut tree, and lit a cigarette, pulling the smoke deep into his lungs. He exhaled, watching glider spiders skim across the sparkling surface of the backwater lagoon, thinking, remembering things better forgotten.

He and Luke had been opposites. Night and day. Black and white. Good and bad, if he believed Old Lady Fielding, the female Gestapo who ran the orphanage where they had spent their formative years.

She was probably right. Ash was always in some kind of trouble. It must have taken a whole damn tree to make the paper for all the demerit slips he'd accumulated in his unflaggingly delinquent childhood. Luke had never gotten a single one.

If he and Luke hadn't been brothers, if they'd just met in a schoolroom, they probably wouldn't have spoken to each other. But since they had no family, they were more than brothers. They were each other's mother, father, aunts, uncles, best friends. But that in no way meant they thought alike.

Ten years ago, when Luke joined the Peace Corps, Ash had told him he was an idiot. Five years ago, when Luke asked Ash to leave the cut-rate safari business he was running in the Florida Keys, Ash hadn't wanted anything to do with it. He told Luke he wasn't a do-gooder. Then, three years ago he'd gotten George's message saying Luke was missing and presumed dead.

The guilt and loss he felt was overwhelming. He should have gone with him to South America. Luke had an irritatingly childlike faith that made him a threat to himself. Blind optimism and the Amazon jungle don't mix. But at that time Ash hadn't been aware of the dangers, hadn't known that hundreds of people disappear in the Amazon every year. To him the jungle was just a place adventurers went to find gold and missionaries went to save souls. He hadn't thought of people dying there, of Luke dying there.

Three years. Few could survive in the jungle three days, let alone three years. But people were made of memories, and it was hard to give up, hard to let go when almost all of Ash's memories included Luke.

Like the day he'd ditched school and spent the afternoon pitching pennies in the alley behind Stubbie's Pool Hall. It was his birthday, and by thirteen Ash had learned not to win too much at a time because if you do, you get jumped on the way home, get your ass kicked.

The wind tunneled down the alley, tugging his hair, licking up his spine, up the back of the flight jacket he'd admired for so long at the Salvation Army store. He'd even considered swiping it, but then for some weird reason the lady who ran the place just gave it to him. It was a little big, but it was the first thing he'd ever worn and liked, first article of clothing he'd ever paid much attention to.

The air smelled of diesel exhaust left by the slush-covered New York City buses. Sewer steam rose from manholes in the middle of the street.

Ash blew on his fingers, more for good luck than to warm them. He had his lucky Lincoln penny. Jerking his head, he tossed a lank strand of dark hair from his eyes, aimed, then pitched the coin, his bony wrist protruding from a shoved-up sleeve. The shiny copper circle arched and spun, catching the light before it hit the brick building and fell to the greasy asphalt.

"All right!" Ash hooted, arm bent, shaking a clenched fist. When he was hot, he was hot. And he wanted to make enough money to get the red Swiss army knife he'd spotted at the pawnshop.

He needed only one more buck when some jerk yelled, "Cheat!"

Everybody cheated, but it was a bad thing when you

got caught. Suddenly fists were flying, knuckles popping, blood splattered from noses. Ash was knocked back against a metal garbage can, sending it and him careening into the wall, the alley revolving sickeningly around him. Rough hands felt inside his jacket, riffled through his pants pockets. Feet pounded away.

Later Ash opened his eyes to find Luke bending over him, his hair combed and Brylcreemed, trousers ironed.

"Took my damn money," Ash muttered up at him. Then he realized he'd never seen Luke in this part of town before. "What're you doin' here?"

"Looking for you," Luke said with wry concern. "You cut school again." He pressed something into Ash's hand. "Happy birthday, little brother," he said, grinning.

In Ash's palm was a red Swiss army knife.

chapter
six

Corey picked up the photograph of the two boys, now noticing that the older boy had his hand on the younger one's shoulder. She turned the picture over. On the back, in cramped, sharp handwriting, were their names:

Lucas Adams, Asher Adams
East End Home for Boys

She turned the picture back over, feeling a poignant sadness. *A family portrait.* She thought about the pain she'd seen in Ash's eyes before he walked into the jungle, and with a jolt she realized she'd wanted to wrap her arms around him, comfort him. She had always been too sensitive, she quickly reminded herself as she put the picture back on the cluttered dresser and sat down on the edge of the bed.

When Mike Jones had mentioned Lucas Adams, the name had struck a chord. She'd never been one to avidly watch the news, but Lucas Adams's story had caught her attention because of the way reporters and newscasters had romanced it by comparing his disappearance to that of Dr. Livingstone. And if memory served her right, Lucas Adams had been a philanthropist known for his work with the poor.

She didn't know what to think of Ash, a man who obstinately clung to the gossamer hope of finding a brother who had been written off as dead by everyone else. Did that make him crazy like Mike Jones said? Or brazenly stubborn? She knew only that most people would have given up a long time ago.

The sound of Mike Jones's departing plane faded to silence, yet she lingered in the bedroom, feeling nervous about facing Ash after what had happened outside. She felt like an intruder, having just witnessed something she had no business seeing.

Corey had been in the small bedroom for half an hour when through the closed door came a series of muffled slams.

Ash was back.

Corey was familiar with his quest for food, having observed his banging and stalking of kitchen cupboards the previous night, after which he had presented her with a concoction of macaroni and ketchup.

Well, she had a report to write, and the sooner it was done, the better. She put on a pair of cotton socks and her white Nikes, then picked up her notebook, took a deep breath, and opened the door.

She passed another small bedroom, probably George Dupree's. That left the combined kitchen-living area and the wide front porch. The structure was more like a rough river cabin than a house, except it wasn't claustrophobic because of all the huge, mosquito-net-covered windows.

"Have a seat, Lily," Ash said when she hesitated in the kitchen doorway.

So, it was still "Lily." Why had she thought he would be subdued and humble after what had occurred outside?

He seemed to have a talent for forgetting things, a sort of selective amnesia, willfully blocking out anything he wanted to ignore. It still galled her that he had dismissed that little episode at the pit so lightly.

"I wish you'd quit calling me that," she told him, unable to keep the irritation from her voice.

"What? Lily? I kinda like it. It suits you."

"Thanks."

"Not Lily as in Lily-Libber. That was yesterday. Now I think of you more like the flower that grows in the jungle. The Amazon lily. Delicate and fragile."

Was he getting poetic on her? She, who had always prided herself on being able to tune into people fairly easily, was having a hard time figuring him out.

"I've been meaning to do a little cleaning," Ash said when he saw her looking around the cluttered room for an empty chair. "Just haven't gotten around to it."

It was obvious a couple of bachelors lived there. The place looked as if they had moved in but never finished unpacking. Pans were stacked on the white enamel gas stove; cardboard boxes full of canned and boxed food sat on the kitchen counter. There were no curtains, not so much as a throw rug, not a single decoration on a wall. The only furniture was a round, wood-topped table with loosely wrapped bamboo legs and four equally frayed chairs. In one corner were stacks of newspapers and thick blue books she recognized as medical journals, several on tropical diseases.

Actually, the place was reminiscent of the cargo area of Ash's plane. Some of the junk, like the baseball and glove, she recognized. Obviously, he'd gotten really industrious and dragged some of the stuff out of the plane and tossed it on the kitchen floor.

He picked up a stack of magazines off a chair.

"George is a *Mad* magazine freak," he explained, looking around for a place to deposit them.

"George?" Who was he trying to fool? She'd seen Alfred E. Newman's face grinning up at her from the table in the air-taxi building, and she didn't think Mike Jones had left it there.

"Well, I am too," he admitted. "It's the only way to be sure of getting unbiased news." He found an empty space on the floor against one wall and dropped the armload of literature.

"Better not put that in your report. It probably wouldn't look good. Tell 'em we read things like *Newsweek* and *Time.*" He pulled up the round-seated bamboo chair and gave it a quick experimental shake before indicating that it was safe for her to sit on.

He had shaved. The blue-black stubble that had made his cheeks appear slightly full was now gone, revealing a well-structured face with a slashing indentation below each cheekbone. Wet hair was combed to lie untrimmed and shaggy against the back of his tan neck. He was wearing a green T-shirt, sleeves cut off. Across his broad chest was the silhouette of a plane, straight-on view. Above that, in faded black letters, were the words: KEY WEST SAFARIS, AIR OR LAND ADVENTURES. His jeans were just as torn and faded as the ones he'd worn yesterday.

"So you decided not to leave with Jones. Good idea. When I was in first grade there were a couple kids who used to spend their time sitting around pulling the legs off flies and eating paste. I always wondered what kind of person they'd turn into. Now I know. Jones would sell his own grandmother for a buck. The guy's a leech. Instead of torturing flies, he takes bored rich people to Amazon villages so they can stare and gawk at the natives, treat them like freaks at a side show."

Ash slammed two cups down on the table, then went back to the cupboard and looked inside. "I hate to tell you, but George is on this fiber kick. We've got 100%

Bran, Bran Buds, and Fiber-All. A good representation of one of the food groups, but which one? Is wood pulp a food group?"

She put her elbows on the table, chin on her fists. "I think cereal belongs to the bread and grain group."

"Ah, here's something straight from the health food store. Cap'n Crunch. So, what'll it be? Bran? Or the captain?"

A smile tugged at the corners of her mouth. "I'll go with the Cap'n Crunch." She flipped open her notebook, thinking that she would ask him some questions while they ate.

"Wise choice. It's a new box, so it might not have any bugs in it yet, and it shouldn't be too soggy. And look at this." He tapped the picture on the back of the box. "A glow-in-the-dark compass inside."

"Fascinating. That should come in handy when you're having trouble navigating."

He laughed and nodded. "That's pretty good." He slammed the box on the table, then strode to another cupboard and came back with two bowls, bowls that had been margarine tubs in their previous lives. "It's a good thing you're a farm girl, because we're having warm goat's milk." He gave her a spoon and a can of orange juice, then plopped down across from her.

"Admiring my tattoo, I see."

She hadn't realized she was staring at it again. She looked from his arm to the faded orange on the juice can. "I . . . ah—" She never had been a good liar.

"There's an interesting story behind it." He opened the cereal box, poured some in her bowl, then his. "One I think you'll appreciate." Next he poured the goat's milk, straight from a half-gallon milking bucket. "It happened about two years ago. I woke up in this seedy hotel in Rio. It had flying roaches as big as bats. Anyway, I couldn't remember where I'd been, or how I'd gotten to the hotel." With an opener he punched a V in the juice can, then poured the juice into the cups. "I was halfway home before I noticed the damn tattoo."

He was kidding, wasn't he? She had the sinking feeling he wasn't. And she didn't know if she should laugh or cry.

"The only thing I halfway remembered was this strange party. Everybody had a bingo card, and there was a guy in a white linen suit calling out numbers. You'll never guess what happened if you got a bingo."

"What?" she asked innocently.

"You got to get it on with one of the caller's lovely assistants."

Corey looked down at the cereal in her bowl. It was starting to get soggy.

Ash wagged his spoon at her. "Don't *you* ever get that drunk, Lily. Or you might wake up and find a damn tattoo on your arm. Or worse, you might find yourself playing bingo with a bunch of strangers." He leaned closer. "Never play bingo with strangers."

She sunk her spoon into the cereal.

"You want to know what happened if two people got a bingo at the same time?"

"No." She looked up at him, eyes flashing. *"No."*

He shrugged, then took another bite of cereal while she told herself to calm down. He was making all of this up just to get a rise out of her. The whole story was ludicrous.

"I almost got the tattoo removed last time I was in the States, but then I decided, what the hell? The natives really get a bang out of it."

The Cap'n Crunch and goat's milk tasted awful. But then, maybe it wasn't the cereal that was creating a bad taste in her mouth.

It occurred to her that there might have been some truth to what Mike Jones had said. A man who drank himself insensible to the point of not knowing he'd gotten a tattoo, who made up wild stories, who smoked vile cigarettes and cigars and lived on a diet that would appall a junk-food junkie *did* need a babysitter. It was amazing he was still alive, let alone in such good physical shape.

She felt sad and had to look away from him, so she focused on a picture that sat crookedly on the cluttered desk beside a multiband radio. It was of a middle-aged couple, the man balding and wearing black-rimmed glasses, the woman dark-haired and tidy.

"George and his wife, Francine," Ash supplied, seeing the direction of Corey's gaze. "I should probably say ex-wife, but they never could make themselves sign the divorce papers. She just couldn't take it here, and George is too dedicated to leave, even for her."

"So she lived here?" Corey jumped at the chance to change the conversation to something normal.

"For a couple months. It's a hard life, especially for a woman. It's not exactly the American dream of a three-bedroom house with a two-car garage. Anybody who stays here long ends up with malaria, jungle rot, or a belly full of amoebas. Or if you're really lucky, you get all three. Disease just comes with the territory, like a fringe benefit. It's a bug-infested, disease-ridden rat hole. And you *can* put that in your report."

Yet he stayed.

"Do you have anything to do with the operation?"

Ash had finished eating, and now he leaned back in his chair. "Flying. George can't fly worth a damn. He takes off and lands like a gooney bird. Scares the hell out of me."

He reached across the table for a pack of cigarettes, then let the chair legs slam to the floor. "The biggest favor anybody can do for the natives is to leave them alone. They have their own religion, their own customs. Why should white people presume that their way is better, more civilized? I like the Indians the way they are."

"You don't think they should be educated?"

"What for? So they can read a dinner menu? Get off

the bus at the right corner? Fill out a W-4 form? This place wasn't started with the intention of converting these people, only saving their lives."

"I was hoping you might take me to one of the villages. But if you're so against my being here . . ."

Ash lit his cigarette, shook out the match, then flung it in the tuna can that served as an ashtray. "We—George is kind of in a bind. He does need money for drugs and vaccines. When the missionaries and explorers came here, they not only brought their God and guns, they brought their diseases to people who had never even had a cold, which means their immune systems are practically nonexistent. Whole tribes have been wiped out by the twenty-four-hour flu. Paradise lost. So, you see, we do need help, but I would prefer to get it from the Brazilian Indian Foundation. They're interested in preserving life here, not saving souls and dressing the natives in cast-off polyester shirts with button-down collars."

"Does that mean you won't take me to a village?"

He bent forward and stubbed out his cigarette. "If you think you can give a shot without twisting the needle, I'll take you to the Tchikao village and you can help with vaccines. But you better take a bath before we go. Now, don't get all huffy. I'm not saying you *need* a bath, but the bugs won't swarm you if you take one right before we leave. I've got some special soap that'll help. And don't use anything perfumy afterward. Not even deodorant."

"I haven't been told to take a bath since I was five."

"I don't know if it should be called a bath. The cistern's cracked, so there's no rainwater to fill the tub in the bathhouse—we don't have a well. I could haul up river water in a bucket. Or you could just wash in the river, like I did." The last words were clearly a challenge.

She shrugged with affected unconcern. It couldn't be much different from swimming in a farm pond, could it?

"You have to be careful of the *piraiba*," he warned.

"Piraiba?" She was probably walking right into this one.

"It's a tiny fish that swims into various parts of the body. And I don't think I need to tell you which parts. It can only be removed surgically."

"If that's a joke, it's disgusting."

"No joke. Just stay in shallow water, and you'll be fine. And watch out for anacondas. Snakes," he explained.

"I'm familiar with snakes," she told him, her confidence returning. "My father taught me how to pick up and hold snakes when I was a child. Even poisonous ones."

"You haven't picked up a snake like this. I've seen anacondas sixty feet long and as big around as a telephone pole. I know a guy who claims to have seen one eighty feet long."

"You've got to be kidding."

He shook his head, and she hoped the queasiness she was feeling in her stomach didn't show on her face. Was he just trying to scare her? She thought longingly of the bathtub, but she wouldn't back down now.

"Just keep your eyes open. They're easy to spot."

"I'm sure they are." It would be like taking a bath with the Loch Ness monster.

"By the way, I hope you aren't going to wear all that typical tourist garbage. We had this botanist here last year, and he had the whole setup. It looked like he'd just stepped out of a 1950s jungle movie. People come here thinking they should cover up, when just the opposite is true. So, if you packed some cute khaki outfit you picked up at a safari store, leave it here, along with the hiking boots. Just wear those tennis shoes."

"I thought my feet and legs should be protected from brush and snakes."

"Workboots start feeling like ten-pound weights after you've gone a half mile. The stuff you have on is okay."

He pushed his chair back and strode to a corner cupboard, pulled out a caramel-colored towel that Corey suspected had once been white, and tossed it at her. "If it'll make you feel any better, I'll wait nearby."

She stood up, clutching the towel to her chest. "You're not going to watch me take a bath."

"I said *nearby.*" He was standing an arm's length away—near enough for her to see the star pattern in his challenging eyes. "Just close enough to hear you if you scream."

He smiled, and every coherent thought but one fled from her brain. She forgot he was a smart aleck, forgot he got into brawls, forgot he got insensibly drunk, forgot about his tattoo, forgot about the bingo party.

She only knew Asher Adams had dimples. One in each cheek. Why on earth did he have to have dimples? Didn't she have enough to contend with? Didn't somebody up there know she was a sucker for dimples?

"Where is this river?" she asked.

His smile widened, and his dimples deepened.

chapter
seven

It was a shame that little Miss Socialized Medicine's bath had gone without a hitch, Ash thought regretfully as he pushed the plane's fuel mixture to full-rich and throttled forward all the way. It had held all the promise of a great rescue scene.

The plane picked up speed. Out of the corner of his eye Ash could see Corey clutching the edge of her seat. Not a peep out of her, just that aggravatingly small hand white-knuckling the black leather for all it was worth.

Good thing she didn't know the plane required a five-hundred-foot runway. He fought back the smile that hovered at the corner of his mouth. And an even better thing that she didn't know the strip they were tooling down was a mere four-fifty.

The climb had to be fast, and he had to keep the nose low or they could stall out. But the real secret was to eliminate the drag as soon as possible.

Ash would never admit it to anybody, but flying was

his life, the ultimate freedom. No ties, no laws. When you were in a plane, you weren't a part of anything.

They were rapidly approaching the thick stand of trees at the end of the strip hacked from the jungle.

"Get 'er off. Get 'er off," he mumbled to himself, the green barrier beginning to loom a little too close.

The plane lurched and they launched into the sky, the struggling sounds of the oil-burning engine roaring in his ears. Ash quickly flicked a switch, simultaneously bringing in the landing gear and reducing the drag, the floor shuddering under his feet. When it looked as if they were going to smash into the wall of trees, the craft surged upward again, the belly barely kissing the swaying treetops.

His copilot blew out a long breath. "Ever thought about making your strip longer?"

"That would take all the fun out of it."

She shot him a rueful glance before leaning forward to take some pictures out the front window. Ash drew his gaze away from her, back to the horizon.

He'd been feeling guilty about the unchaste thoughts he'd been having. Lusting after Corey McKinney seemed a little too much like lusting after Joan of Arc. If only that pit business hadn't happened, then he wouldn't have such vivid, hot memories of her body lying so damn sweetly under his. To him the whole experience had been a little like the first time he'd soloed. What a rush! Or the time lightning had struck a few feet from him.

And what had he done? Instead of enjoying a little bungle in the jungle, he'd gotten up and walked away. Sometimes he couldn't figure himself out.

Damn George and his bright ideas. Ash had been against this whole thing from the beginning. He didn't like to beg alms from anybody, and the last thing they needed was a bunch of holy rollers butting in. Just what he thought would happen, happened. He was turning into a damn babysitter. Well, she had to be made aware that a stroll in the jungle wasn't a stroll in Pleasantville.

She didn't belong here. Not with the kind of skin the strong Amazon sun loved to devour. She belonged in her sleepy little town, sitting on a white porch swing, making small talk with any neighbors who happened by.

And no, he told himself sternly, he wouldn't have casual sex with Miss Small Town America, because it wouldn't be casual to her. Females, especially *her* type, thought about sex differently than guys. She wouldn't be content to have a few hours of fun, then forget about it. Afterward, she'd go around flogging herself and wearing a hair shirt. He didn't need that kind of thing on his conscience. He had enough to worry about. All he had to do was forget about how soft her skin had felt under his hands, how great her legs—

"It's like one of my grandmother's crazy quilts," Corey said, interrupting his hot-blooded thoughts.

Cripes. He'd been thinking about how great her legs had felt locked around him, and she was thinking about a damn quilt. That was their whole problem. They were running on two completely different tracks—on two completely different continents.

"What looks like a quilt?" What the hell was she talking about?

"The treetops. They look like a crazy quilt. It's a quilt made of odd-shaped fabric scraps."

Great. She had a grandmother who made quilts. It didn't surprise him. Mentally he placed the grandmother on the porch swing next to Corey.

"I always thought they looked like green cauliflower, myself." Put that in your poetry notebook. He took out a cigarette and started to light it, then remembered that smoking bugged her. With an exasperated sound he stuffed the cigarette back in his T-shirt pocket. It was pretty bad when a guy couldn't even smoke in his own plane. Good thing he'd never gotten married. He couldn't imagine having a wife harping at him for every trivial thing. Why is it women think it's their God-given duty to go forth and civilize, to the point of making life a damn stiff collar?

Five minutes later they were flying over a cluster of haystack houses set in the middle of a cleared area. The footpaths that fanned out in every direction always made Ash think of veins. "Look down there—" He pointed. "See that landing strip?"

"Landing strip? But . . . it's full of stumps. . . ."

"Yeah, I know." He gave a pained laugh. "The Tchikao tribe built it so I could land closer to their village. But they didn't know the stumps had to be taken out. And I haven't been able to break the news to them."

Ash knew it had to have taken them weeks to hack out that path with their primitive tools—tools far too crude to even begin to tackle the remaining massive tree stumps. What really hurt was the way Barari had looked when he told him about the strip. The chief had been just proud as hell.

Another five minutes and they were landing on a dried riverbed that ran parallel to a tributary of the Amazon. The propeller had barely stopped turning when Corey opened her door and stepped out, keeping a tight hold on the camera slung around her neck.

"Don't get out of my sight," Ash told her, handing down the stainless steel medical case.

"Are the natives dangerous?"

He had to admit it—she had guts, and she was good at hiding her fear. But more than once he'd detected the barest flicker of it in her soft eyes. And more than once he'd wondered what she was afraid of the most—the jungle, or him.

"There are hundreds of different tribes in the jungle. Some not very friendly. But the tribe we're visiting today, the Tchikao, haven't learned to hate white people. Not yet anyway. It's the jungle you'll have to worry about."

He picked up the army-green backpack, then, bent at the waist, he stooped through the doorway and onto the wing. "Never take the jungle lightly. Every year people come into the Amazon"—he grasped the door latch—"and every year even less come out."

Like Luke. His fingers tightened on the handle until his knuckles showed white, then he slammed the door shut. "If you get lost, you'd just become another jungle statistic. The Brazilian government wouldn't even bother to look for you," he added with bitterness. With a fluid movement he jumped down beside her.

She was staring at him, watching him with those curious, animal eyes of hers. He was surprised and puzzled by the pain he saw there. And for a flashing of a millisecond, he felt a strange shock of recognition, like when you realize the fleeting glimpse of a stranger in a store glass is really your own reflection.

He knew she was curious about Luke, but Ash didn't bare his soul to anybody, sure as hell not to some do-gooder. Deep down he knew that someday he was going to have to admit to himself that Luke was dead. But he just wasn't ready.

He took the medical case from Corey. In a few days she would be gone. And when she returned to the States, he didn't want his brother's story to be featured in her Jungle Adventure Presentation. He didn't want her talking about Luke to a bunch of strangers, strangers who wouldn't give a damn. And why should they?

When a guy reads the obituaries, he doesn't get all choked up over somebody he never knew. Yet . . . it always made Ash feel funny to read those cold, impersonal words, knowing that somebody, somewhere, was crying his heart out over a name that was being skimmed with detachment by thousands of indifferent pairs of eyes.

Maybe Jones is right. Maybe I am going nuts. . . .

"What about the natives?" Corey asked. "I would think they would be helpful in finding somebody who was missing in the jungle."

"Oh, they *like* to help. That's the whole problem. You

can't believe half of what they say. Lies are their entertainment. The bigger the better. And they're always trying to outdo one another. Also, they have no perception of time. If they say they've seen somebody, it could have been years ago."

He adjusted his cap and looked sternly down at her. "So, just remember, if you want to get back to Dudley Do-right and Sleepyville, don't wander off."

He turned into the jungle, foliage brushing his broad shoulders as he went.

"Do you always make fun of people?" Corey asked, coming up behind him.

"Habit. Purely habit."

Dudley. *I'll bet he's boring as hell,* Ash mused. Probably one of those generic kind of guys you couldn't quite remember when he wasn't around, whose face just became kind of a blurry smear. Why was it those kind seemed to attract women?

"You don't even know him," she argued. "And for that matter, you don't even know *me.*"

So, his name-calling was getting to her. Well, he wasn't going to quit just for Corey McKinney. Name-calling was a fine craft he'd been cultivating since grade school. And he *did* know all about prom queens like her, and had learned to steer clear of them a long time ago.

"I've got your number," he shot back over his shoulder. "You had the traditional church-on-Sunday, Kool-Aid-and-homemade-cookie kind of childhood. I'll bet you took piano lessons and ballet lessons and singing lessons. In the summer you played on a wide front porch with your dolls."

He stopped to hold a huge palm leaf aside for her, waiting until she was even with him before letting go.

For a second it seemed as if they were enclosed in a cocoon of thick green fronds, the musky peat smell of the jungle saturating the air around them. Some people found the heavy scent oppressive, but Ash liked it.

Behind her was a jagua tree. Witch doctors claimed its fruit was an aphrodisiac. Around the tree's trunk was a vine referred to as soul vine, its shiny leaves producing a narcotic similar to opium.

"Stuffed animals," Corey stated, looking up at him, directly into his eyes. There was a smile in her voice.

"Stuffed animals?" he asked blankly.

"On the porch." Her voice was slightly breathless from hurrying to keep up with him, and he made a mental note to take it slower.

"I didn't play with dolls. I played with stuffed animals."

She was smiling now, and she was near enough for him to see the golden tips of her long lashes, the light spray of freckles across her nose. Some of her hair had come loose from the rubber band at the back of her head, curling around her face like a halo.

And he wanted her like hell.

Ash decided right then and there that he'd been in the jungle, away from female companionship, for too long.

His scar was itching. Sweat was running down his back like a river, washing away every trace of insect-repellent soap. His shirt was clinging to him like a leech, and the bugs were eating him alive. And he still wanted her. Right here. Right now.

"And you—what kind of childhood did you have?" she asked naively.

He thought about how she had grown up, and he thought about how he had grown up, and the cynic in him resurfaced.

Miss Norman Rockwell wouldn't be able to fathom the kind of childhood he'd had. If he told her about sleeping on city streets and in abandoned buildings, about skipping school to gamble, she wouldn't believe him. He could tell she didn't believe half of what he said anyway.

"Let's just say, if I'd lived in your neighborhood instead of New York City, I wouldn't have been invited to your birthday party." He turned and continued walking.

When Corey and Ash stepped into the clearing, they were immediately surrounded by a group of men, women, and children, all with mahogany skin, ebony eyes, and perfect white teeth. Their straight, gleaming caps of coal-black hair were trimmed neatly into what Corey would be able to describe only as bowl cuts. Around their necks they wore string after string of necklaces consisting of nut shells, feathers, beads, and empty shotgun shells. And that was all they wore.

Corey now knew the true meaning of the phrase "out of your element." She was living it.

Instead of being embarrassed by the nudity of the Indians, she felt awkward and out of place, like somebody who had worn an evening gown to a beach party.

Ash was watching her, gauging her reaction. "Feeling overdressed?" His aviator sunglasses hung over the sweat-soaked neck of his T-shirt, and she could see the slight indentation they had left on the bridge of his nose.

He slipped an arm around her slim shoulders, a familiarity she would normally have rebelled against, but now the tingling warmth of his body was welcome, giving her the security she needed.

"I told you, the less you wear in the jungle, the better off you are," he reminded her. "Just wait till the soles of your feet start peeling, and you get gall under your arms. Then you'll know what I'm talking about."

"I can hardly wait," she murmured unenthusiastically.

He gave her shoulder a brotherly pat, then dropped his arm. "As for myself," he began blandly, "I usually strip down to a loincloth, but for your sake I left it at home this trip."

She couldn't stop the irritated clicking of her tongue

as she watched him saunter away. Here they were, in the middle of the jungle, surrounded by primitive tribesmen, and he couldn't be serious, not even when the situation called for it. Demanded it. But she wasn't surprised. Nothing about him would surprise her anymore.

Her irritation slowly changed to curiosity as she watched the scene that was unfolding before her.

One of the native men, face open and friendly, eyes black, alert, and intelligent, was talking to Ash in a deep, guttural tongue. The pilot shot a glance at Corey, shook his head, then further surprised her by answering the man in the same strange language. When a small boy darted up, Ash bent down and swung the child onto his shoulder while he continued to talk to the gesturing man.

What on earth could the two men have in common to talk about so intently?

Corey had expected to find the natives suspicious, shy, and unresponsive. Instead, the Tchikao were acting as if a favorite relative had come to visit. The very friendliness, the very calm amicableness of the atmosphere, the very ease of Ash's interaction with the native man and child, didn't fit the typical mental image Corey had of a white man meeting primitive Amazon Indians. Of course, Asher Adams was by no means typical.

As she watched, Ash laughed deeply, then set the boy back on the ground. The child, who was now wearing Ash's New York Yankees baseball cap, skipped away to join his playmates.

Ash made a remark in a dry voice, and the man answered, the conversation quickly becoming seasoned with varying degrees of snickers and snorts, until their laughter grew to the point that the two men were practically supporting each other.

Ugly suspicion as to the subject of their conversation sifted into Corey's mind, their furtive glances in her direction making her think of two schoolboys exchanging vulgar jokes. She crossed her arms in front of her and shifted her weight to her other foot.

Ash must have recalled her existence, because he and the native finally stopped their clowning and came over to her.

"This is Barari," Ash said by way of introduction, traces of laughter still in his voice. "He's the chief of the Tchikao tribe." Then he rattled off some words to Barari, the only English one being "Lily."

"What were you two talking about?" she asked after she and the chief finished nodding and smiling to each other.

"You don't want to know," Ash assured her.

"But I do."

That was all the persuasion it took. "Well, he asked if I'd taken you to . . . Ah, these people are very earthy, you have to understand. He asked if I'd taken you to . . . ah . . ."

Ash tilted his head back and gazed skyward, hand on his chin in exaggerated thoughtfulness. "How can I put this delicately . . . ?"

Corey mentally bet that Asher Adams had never put anything delicately in his life.

He looked squarely at her, humor lurking in the depths of those unusual eyes of his. "Barari asked if I'd taken you to copulate with and be the bearer of my children," he finally stated, seeming quite pleased with his choice of words.

Corey glared at him. "Ha, ha, ha."

"Don't worry. I told him no."

"Then what was so hilarious?"

"When he asked me why I hadn't taken you to—"

She gave him a hard look, firmly halting the repeat of his earlier statement.

"Well, I told him you were too short for me. And *he* said it wouldn't matter, not as long as we were both lying down."

She sucked in her breath, eyes shooting sparks.

But it seemed Ash was just getting warmed up. "Then Barari said that even though the sun has faded your skin and hair—" Ash moved closer to lightly trace a finger along one of her flushed cheeks.

The flame that shot through her was red-hot anger—wasn't it?

"He said that wouldn't matter either, as long as there was no sun or moon in the sky. Or if I kept my eyes closed."

She smacked his hand away, dimly aware of the burst of half-smothered giggles from behind them. "Oh, *grow up!* I realize it was my choice to come here," she hissed, "but I didn't realize I'd be accompanied by an irresponsible smart aleck spouting bathroom humor."

"Yeah." He sighed with exaggerated pride. "I can be a real potty mouth."

He was laughing at her. Straight white teeth in a tan face. And those damn dimples. But even they couldn't save him this time.

"I knew you wouldn't think it was funny. You know what your problem is?" he asked. "You don't have any sense of humor."

"That's not true," she protested sharply. "It takes a certain kind of mentality to laugh at juvenile vulgarity."

"What do you laugh at? What do *you* think is funny?" In his voice was a dare.

"Not *Mad* magazine."

The natives were inching closer, seemingly fascinated by the dressed, arguing white people.

"The Three Stooges. Have you ever laughed at the Three Stooges?" he asked.

"I . . . well . . ."

"Aha! See? You have. Admit it."

"This is ridiculous."

Corey became aware of the natives closing in on her

and the fact that she alone seemed to be the focus of their very deliberate attention.

The argument was forgotten. "What do they want?" She inched slightly closer to Ash. "Why are they all staring at me like that?"

"I doubt if they've ever seen an angry white woman before. And you're a double treat. An angry white woman with blond hair. Luke had blond hair, but it wasn't nearly as light, and it was straight, not curly."

Corey froze as Ash reached out to slowly thread his fingers through the loose tendrils of hair around her face. A crease formed between his gray eyes when he found a tangle, which he carefully fingered until it was smooth.

She was poised to step back, when she noticed the rapt attention in the faces around them. The Indians had fallen silent, as if breathlessly anticipating the pilot's next move.

Quite obviously Ash was a ham as well as a clown. He turned to his audience and lifted the silky strand of Corey's hair so it caught the light. Then he said something in that strange, guttural language, and the crowd let out a unanimous sigh.

"What did you say this time?" she demanded, bracing herself for more of his childish insults.

"Just something from an old Tchikao legend."

"What?"

For a fraction of a second Corey had the extreme pleasure of seeing Asher Adams looking uncomfortable. Then his expression calmed, became neutral.

"The Indians have a legend about a goddess with hair spun from moonbeams. But only special moonbeams. Only ones that have journeyed through the tree branches and vines to finally warm the jungle floor. I said that the goddess's hair must have looked like yours."

There. He'd done it to her again.

Just when she was sure he needed his knuckles rapped with a wooden ruler, he said something nice.

Before she could think of an adequate reply, a native man drew Ash to the edge of the crowd. They talked briefly in quiet tones. The next thing Corey knew, Ash was disappearing into one of the huts, deserting her, leaving her surrounded by pairs of curious black eyes.

But then, seconds later, Ash stuck his head out of the hut. "Corey—come here," he called sharply. "And bring the case."

Miracle of miracles. He'd called her Corey. But she had also detected the underlying urgency in his voice, so all she could do was apologetically wade through the throng of people, case in one hand, camera steadied with the other.

After her eyes adjusted to the dimness inside the hut, she could see an Indian woman lying on a straw pallet. Ash was kneeling beside her.

"This is Para," he told her. "She had an accident a couple of weeks ago, and now her leg's infected."

Corey moved closer to set the case on the ground near him while Ash rapped out some rapid-fire Tchikao, causing the faces in the doorway to scatter, leaving only the native man standing anxiously behind his wife. He said something to Ash in a quiet tone, his words faltering, his breath catching in his throat.

Ash's answering voice was low-pitched and soothing, all trace of the clown gone.

He looked up at Corey. "He feels guilty because he didn't come to get me. But I told him infections can set in fast."

He snapped open the case, removed the lid from a bottle of alcohol, and began pouring it onto his hands.

"What are you doing?" Corey whispered with frank dread.

"Giving her a tetanus shot."

Bottles clinked and paper rustled, then he was filling a small syringe. He gave the woman a shot, then rummaged through the case once more. "Then I'm going to cut the wound open and drain the infection."

"You're no doctor." Corey knelt down beside him on the earth-packed floor.

"Do you think these people give a rip whether or not I have a diploma or have taken the Hippocratic oath?" he asked as he casually filled another syringe.

"Have you ever done anything like this before?" She couldn't disguise the anxiety in her voice.

"I took a correspondence course in taxidermy when I was fifteen," he said with exasperation. He returned the bottle of anesthetic to the case, then looked at her levelly. "Now, are you going to disinfect your hands and help me, or not?"

"Taxidermy," she sputtered. How could he make jokes now?

"Lighten up," he complained. "If it'll make you feel any better, I've had all the basic emergency medical training stuff."

Emergency training stuff? What was that supposed to mean? Considering the source, it could mean a boy scout merit badge.

She mumbled something about not liking the idea of his playing doctor.

"Either I play doctor—see if there's any injectable combiotic in there—or she dies from blood poisoning."

Corey knew Ash was right. One look was enough to make her worry that they were too late. The infection might have already spread through her bloodstream.

While Corey searched through the case for combiotic, Ash talked to the sick woman. How could a voice as rough as his sound so compelling and soothing all of a sudden? How did he do it?

Corey looked up to see that the woman had visibly relaxed. And somewhere in the last few minutes Ash had made the transition from class clown to doctor with great bedside manner.

In the dim mustiness of the primitive Tchikao hut, lethargic flies clung drunkenly to sweaty skin. Ash poised the scalpel above the wounded leg while Para calmly watched him with trusting eyes.

Corey saw Ash's hand tremble slightly, saw the taut rigidity in the broad shoulders that filled his sleeveless T-shirt. Cutting human flesh was a hard thing to do, and she doubted she could ever do it under any circumstances.

She heard him take a deep, steadying breath, saw his hand still and become sure.

"Hope you have a lot of gauze ready. This is gonna blow like Mount St. Helens."

Spoken like a dedicated surgeon. She brought the gauze closer.

The scalpel came down, and Corey was distantly aware that Ash was left-handed, and that the hand wielding the surgeon's blade was attached to the very arm that blatantly shouted: BORN TO RAISE HELL. There had to be some symbolism there somewhere.

When it was all over, Corey gathered up the blood- and infection-soaked bandages before they could draw more flies.

"We'll leave some disinfectant, gauze, and antibiotic tablets with her, and just hope she doesn't take them all in one day," Ash told her as he covered the leg with a loose bandage, then gave Para a shot of the combiotic Corey had prepared.

"Nice work, Nurse Kildare," he stated evenly. "You're a better assistant than George. He always gets queasy on me and ends up running outside to puke."

Corey could feel the sweat on her upper lip, the perspiration on her forehead, escaped tendrils of limp hair clinging like itchy seaweed to the back of her neck. And there was Ash, just as sweaty, squatting on his heels, one knee through his faded jeans.

She'd never known anybody like him before, and she felt an overwhelming curiosity. She had accused him of acting like a child, and she had believed him when he told her he had nothing to do with the reserve, that he only flew for George Dupree. But it wasn't true.

What he was, was a fraud.

She felt ashamed of her pomposity, ashamed of her desire for professionalism. Ash's method was better. Except it wasn't a method at all. He was just being himself.

"What are you smiling at?" he demanded suspiciously.

"You. I'm smiling at you. At you and your name-calling, and your complaints about social workers and do-gooders. You led me to believe that you weren't involved with these people, that you just flew for George. When you are a part of them. When you're a humanitarian." Her words surprised her even as she spoke them.

He looked stunned, then snapped the case shut with a loud click. "The hell I am!"

chapter
eight

Corey snapped the metal case shut. It had taken a little less than three hours to give vaccinations and treat an array of disorders ranging from infected cuts to skin funguses. With a weary gesture she pushed loose tendrils of damp hair from her face, then stood up, legs stiff and cramped from crouching for so long.

No wonder the Tchikao were afflicted with so many parasitic skin diseases, she thought as she slapped at yet another blood-sucking mosquito, hoping the malaria tablets she was taking would keep her free of the sickness. The Indians needed so many little things. They should have nets over their doors; insect spray should be used inside the huts.

Lazy cigarette smoke floated her direction. "We've been invited to stay for a little wingding," Ash announced. "A wedding ceremony." He had his cap back on, his sunglasses folded over the frayed neck of his T-shirt.

A wedding ceremony. Corey couldn't believe her good

luck. "I'd love to stay," she said, unable to hide her eagerness. Then her smile dimmed. "What's wrong?"

"I have to warn you, these things start out tame enough but can end up getting pretty wild. But we don't have any choice. They'd take it as an insult if we didn't accept their invitation." He took one last drag off his cigarette, then flicked it to the ground just as a small form darted between them.

"Beat it, you little outlaw."

Before Ash could stop him, one of the youngsters picked up the still-smoldering cigarette and took a knowledgeable puff.

"Come on. Fork it over."

A chorus of childish giggles could be heard coming from a nearby hut as Ash pried the cigarette from the boy's tight grip. Undaunted by the reprimand, the child skipped off to join his buddies.

Corey was still worrying about what Ash might define as "wild." She had known him less than twenty-four hours, yet it had been long enough for her to realize that what was wild to Asher Adams could very well be something totally unthinkable to her. "How wild is wild?" she ventured.

He rubbed the back of his neck. "Well, for one thing, they like to get drunk, then play this game, it's a lot like football, only rougher. And they don't consider it a success unless they break some bones and bash a few skulls. I made the mistake of telling them I preferred baseball. Of course I had to explain about baseball. Next thing I knew, they were cutting a tree branch for a bat, and using a fist-size rock for a ball." He shook his head. "What a bloody mess. They can't comprehend a sport unless the objective is bloodshed."

Just then an excited young man came up and grabbed him by the arm. "This chap's the bridegroom!" Ash tossed the words back to Corey as the native dragged him toward an open, thatched structure near the edge of the clearing. Ash motioned for Corey to follow. "Come on."

Soon she was sitting cross-legged in the shade of the thatched building while Ash lounged on the ground a few feet to her left. A smiling native woman thrust a flat, tortilla-like substance into Corey's hand, followed by a black clay cup of amber-colored liquid.

Ash held up the flat piece of bread he'd been given. "This is *beiju*—their mainstay."

Corey looked at the food in her hand, then took a timid bite. It was chewy but mercifully tasteless. The only problem was that as she chewed, the piece of bread became tougher, taking on the combined consistencies of beef jerky and gum. She tried not to think of the conditions under which it had most likely been prepared, or what kind of rating a U.S. food inspector would give a Tchikao kitchen.

Ash didn't seem to have any qualms about thoroughly enjoying his role as pampered guest. He was leaning back, one elbow on the ground, the hand holding the half-finished *beiju* dangling over his bent knee. "They make it from poisonous manioc root," he informed her, talking with his mouth full.

Corey's jaw stopped as she stared at him.

"Take it easy." He lazily waved his hand, as if to say eating poison was nothing. "It's been boiled. For some reason, boiling takes out the toxins."

"And what's this?" Doubtfully, Corey looked down at her cup, talking with the bite of bread safely lodged at the side of her mouth.

"Kasili. It's not too bad. Reminds me of warm beer."

She shooed the fly from the rim and took a suspicious sip, the cup tasting like damp clay against her lips. The drink was tolerable anyway. She used it to wash down the *beiju.*

"All their pottery is black," Ash told her. "They say it reflects the spaces between the stars."

Corey looked closer at the cup in her hand, noting its primitive, simplistic beauty. "What a lovely belief. How is it you know their language so well?"

He shrugged. "Barari helped me. It wasn't too tough. They don't have a very big vocabulary. What do you think of the *kasili?*"

"It's really not too bad."

"It's kinda weird how they get it to ferment." Head tipped back, Ash drained his drink. The woman snatched up the empty cup, chattering and motioning for a younger girl, obviously telling her to hurry and refill it.

"Instead of using yeast, they use bacteria from their own saliva."

Corey had just finished the last swallow.

She glared at him over the rim of her cup, calling him a liar with her eyes. Couldn't he ever be serious? She saw amusement in the electric gray eyes regarding her, saw the laugh lines around the corners of his mouth. He was just getting back at her for calling him a humanitarian.

"It's true." He laughed, accepting the refilled cup from the Tchikao woman.

"They *spit* in it?" She had to know.

"Yeah. Bet your church group doesn't have any recipes that call for a cup of spit."

"No," she said levelly, determined not to let him see her revulsion. It would only amuse him more. Instead, she would show him that she could easily return his crude banter. "I can't say I remember coming across one requiring more than a teaspoon or two."

The glimmer in his eyes brightened, and for a flash of an instant she felt an absurd camaraderie, then his gaze shifted away from her to focus on the people gathered in the clearing. It took a few moments for Corey to realize that the boisterous group had changed, become subdued.

Barari began speaking to the bride and groom. His voice was a chant, and even though Corey couldn't understand what he was saying, there was a melodiousness to his words, a singsong quality that hinted of decades gone, of tradition and beliefs passed down through generations of Tchikao people.

Ash's deep, rasping voice startled her as he leaned close to whisper in her ear. "He's saying that the gods are mighty, but mightier still is the jungle," Ash explained, his breath caressing the skin of her neck. "Now he's going into the story of their creation." He shifted closer, his chest brushing up against her arm. "They believe that in the beginning there was only jungle. Then the son of a bat flew through the darkness and fell in love with the daughter of a *jatoba* tree. Out of this love came the first people. And the jungle was pleased, so it made the man sky fire that lights the day, and the woman sky fire that lights the night."

As she listened, Corey was intensely aware of the life around them, the heartbeat of the jungle. Monkeys chattered, birds squawked, along with the never-ending hum of a billion insects. The man beside her smelled like jungle and the cockpit of an airplane. And she was caught up in the magic.

Barari stopped speaking and there was a unanimous shout and cheer, then everyone started moving back toward the vat of *kasili*. The entire ceremony had lasted no longer than two minutes. Corey now assumed the couple in the center of the clearing were man and wife.

People began to dance to the beat of tomtoms, flutes, and rattles made from gourds and shells. The alcoholic drink flowed freely. Women as well as men puffed enthusiastically on filterless cigarettes, most likely supplied by Ash. Although still magical and mysterious, the mood of the gathering was quickly changing, building to a noisy, confusing frenzy.

Corey was about to suggest they leave, that surely they had stayed long enough to satisfy Amazonian etiquette, when to her distress she found that Ash had silently disappeared. But she hadn't been left unchaperoned. A young

Indian man planted himself in front of her, a cup of *kasili* rigidly extended in his outthrust hand.

Corey smiled uncomfortably and shook a head that was slightly befuddled.

He pushed the drink at her, his voice conveying urgency. Rather than antagonize him, she accepted the cup. Not wishing to imbibe any more of what she now realized was fairly high-proof booze, she merely held it while politely waiting for him to leave.

Instead of leaving, however, he made it fiercely clear that he expected her to drink the vile brew. He was so adamant that she decided she had better drink it before her refusal brought on the censure of the entire tribe. Taking a deep breath, she put the clay cup to her lips and downed the contents, hoping the gag that followed wasn't too obvious.

She thought he would be satisfied, and the whole thing would be over, but she was wrong. After taking the empty cup from her hands, he remained firmly rooted in front of her, his face expectant.

What did he want?

To her further alarm he reached out and pulled her to her feet. Just as Corey was wondering if it would be overreacting to scream at this point, Ash made a well-timed appearance.

"Where have you *been?*" Corey asked in breathless relief, her eyes sidling toward Ash, then back to the young man in front of her. Fortunately he had dropped his hands from her arms, but that was the only move he had made.

"Had to powder my nose," Ash explained casually. He spoke to the Indian, and the young man frowned, then returned an answer in his clipped tongue.

"I don't know what you did, Lily. But for some reason Takari here thinks you're his date for the evening."

"What?"

"And we're not talking about pepperoni pizza followed by a game of miniature golf, followed by a good-night peck on the cheek. This guy's hoping to fondle your horizontal hold."

"Tell him I'm not interested," she ordered, latching on to Ash's upper arm with both her hands. *"Tell him to leave me alone!"*

"That might be a little tough. See, they haven't heard of the ERA here, and women's lib hasn't gotten this far south yet. But I'll see what I can do."

Unconsciously Corey tightened her grip on Ash while he rattled something to the man standing belligerently before them.

Takari shook his head, his face remaining stubborn.

"Maybe he'd be willing to make a trade. You for something of equal value." Ash reached into his T-shirt pocket and pulled out a recently opened cigarette pack, complete with a new book of matches. The native snatched them from him, then shook his head, indicating that the exchange wasn't satisfactory.

"How 'bout a cap?" Ash pointed to the cap slanted back on his head.

That drew another negative response.

"Pair of shades? Come on, they're polarized." Ash blew out his breath in frustration. "You're more valuable than I thought, Lily." Seeming to come to a decision, he dug deeply into the front pocket of his tattered jeans and pulled out a neon-green rabbit's foot, which he dangled temptingly before Takari's slowly responding face.

"Think we got a nibble." Ash spoke with the hushed voice of a fisherman ready to set the hook. Then Takari's expression shuttered closed, causing Ash to let out a loud, disgusted sigh.

"What about my camera?" Corey suggested, silently cursing the note of hysteria she couldn't keep from her voice. "Would he maybe want that?"

Ash shook his head. "He might if it was a Polaroid."

A curious light came into Ash's gray eyes as he looked down to where the front of his shirt was being drawn into a tight ball by Corey's fist. "Whew, Lily! You're a mess. Lighten up, will you?" Carefully, as if the ragged T-shirt were his Sunday best, he untangled her tense, clutching fingers. "You're mangling my shirt."

She hadn't even been aware of what she was doing. Now she focused guiltily on the wrinkled circle she'd left at his chest. "I'm sorry," she mumbled, her gaze climbing to his face.

He was studying her. "Relax." He gave her shoulder an awkward pat. "We'll figure something out." Then his expression changed, as if a surprised thought had suddenly popped into his head. "Hey, you're not lily-white, are you?"

It took a second for her to comprehend the intimacy of his question.

"You are, aren't you?"

She had a quick flash of the times she and Todd had been intimate . . . and the emptiness she'd felt afterward. Before she could choke out a response, Ash continued. "Take it from me—" He let out a gusty sigh. "The loss of one's virginity is completely overrated."

How could he be so crude? Disgust mixed with her fear. Didn't he take this seriously? Did he take anything seriously?

"It's a joke, Lily. A *joke*."

"Ash, please . . ."

He flashed her a sympathetic grin before his face became contemplative, brows furrowed in thought as his eyes focused on some point above her head.

Takari had obviously grown tired of waiting for what he deemed rightfully his. Suddenly he reached out and jerked Corey toward him so that she found herself planted against a painted barrel-shaped chest.

"Ash!" she begged, pleading at him with her eyes.

Beginning to show signs of concern, Ash agitatedly held his hands up. "Okay, okay. Everything's cool. No sweat." He fumbled in his pocket again while Corey tried unsuccessfully to twist away from the Indian's viselike grip.

With obvious reluctance Ash pulled out a red Swiss army knife. Fanning the blades open, he verbally catalogued each accessory. "Here you've got your big spear blade, small pen blade, can opener, regular *and* Phillips screwdrivers, corkscrew—that'll come in real handy for those champagne dinners you're always throwing. Oh, and here's a nail cleaner and fish scaler."

Ash held the paraphernalia-laden knife between his thumb and forefinger. "Beauty of a knife, isn't it?" To demonstrate the largest blade's sharpness, he deftly shaved a small patch of hair from his forearm. Even Corey was impressed.

That must have been the clincher, because Takari let go, forgetting Corey like an old toy at Christmas.

Ash snapped the appendages back into place, then looked from the native's outstretched hand to Corey's relieved, upturned face. "Sure you wouldn't be interested . . . ?" He wagged a finger between the two, indicating that maybe they *might* enjoy each other's company.

Corey glared up at him.

"No. Guess not." Face resigned, Ash slapped the folded knife into Takari's open palm. "There you go, bud."

"I'll pay you for it," Corey promised as the native strode away, head bent, examining his new possession.

Ash's face, as he watched him leave with his knife, was hurt, mournful almost.

Corey couldn't help but feel offended. "For heaven's sake! It's only a knife!" He was acting as if he'd lost a dear friend.

He was quiet for a minute. "Yeah. Guess that's a pretty good trade." One corner of his mouth crooked up, and his voice came out an ugly sneer. "A pocketknife for a lay."

Her anger bubbled. Asher Adams was lacking in one basic thing: human sensitivity. The man was emotionally illiterate, socially retarded. When she spoke, her voice was brittle as glass. "I said I'd pay you back, *in cash*. Believe me, I wouldn't sleep with you if we were the last two people on earth and the continuation of the human race depended on it."

"Let's get out of here," he snapped, ignoring the insult to his male ego. "Before Romeo changes his mind, or you start coming on to some other guy."

Corey opened her mouth to protest, then realized how useless it was to argue with him. To him, being obnoxious and crude was an art form, a way of life. She could never compete against his perfected craft. She was like a child futilely swinging her fists while her adversary safely held her by the head an arm's length away.

chapter
nine

On the way back, Ash's only communication with Corey was an occasional grunt or monosyllabic utterance, which, as far as Corey could tell, had absolutely nothing to do with their immediate situation. His pouting, petulant silence was just fine with her, because she knew by now that whenever he did speak at any length, it was usually something she had absolutely no desire to hear.

By the time they finally reached the plane, Corey had a stitch in her side and a throbbing headache.

Holding her camera so it wouldn't get bumped, she stepped up on the wing, then into the cockpit. After settling in the seat, she located her canvas bag and made a quick search through it until she found a bottle of aspirin. Using stale water from the blue thermos, she managed to wash down two chalky, bitter tablets.

She was screwing the lid back on the thermos when Ash ducked in, put the medical case in the cargo area, then plopped down on the seat beside her. The door slammed, and he jerked the shoulder harness across his chest, latching it with a firm click. Deftly he flicked a series of switches on the dash before pushing the red start button. All it produced was a repetitious grinding sound. He tried again and still the engine wouldn't turn over.

Ash slammed a palm against the control wheel. "Shit!"

She had to wonder if he would ever speak a complete sentence again.

With quick, angry movements, he threw his cap down, unsnapped the seat belt, then shoved his shoulder against the door and ducked back out, muttering something about fuel.

Corey's head was still throbbing, and now her stomach was beginning to churn. Trying to ignore her physical discomfort, she stared glumly ahead while Ash wrestled the engine cover open, then stuck his head inside.

A minute later he was glaring up at her through the bug-splattered windshield as if the whole problem were somehow her fault. "Bring the toolbox here!" he demanded before turning back to the engine.

Elbow high, Corey gave him a clipped salute. The man must be humored. Then, heaving a stoic sigh, she unlatched her seat belt and stood up, leaving her camera on the ledge of the control panel.

With head bent she stepped back to the cargo area. It took quite a bit of foraging to locate the toolbox, but she finally discovered it under the sleeping bag. To her further annoyance, she found that the box weighed a ton. It couldn't have been heavier if it had been filled with lead shot. Like an instrument of torture, or something deliberately devised by Ash for just this very occasion, it banged and bruised the side of her thigh as she struggled out the door with it. Instead of attempting to climb down the wing with the box, she simply gave it a heave. It hit the ground with a loud thud.

Stepping down after it, she said, "Surely we aren't

going to be stuck here, are we?" Her voice held all the icy disapproval of a two-hundred-year-old schoolmarm.

"Look—" Ash strode over to the toolbox, hunkered down, and flicked it open. "I never said I was Sky King, or Indiana Smith, or whatever the hell his name is."

It took her a little while to figure out what he was talking about. When she did, she let out a disdainful snort. "*Jones*," she corrected mockingly. "Indiana Jones."

"So I haven't seen a movie since *Easy Rider*," Ash growled into the toolbox. Finding what he was looking for, he stood up and walked back to the plane. "I need the four-inch extension shaft," was his next command, this one muffled since he hadn't bothered to turn around.

Feeling like strangling him but knowing a dead pilot was no pilot, she knelt down to look into the box. Using a suspicious finger, she nudged aside greasy tools, recognizing a pair of pliers and a couple of screwdrivers. She pulled out a thin, bent piece of metal that was about four inches long.

"This thing?" She held it up for his inspection.

He looked around at her, his lean, hard face registering annoyance and disgust. "No," he bit out. "That's an allen wrench. Cripes, Lily. Don't you know what an extension shaft looks like?"

She abandoned the toolbox to stand up straight. "No." Fingers bent, she coolly examined her cuticles. "It's been quite some time since I overhauled an engine."

He stomped over to her, and she casually looked up from the critical inspection of her nails. There was a smudge across his nose, which somehow belied the ferocity of his anger.

"This"—he picked up a length of steel and held it so close to her eyes that she blinked and drew back—"is an extension shaft. It fits on the socket wrench handle"—he slammed the tools together—"like this." After that thoughtful lesson in mechanics he stomped back to the plane.

She watched him as he leaned into the engine, taking in the way his damp T-shirt clung to the corded muscles of his strong back, the way his hair lay shaggily against his brown neck, begging for a trim.

Too bad he was such a jerk.

Yet she had to be honest with herself—there was something about him that drew her, something about his rasping whiskey voice, about the way it sometimes cracked at the end of a statement that touched her heart. Maternal instinct, she decided. Maternal instinct was what she was feeling for the Peter Pan boy.

A muffled oath brought her out of her daydreaming. "The damn fuel pump's shot."

With a squeaking of metal he slammed the engine cover shut, then tossed the tools back into the box, kicking the lid closed with his foot.

The throbbing in her head hadn't stopped, and Corey was still trying to ignore the peculiar way her stomach felt. All she wanted was to get back to the reserve and lie down. "Can't you fix it?"

He rubbed his hair, jammed his hands into the front pockets of his jeans, looked up at the rapidly dimming sky, then blew out a long, exasperated breath. His eyes, when he looked at hers, were accusing. "You don't fix fuel pumps. You replace them."

"Oh." Then, "You have another one?"

"Sure. I have another one."

She let out a relieved breath.

"Back home at San Reys."

"You mean we're stuck here?" she asked in total disbelief.

"Yeah, we're stuck here."

She passed a fatigued hand across her eyes. "So what do we do now?"

"Well, if I was by myself, I could walk to the reserve in about six hours. But with *you* along . . ." He shook his head. "It'll be like dragging a damn ball and chain with me."

Headache and queasiness were instantly forgotten. Corey took a defensive stance, placing both hands on her hips, legs braced apart. "This asinine predicament isn't *my* fault. I'm not the one who didn't put in a new fuel pump. I'm not the one who let your plane fall into disrepair. Tell me, have you ever heard the word *maintenance?*"

She marched over to the plane and ran an irate finger across a thick glob of oil. "This"—she extended the black forefinger toward him—"this looks like something that could have come from the LaBrea Tar Pits. How long has it been since you changed the oil, Mr. Bush Pilot?" Sarcasm dripped from her voice as she sauntered up to him. "I'll bet you can't even remember."

His eyes followed her hand as she reached out, then wiped the smudged finger across his chest, leaving a grimy trail. "For the life of me, I don't know why I ever got into that scrap heap with you. Obviously I was suffering from temporary insanity. Jungle fever." She pivoted on one heel, then started walking toward the jungle.

"Just where the hell do you think you're going?"

Stopping, she swung around and looked at him. And she didn't like what she was seeing, afraid maybe she'd gone too far.

His arms were crossed over his chest, and there was a cruel twist to his lips, a gathering tempest in his stormy eyes. She hadn't felt afraid of him for some time, but she was afraid now.

Her chin lifted a bit higher. "Walking back to San Reys."

He shook his head, his sinister smile frightening to see. "Can't." He pointed skyward. "It's gonna be pitch-black in another fifteen minutes. And anyway, San Reys is east of here, not north." He unfurled his arms and started walking toward her, stalking her.

Corey turned to run, but she wasn't fast enough. His

hand flashed out, long brown fingers curling around her arm, jerking her back, spinning her around to face him.

"We'll have to wait it out till morning. Just you and me. You don't mind, do you?"

His voice was alarmingly smooth, as smooth as sin. Like the shadow lurking in a dark hallway. "Seeing as how I paid for you—a knife for a lay, remember? You owe me."

"God, how I hate you!" she said through gritted teeth while attempting to kick him.

He agilely dodged her swinging foot. She wrapped her fingers halfway around his strong wrists, trying to drag them from her arms, but it was as if they were welded there. "Let go of me!" she demanded. "I would have been better off with Takari. At least he didn't know he was doing wrong. What you're talking about is rape."

She heard his quick intake of breath, felt the rigid tautness of his arms.

"You self-righteous little hypocrite. Have you forgotten about yesterday? Forgotten that you were mewling under me like a sex-starved cat? You wanted it. Wanted it *bad.*"

Corey blanched at the taunting truth of his crude, brutal words. Hadn't the wicked memory of the way her body had responded to the tempered rock-hard length of him shamed her more than once today?

She let go of his wrists to flail small white hands against the steel of his chest. "Oh, you cruel, sadistic bastard."

In her hurt confusion she was only dimly aware of the tears streaming down her cheeks. Corey McKinney didn't cry in front of people. She didn't like people to see her cry. *Nobody* had seen her cry in years and years. And now, this *beast,* this pig of a man was watching her with his devil eyes, seeing the salty wetness that trailed unchecked down her face, onto her neck. His expression was camouflaged by a blurring haze. But she didn't have to see his face to know that it would be mocking and contemptuous, maybe even gloating.

Suddenly her stomach lurched again, and she let out a low moan. With no warning the jungle had quickly become a spiraling, spinning blur. Her body felt like dead weight. Instead of tearing herself away from the devil man, she reached up, clutching iron biceps to keep herself from falling to the dry floodplain.

"Is this what is commonly referred to as the maidenly swoon?" his voice taunted.

She tried to give him a haughty stare, tried to tell him just where he could get off, but she couldn't seem to focus, couldn't seem to get her tongue to work. The harder she tried, the queasier she felt, so she gave up and let her eyelids fall shut.

"Lily?"

Was that a note of worry creeping into his gravelly voice? Hah! It'd be a snowy day in the Amazon when Asher Adams worried about her.

"What *the hell's* the matter with you?"

Her stomach. Oh, God, her stomach . . . She felt so sick. . . . She was afraid to open her mouth, afraid if she did, she might throw up.

"Corey." He shook her until her head snapped to attention, her eyes still safely closed.

"Leave . . . me alone . . ." she finally managed to croak. "I . . . don't feel . . . so good . . ." Her voice was small and slurred.

Raising delicate, trembling fingers, she was surprised to find that her forehead was clammy and beaded with sweat. Then both her hands became incredibly heavy, as heavy as that damn toolbox, and she let them drop uselessly to her sides. Her knees buckled, and Ash caught her to him, his left arm wrapping around her.

Her jaw was taken in a firm grip, her chin tilted up. "Open your eyes," he demanded sharply.

"No . . . you . . . pig. Pig of a man." She tasted

the saltiness of her tears, dimly recalling that he'd been mean to her. He was always mean to her. Except for those few times . . .

"Open your eyes, damn you!"

Like someone in a deep hypnotic sleep, her eyelids opened against her will. The world was a tilted, tear-washed blur, but she managed to catch a glimpse of wild red sky and gunmetal-gray eyes.

A calloused thumb moved across first one cheek, then the other, wiping at the trailing wetness. "Cripes," he muttered, almost to himself. "I can't even see your irises. Corey—Corey! Listen to me!"

"Don't . . . shake . . . me. . . . Makes me feel worse. Seasick. Get seasick . . . you know? I have to lie down. Gotta . . . lie down . . ."

"After you answer me, then you can lie down. Okay?"

For once his voice was serious, more serious than she could ever remember hearing it, and she forgot to be mad at him. She nodded, letting her forehead drop against the solid wall of his chest, vaguely aware of the comfort she was deriving from the strong arms that encircled her, vaguely aware that she felt safe.

"I want you to think. Do you remember being bitten by anything? Or did you touch anything strange when we were walking back here? Okay. Think. Did you touch anything?" His voice was intense. "A bug, a sharp leaf, a caterpillar? *Anything?*" He shook her again. "Get your act together, Corey. This could be real important."

She liked the way he said her name. So much nicer than Lily.

A lot of times he sneered when he called her Lily. She shook her head and could hear a sound like waves crashing against a rocky shore. "Maybe I just drank too much . . . ah . . . too much of . . . that stuff. . . ." She shuddered, recalling the awful brew Takari had given her.

"That couldn't be it. You had only one cup." With a

long finger he brushed a mosquito from her thought-fur-rowed brow. "One cup wouldn't make you feel like this."

With more care this time, she slowly moved her head from side to side, but it didn't help. The waves were just as bad. "Two . . . had two cups. Ta-Takari gave me one." Her head dropped back to his chest.

At first there was just the steady roar of the ocean. Then it changed, combined with a low, rhythmic thunder. Ash's heartbeat.

This was nice. Very nice. She didn't feel quite so sick to her stomach, but now there was a heavy, languid warmth stealing into her already weak limbs. If Ash's arms hadn't been wrapped around her, she would have melted onto the ground.

"No wonder Takari thought you belonged to him for the evening."

Ash's voice sounded strange to her, as if he'd been running, or maybe more as if he were trying not to laugh.

"The jungle's a regular pharmacist's delight," he said, his voice rumbling in his chest, under her ear. "There's a drug out there for every conceivable problem, and some not so conceivable ones. It's my guess, knowing the horni-ness of the Tchikao, and their penchant for drug-induced orgies, that your *kasili* wasn't straight *kasili*—that you've just been initiated into the Amazon with the Tchikao ver-sion of Spanish fly!"

There was no exact moment when Corey realized her brain wasn't functioning at full capacity. But through a haze she knew. Her mind struggled to comprehend what he had just said. But she could handle only one thing at a time. And in her single-mindedness she was aware only of the return of Ash's good humor, miffed to know that she, for some reason, was the cause of it.

"This is great!" He tipped his head back and his laughter rocketed skyward, startling a flock of birds nest-ing in a nearby tree. "By God, Lily!" he gasped. "You're in heat!"

chapter
ten

He shouldn't have laughed. But the whole thing suddenly struck him as so damn funny. Here she'd been highbrowing it around, trying to ignore the fact that their bodies had been talking to each other all day. And more than once he'd caught her looking at him with a puzzled expression in those doe eyes of hers. Oh, he knew what she was doing. She was trying to figure out what made him tick, trying to figure out why her body was so in tune to his. He could explain it in one word. Sex. It was that simple. Man was, after all, an animal, and animals have instinctive urges. A primal drive to fornicate.

But she certainly wasn't hearing any call of the wild right now. No, she looked ready to pass out.

He slipped his left hand around her back, his right under her knees, and picked her up. Two childishly small hands came up and trustingly wound around his neck, her compact body burrowing closer.

Great. Just great.

Trying to ignore the tightening in his chest, not to mention the tightening he was feeling somewhere else, he carried her through the soft dusk toward the plane.

He should have watched her more closely. But who would have thought a white woman would be slipped the ol' Mickey Finn by a Tchikao? He was sure she'd drunk what the natives affectionately referred to as "mating potion." It was usually prepared for the bride, who was expected to be a shy virgin on her wedding day. But it was also given to women with no family to protest their having sex out of wedlock. Most of the natives, male and female alike, were just plain copulation crazy. And Ash suspected that any claim to virginity by anyone over the age of thirteen was made more in the spirit of carrying out tradition.

Only a month ago he'd been attacked and his clothes practically ripped to shreds by the very "virgin" of today's wedding festivities. She'd jumped from a tangle of bushes, shrieking that she wanted to find out what he was hiding in his pants. Only she hadn't called them pants. She'd called them "bamboo you stick your legs into." He had escaped her frenzied grip by threatening to tell her father, who in turn would have been forced to publicly beat his daughter in order to save face. Saving face was very important to the natives.

By the time he got to the plane with his semiconscious burden, an angry cloud of mosquitoes was swarming above them. The sun was long gone, and a heavy fog had moved in, clinging to low-lying vegetation. The moon was almost full, but it would soon be eclipsed by vaporous clouds, making for a black, shadowless Amazon night. But that was good. A dark night meant fewer bugs.

He shifted Corey slightly, then stepped up to the plane wing, all the while intensely aware of the warm body in his arms. He could feel her soft breath against his neck, feel the soft globe of one breast where it pressed against his chest. And he could swear he felt the pliant tip of a nipple through the three thin layers of damp cloth that separated their skin.

Don't even think about it, he warned himself. She was right. He was a jerk. At least he'd felt like one when she'd started crying. And the worst of it was, he'd *meant* to punish her, *intended* to hurt her.

Bracing her body against his knee, he managed to open the plane door, then step inside.

What had set him off was his giving Takari the pocketknife Luke had given him. Ash treasured that knife. And later it seemed as if she just wouldn't stop nagging him. That remark she made about his plane being junk. He and his plane had been through a lot of tight spots together. It was a part of him. When she cut down his plane, she cut him down.

But he'd never meant to make her cry. When he saw those sad brown eyes fill, then overflow, he desperately wished he could take it all back. Every rotten thing he'd said. Yeah, no doubt about it, with very little effort he could be a real first-class bastard.

He put her down in the seat and she groggily mumbled his name.

"Wait here," he whispered, unlocking her hands from behind his neck.

Why the hell was he whispering? This whole thing was getting to him. Frazzling his nerves. "I'm gonna fix a place so you can lie down."

In the time it had taken him to get her inside, darkness had fallen. And there is nothing darker than an Amazon night when low-lying clouds roll in, obliterating stars and moon.

He groped under the pilot seat for the flashlight he'd seen there a couple months before. When he found it, he pushed at the rusty switch. It gave out a weak ray of yellow light that seemed to grudgingly pierce the heavy air, making strange shadows. He was surprised it worked at all.

He put it down beside him, then started shoving things around to make more room, crates scraping against the gritty metal floor.

She shouldn't be here, he told himself as his fingers touched the zippered edge of the nylon sleeping bag and pulled it toward him. She should be home making those lacy jobs old ladies like to put on tables and couches and anything that didn't move too fast. She should be home, making love to a window full of African violets.

He unzipped the sleeping bag and spread it out in the area he'd cleared, then grabbed the pillow. No pillowcase. But then, he wasn't running a hotel. He tossed it down at the head of the bag. And he wasn't any damn maid. He gave the corner of the sleeping bag an irritated tug, then stood up, careful to keep his head ducked.

It would be nothing less than rape if he took advantage of her now, no matter how much she begged for it, he told himself as he made his way to the front. And she would beg. From times he'd witnessed Tchikao ceremonies, Ash knew the drug had three stages, and right now she was in the eye of the storm. Next would come the part he was dreading.

He quickly came to the conclusion that trying to tote a warm, sexually awakening female from the cramped cockpit to the cargo area wasn't exactly a stroll in the park. He had a hard time maneuvering his own frame through the small area under normal, less stimulating circumstances.

He put her down on the bag, then attempted to stand.

"Don't go," she whispered in a husky voice, clinging to him with a body soft, warm, and languorous.

Gently but firmly he disentangled himself. "I'm going to sleep in the front."

"Don't go."

Panic shot through his heart, and he had to quickly reassure himself that he didn't have a heart. Jeez! How could she look like that? So damn sexy and innocent at the same time? Her dark, slumberous eyes reflected the light, holding sweet promises of ready-to-be-awakened passions. Her lips were moist and parted, inviting him to—

He'd died and gone to hell, that's what had happened. Because the devil himself couldn't have devised a more sadistic form of torture than having a beautiful body, eager and begging to be laid. But there was a catch —a moral catch.

No, you don't take off with the wind at your rudder, you don't go into the jungle without antivenin, and you don't play bingo with someone who's not using all her chips.

What was so frustrating was knowing there was no way he could come out of this looking anything but bad. Guys always got the blame when it came to sex. She could crawl all over him tonight, but come morning, whose damn fault would it be if he finally gave in to her demands?

His.

Well, he might be a lot of things, but he sure as hell wasn't a rapist.

"Just go to sleep," he told her roughly, pushing her away and standing up. He moved to the front and plopped down in his seat. The air around the plane hummed with small insects, joined now and then by a hard-shelled beetle dive-bombing the windshield, futilely attempting to reach the light.

He lit a cigarette, then switched off the flashlight. It was his conscience again, he decided, staring at the glowing tip of the cigarette, trying to ignore the sounds of slight movement behind him. So near, and yet so far.

Maybe she'd just pass out. If she'd just pass out, everything would be okay. He took a drag, then stubbed out the partially smoked cigarette, leaned back, and closed his raw, tired eyes. Better not let his guard down. He'd just rest a few minutes.

He struggled to stay awake, but too many sleepless nights and the ever-waiting malaria tugged at him, pulled him down. His mind drifted, disjointed thoughts flowing in and out like the tide. Bobbie. Shouldn't have left Bobbie at San Reys. But the natives don't understand pets. They think dogs should be the main course. Elvira. Elvira needed to be milked. Don't milk her, and she could get mastitis. And the chickens— Chickens need to be fed. . . .

Most of the time, Ash didn't dream. He just kind of OD'd. But this dream, it was nice. Real nice. In fact, he wished he had dreams like this every night. Of course, if he did, he wouldn't ever want to wake up.

The heat was incredible. But heat was okay. He liked things hot. Especially when that heat was body heat.

Someone soft, pliant, and definitely female was pressing against his chest. Light kisses were being trailed across the sandpaper of his jaw. A small hand was working its way under his T-shirt, then up his ribbed side. The touch was whisper-light, making his hot skin feel as if it were charged with static electricity. One finger lazily circled a flat nipple, then trailed lower, following the jagged scar all the way to where it disappeared into his jeans.

Ash came surfacing from the invisible recesses of deep sleep.

"What the—?"

He jerked away, but not very far, the back of his head slamming into the headrest of the leather seat. It was too dark to see anything, but he could sure feel. And what he was feeling he was liking way too much.

He let go of the body that was draped across his

aching lap. "Stop it!" He caught the busy hands, trapping them in a tight grip.

"I want to see where your . . . your scar ends. . . ." Corey's voice was husky and slurred.

"You don't want to know."

"But I do. I'll be gentle. I promise," she breathed, leaning into him. "Tell me how you like it. Fast . . . or slow? I like it *slow*. Slow, and easy. You'll like it that way too. I promise." Her breath caressed his ear, the soft roundness of her breasts pressing against his hardness, their hands clenched at his waist. She kissed his earlobe, then her lips followed a leisurely path from his stubbled jaw to his chin, to his mouth.

She kept her promise. He had to give her that. He was a firm believer in keeping promises.

It was slow. Real slow.

Her lips were soft and moist and coaxingly gentle. He would never have guessed that slow could feel so good. Then, with mouth relaxed, her tongue moved over his top lip with lazy deliberation. Then the bottom lip, leaving his mouth wet and agonizing for more. Just when he thought he'd go off the deep end, she took his bottom lip between hers and began to suck with unhurried ease.

God! Where had she learned something like that? Necking on the front porch with Dudley?

Unreasonable red-hot anger flared in him, then died as he felt her small tongue easing its way between his lips and teeth. There was a roaring like a giant propeller in his ears, and his brain spun.

He released her trapped hands so he could put his arms around her, hold her, feel her, his mouth and tongue meeting hers. In the inky darkness he was completely wrapped up in her, surrounded by her: the taste of her wet, clinging lips; the incense of her musky skin; the incredible softness of her hair where it brushed against his neck; the small delicateness he thought of as Lily.

Her sweet, agonizing slowness was like a drug to him. He'd never known anybody so sexy. So sexy and so sweet.

She broke their kiss, bringing him to a befuddled state of dawning awareness. Like a stall-out indicator light, a red warning flashed in his mind. "We gotta stop," he rasped, his voice sounding like a rusty gate hinge.

"No! Not now. Not *now.*" It was a hoarse, desperate plea. "You don't know how I feel. I have this aching . . . deep inside."

He let out a low groan. "Tell me about it."

It wasn't until he heard the rustle of fabric that he realized what she was doing. She was taking off her damn shirt! His hands flew up to stop her. "Don't do that!" His fingers came in contact with the silkiness of her bra, then moved to quickly tug the unbuttoned edges of her blouse back together. She let out a whimpering protest, then shifted her weight.

Damn her. She was intentionally rubbing against a very vulnerable spot. A spot that was aching like crazy already. "Corey—"

"You talk too much," she told him in a low whisper. "I'd like you better if you didn't talk at all."

"I never asked you to like me."

She lightly touched his lips with one finger. "Don't talk."

"I—"

"Don't talk."

He fumbled until he found a button on one side of her blouse and a buttonhole on the other. Not caring if they matched, he jammed them together. He had another fastened, when he felt a tug at the front of his jeans, then heard the zipper going down.

His hand flew to where she was gently stroking the throbbing bulge of his shorts. "Corey—" he rasped, closing his eyes tightly, stilling her curious hand. "Dammit! That's enough!"

"Ash, please—"

He knew his brain would completely shut down any second, leaving his body on automatic pilot. And it's a bad thing to be on automatic pilot when you're approaching turbulence. He had to rally himself, get his act together so he could tough this out.

His eyes came open. With great reluctance and more self-control than he knew he possessed, he lifted her hand away.

"Make love to me."

Tough it out, Adams.

"Make *love?*" The ever-faithful sneer was back. "You have a funny way of putting it. Is that how you justify the sex act—by using the word *love?* Well, let me tell you something, honey. If we did *it,* it would be called having sex, or getting it on, or—"

He broke off, surprised and angered at finding he couldn't say such a crude word—not to her. "Whatever you want to call it, it sure as hell wouldn't be called *making love.*"

He knew when his brutal words sunk in, because he felt her abrupt stillness. Then, with stiff, awkward movements, she pulled away from him and moved back to the sleeping bag.

He zipped and snapped his pants, then strained to hear . . . what? Her raging anger? Tears?

There was nothing but the sounds of the jungle.

He worried for a half hour, then flicked on the light. She was lying on her side, knees drawn up to her chest, asleep, or passed out. One arm was crossed protectively in front of her so that her hand lay over her shoulder. Her hair had come loose from the rubber band. On her flushed cheeks were damp traces left by quiet tears.

With very little effort he could be a real bastard.

He found his focus drawn back to that pale hand. It was cupped, half-open, fingers gently curved, as if holding something fragile and delicate. There was an unfamiliar stirring in his chest, followed by a deep foreboding of personal danger.

Silently he took out a cigarette and book of matches, then flicked off the flashlight. For a long time he sat there in the dark, unlit cigarette between his fingers, listening to her shallow, steady breathing.

chapter
eleven

Maybe she'd died and nobody had told her. Maybe that's why she felt so awful. Worse than awful. Rigor mortis should be setting in any time now.

She'd been to a party, that much she knew. A New Year's Eve party. A bunch of nurses had gotten together and thrown a New Year's Eve party in one of the dorm rooms. Of course, most of the party had ended up in the hall.

Usually Corey never drank more than one or two glasses of wine once or twice a year. But this time she'd become caught up in the noise and revelry and crowded confusion.

Like overflowing treasure chests, coolers loaded with ice and liquor of every kind filled the bathroom. From this almost endless supply, glasses were never allowed to dip below half full.

Todd hadn't been there. He was working nights, getting in his hospital hours on the surgery floor of St.

Mary's. So there was no one to tell Corey when she'd had too much, nobody to gently tug the glass from her relaxed fingers and steer her in the direction of the door and fresh, head-clearing winter air.

Carefully Corey opened her eyes just a slit, bracing herself for the brash morning light. But instead of seeing cheerful sunlight filtering through white eyelet curtains, she saw the shadowy gloom of predawn. And instead of seeing the ceiling of her bedroom, she saw sheet metal.

Oh, Lord.

She squeezed her eyes shut.

Oh, *Lord.* This isn't real. I'm dreaming.

She wasn't really stretched out on a sleeping bag in the cargo hold of an airplane in the Amazon jungle. And yesterday she hadn't really drunk some brew made with spit. And right now she didn't really have the worst hangover she'd ever had in her life. Lastly, and most important, it wasn't true that she couldn't recall any of last night, or how she'd gotten here.

With infinite care she rolled to her side, the easy movement causing her abused stomach to lurch and churn dangerously. Then very, very slowly, so as not to stir the tidal wave in her stomach, she shifted to a sitting position. Like someone who had recently undergone major surgery, she sat there for a while, collecting herself.

Work, brain. Work. *Think.*

Sluggishly her mind shifted gears and picked up speed. She went back over the events of yesterday: the walk back from the village, the plane not starting, feeling sick. Ash. . . .

A spark of memory flashed across the screen of her mind. And the memory was of Ash. He was holding her against him while his mocking laughter boomed around them. What had he said? What had he thought so funny . . . ?

Heat flooded her face, and a fine sheen of sweat broke out on her body. Quickly she looked to the front of the plane, but both seats were empty. She let out a relieved breath. She didn't want to face him now. She had to gather her thoughts, figure this out.

An aphrodisiac. He'd claimed she'd drunk an aphrodisiac.

Surely not, an inner voice scoffed. Another of his tasteless jokes. There weren't such things as aphrodisiacs, were there? Oh, sure, down through history people had always claimed knowledge of magical potions. Corey could even remember reading that ground deer antlers were as valuable as gold to many Chinese. But she had never believed the stories. In her opinion, aphrodisiacs fell into the same category as placebos, good luck charms, and the tooth fairy.

So how did she explain coming up blank when she tried to recall the events of last night? Why couldn't she remember what had happened after her stomach started to churn?

She brought bent fingers up and gingerly ran them across her mouth. Her lips were tender and swollen, as they might be after a night of lovemaking. Recalled sensations flitted in and out of her head, haunting and teasing her like wispy ghosts in the night, vanishing before she could be certain she'd seen anything at all. And then a memory flickered back, the memory of a mouth that was sometimes mocking, sometimes gentle, moving slowly over hers. . . .

She moaned and buried her face in her hands. She didn't want to have to deal with this now, didn't want to have to deal with *him* now, when she felt so awful. When she was grimy and confused, and deathly sick. When she couldn't think clearly enough to defend herself.

Her bug-bitten skin itched and her blouse felt like a limp, twisted rag where it clung to her rib cage. She tugged at the hem, trying to straighten it out, but it wouldn't budge. She looked down, loose tangled hair falling against her cheeks.

Oh, God! Her hands flew up to clutch at her blouse front. It was buttoned all wrong. A million jumbled thoughts flew in and out of her head, none of them good. Her shirt must have been off sometime last night. If her shirt had been off—she quickly looked down at her jeans, then let out a thankful breath. Her pants were okay, but she had to fix her shirt.

Her shaking fingers moved down the blouse, undoing the buttons. She had the last one unbuttoned, when the pilot door flew open.

"You up?"

Ash's hands clung to the top of the doorframe as he leaned in the opening. "We've got to get going if we're gonna make it to the reserve by tonight."

Corey shifted to her knees, clutching the edges of her blouse together. "I want to know what happened last night." Her voice quivered.

He didn't answer immediately. "You don't remember?"

"N-no."

Ash let go of the doorframe and stepped inside, blocking what little light there had been. "Nothing. Nothing happened."

"Nothing?"

She knew better than that. What did he think she was? Brain dead? "I wake up to find my clothes on wrong, and you tell me *nothing happened?*"

His eyes flickered over the front of her blouse, then one corner of his taunting mouth turned up in a half smile.

The interior of the plane was too small. She was much too aware of him. Of the sweat-tinged aroma of his bronze, satiny skin, of the piercing eyes that watched her so intently. Then, like something subliminal, an erotic impression flickered through her mind: that of her fingers trailing across his damp, hot skin. Oh, God, no!

She ducked her head and started struggling with her

blouse. The buttonholes seemed to have shrunk, and she was trembling so badly she couldn't fasten a single button.

"Just forget about last night." He moved toward her. Even with his head bent under the ceiling, he looked big.

Just forget about last night? Forget what? her brain shrieked while she inwardly rejected the conclusions her innermost thoughts were drawing.

He squatted down in front of her. "It wasn't your fault, okay? So just forget it."

She was too upset to take note of the gentleness in his usually harsh voice. He moved her fumbling fingers aside to grasp the edges of her shirt. She froze, expecting to feel one of his large hands graze her breast. And with that thought came another mindrocking flashback: her fingers were once again moving over his smooth skin, this time tracing the scar on his chest. Following it down, down, below the waistband of his jeans. And she remembered more. How he had felt—so hard and hot.

She started, staring in shocked horror at the bent head in front of her. "You raped me, didn't you?" she finally managed to rasp out, hardly crediting how inappropriate her accusations were when compared to the flashing mental pictures she was receiving.

His dark head came up and his hands stilled.

"You *bastard!*" she spat out. "I knew you were a no-good lowlife, but this, this—" There were no words to describe what she felt—the combination of shock, hurt, anger, and humiliation.

He had released her shirt, and now he straightened up. Something flickered across his hard face, flickered, and as quickly vanished. Distress? Followed by anger? She quickly dismissed the thought. She had been hurt, not him. Hurt and betrayed.

For a long minute he just stood there, his expression closed, controlled, unreadable. To Corey, his stony silence was an admission of guilt.

"You did, didn't you?" The words hurt her throat.

Finally he spoke. "There was no rape to it." His cold voice sent a chill down her back. It held that impersonal, dangerous quality she remembered hearing yesterday, right before he'd come after her. Right before he'd threatened her, claiming she owed him a "lay" for his precious knife.

So it was true. It *had* happened. She felt a pain deep inside. And it didn't stop. It just stayed there, lodged below her heart.

"Let me refresh your memory. You were begging for it. Begging."

"I don't want to hear this." She covered her ears with her hands. "I don't want to hear this."

"Please," he mimicked cruelly, his knees only inches from her bent head. "Make love to me."

She gasped, her breath catching in her throat in a half sob. She brought her hands down to clench them against her stomach, then looked back up at him. "How could you? How could you do something like that to me? What kind of person are you?"

"I'm a pig. Remember?"

No. No, she couldn't remember. She had been intimate with someone, and she couldn't even remember. This was a bad dream. But her bedroom—that had been a dream. This—this was real.

Had it been less than forty-eight hours since he had snarled those very words at her in the air-taxi building in Santarém? *This is real.* But he'd left something out. It was not only real, it was cruel and ugly. The bugs she could have taken, and the heat, and needing a bath and a toothbrush, and having no toilet. All those things she could have taken. But human cruelty overwhelmed her, left her bereft and defeated.

"You just had an itch." He bent over, picked up his cap, and slapped it on his head. "When somebody's got an itch, I try to oblige them by scratching it." He moved to the door, then paused. "Be outside ready to go in two minutes, or I'll come back and drag you out."

After he had gone, she looked down. Through a haze of hurt and confusion she saw that two of the buttons on her blouse had been buttoned—correctly.

A minute of her allotted time passed with her staring blankly at the wall in front of her. She had to move, to put confused thoughts on hold while she collected herself.

She finished buttoning her blouse, then struggled to the front of the plane in search of more aspirin. She had three in her hand before she realized the blue thermos wasn't anywhere in sight. Ash must have taken it, and she would never ask him for water, not if she'd just crawled across the Sahara Desert. Recklessly she pitched the tablets into her mouth and chewed quickly, shivering like a wet dog as they went down.

There was absolutely nothing she could do but go with him. Under normal circumstances, any halfway sane person would walk away and never look back. But these weren't normal circumstances. And being here was enough to make her doubt her own sanity. She was just plain stuck with him. At least until they reached the reserve. Then maybe Mike Jones would show up and fly her to Santarém. Why hadn't she left with him yesterday?

As she stuffed her camera into her bag, she thought about the kissing . . . and the touching. . . . Funny, she couldn't remember more. The logical part of her brain was kicking in, beginning to function once more.

Unless he was lying. Unless nothing *had* happened. Let's face it, honesty probably wasn't a habit with Asher Adams. Wasn't it possible that he might have lied just to watch her squirm? Just to torment her?

Like lightning zigzagging across her mind, the next revelation came to her: Sure, her mouth felt as if it had been kissed, and her body ached. But couldn't the soreness and stiffness have been caused by a night of sleeping on a hard metal floor rather than by a night of passionate lovemaking?

Why, he was lying *about the whole thing*. She just knew it. Just to make her suffer. That had to be it, she told herself with more conviction than she felt. She slung the bag over her shoulder and shoved the plane door wide.

Dawn had come on like a raised curtain, the jungle awakening with it. A tidal wave of sounds washed toward her from the green wall of growth that marked the edge of the clearing: bird calls, monkey chatter, the harsh clicking of cicadas, and the never-ending drone of insects. A hazy sun was burning off fog that clung to the ground in misty swirls, making the air feel like a heavily vaporized room.

And there stood the pathological liar at the edge of the clearing, where the floodplain gave way to solid jungle. He was wearing the army-green backpack and holding a revolver. His head turned her direction, but she couldn't see his eyes behind the dark sunglasses. Then he looked back down at the gun, clicked the cylinder into place, gave it a spin, and stuck it in the waistband of his jeans.

She would just bide her time. Wait until she felt up to a fight. It was hard enough to keep up her end of a verbal conflict with him when her mind was sharp and alert, but now it was dull and sluggish.

She stepped off the plane wing, inwardly wincing as the movement jarred her throbbing head. A hangover was partially caused by the brain actually swelling against the skull. But knowing that certainly didn't make her feel any better.

"Come on," Ash said, not bothering to look at her. "Let's go."

"Am I allowed a trip to the bathroom?"

"Hurry up."

She didn't go very far into the bushes this time, and was careful of where she stepped and what she touched. When she returned to the clearing, Ash barely glanced in her direction before he started walking, never bothering to look back, never bothering to see if she followed.

Even though the pace he set was cruel, Corey couldn't help but soak in her surroundings. She had never seen such trees in her life. Some had to be as tall as fifteen-story buildings. They were so huge that their limbs creaked and groaned with the weight. Their broad trunks were surrounded by clusters of lush green palms and smaller hardwoods, many bound together by huge coiling vines. Clumps of flowering air plants grew on trunks and branches, drawing moisture from the saturated atmosphere. Between many of the trunks, some enveloping whole trees, hung glistening, dew-laden spider webs. Enormous hairy spiders darted in and out, spinning silken death cases for the strange-looking insects tangled within their beautiful traps.

Corey shivered, extremely thankful they were so far away. Spiders were one of her least favorite of God's creatures. Even harmless daddy longlegs scared her.

Even though the actual temperature was probably no more than the high eighties, the humidity and suffocatingly heavy air made it feel more like a hundred. Condensation dripped from huge leaves, soaking into her clothes. Her jeans chafed her waist, and her wet arms were soon covered with a strange white powder. Assuming it was pollen falling from the trees, she tried to brush it off. That only embedded it into her skin, causing her arms to itch horribly. She would have asked Ash what it was *if* she were talking to him.

To round out her misery, an occasional black bug, not unlike a housefly, landed on her, its bite vicious and stinging, leaving a huge welt.

They had been marching for two hours, when Corey realized they'd have to slow down, or she would never make it. At this rate, she would burn out within another two hours. Maybe under normal conditions she could keep up, but her hangover—or whatever her malady was called—was a definite handicap.

Her head reeled from the heat, and her stomach was feeling increasingly queasy. What she needed was a good stiff dose of straight oxygen. Finally she dragged to a complete stop. She couldn't go any farther; she had to rest. A ball and chain, he had said, and that must be what she was. A ball and chain.

Looking ahead, she could just make out the green of Ash's shirt mingling with the jungle, then disappearing completely. He had given her no more thought than a snake would give for its shed skin.

Well, she could hardly be a ball and chain if he didn't even slow down for her. Feeling too sick to shout after him, she just stood looking in the direction he'd gone, water and sweat dripping down her face, hair clinging to her cheeks like strands of wet seaweed.

For the last several minutes a bitter taste had been stirring in her throat, and now it settled on the back of her tongue.

She was going to throw up.

She doubled over, hands braced on her knees, heaving until tears came to her eyes and the top of her head felt like it would explode. After she was done, she took shaky steps toward a solid tree trunk that stood a few feet away and collapsed against it, clammy brow resting on her forearm.

From behind she heard rustling. Too miserable to lift her head, she forced her eyes open a slit to peer under the crook of her arm. There they were. The ratty blue tennis shoes. Her gaze traveled upward to the horizontal rip above his left knee, where his jeans had once been repaired but were now torn again.

When she spoke, her voice sounded like a cranky child's. But she couldn't help it. She had every right to be cranky. "Get away."

"You should have told me you felt sick."

"Why? So you could call a cab to take me home?"

She straightened from the security of the tree, relieved to find that she felt better now that she had thrown up. Without thought she scratched her itching arm, then immediately stopped, remembering how scratching only made it worse.

With a quick movement Ash's hand lashed out, callused fingers just skimming the surface of her arm as she drew back.

"That white stuff's *isango*." He swung the backpack from his broad shoulders to the ground, unzipped it, and produced a small tube. "Hold out your hand."

"Go to hell."

She hated him. Hated his handsome face. Hated the rip in his jeans that made her think of a boy. Hated him for his lying, if it was a lie. Hated him for the truth, if it was the truth.

"Go to hell," she repeated. She liked the sound of the words. Liked saying them to him.

"I heard you the first time. But you might be interested in knowing that *isango* is a tiny bug. A bloodsucker."

She looked from his bland face to her powder-covered arms. *Bloodsuckers?*

Ash made an impatient sound, then grabbed one of her arms and began to roughly rub the cream-colored paste onto it. He dropped the finished arm and picked up the other.

When he was done, he screwed the cap back on the tube. "That should kill them."

She had no difficulty interpreting what was stamped on that hard face: annoyance, pure and simple. And she couldn't help noticing that his skin was free of the powder. Apparently the little bloodsuckers didn't care for thick skin. In that, they weren't alone.

Ash produced the previously missing thermos. They drank from it, then started on their way again. Corey opened her mouth to ask if they couldn't rest a little longer, or at least slow down, only to clamp her jaw shut. She wouldn't ask him for anything. Either way she looked at it, he was a low-life scum, whether he'd forced himself on her or he was lying just to hurt her. Neither made him look good. And the faster they walked, the sooner she would be free of his so-called company.

So, in a rapidly increasing stupor she plodded along behind him. To her relief, he had slowed somewhat, but she was still fighting exhaustion. And like her grandmother had always said, bless her heart, when you're outta gas, you're outta gas.

Just when Corey thought things couldn't possibly get any worse, just when she thought there was no way to be more miserable, it started to rain. It began as a few widely dispersed drops tattooing down on leaves and skin, gradually picking up momentum until it became a full-fledged downpour.

She hunched her body against the wetness, squinting her eyes to peer ahead through the sheeting rain. Ash was still going. Naturally.

She trudged after him, the spongy ground getting spongier, her tennis shoes beginning to sink and pull out with a sucking sound.

Had she ever been more miserable in her life? Perhaps the summer she had detasseled seed corn, winding up with her face and arms slashed from the razor-sharp leaves, her clothes in rotten tatters. No, even that had been a Sunday stroll compared to this.

Something struck her shoulder. Something larger and heavier than a mere raindrop. Then another something plonked onto her head. She froze.

Like the rain, huge, hairy, thick-bodied spiders were falling on her, being knocked from the trees by the hard-hitting drops. She could feel the horrible things moving across the skin of her arms. One was in her hair, another on her shoulder, moving down her back.

She screamed. And screamed. And screamed.

"Corey! They're harmless!" Ash shouted through the pelting rain. Then he was there beside her, brushing off the spiders with his cap.

"I . . . I . . . don't care," she sobbed. "I don't like spiders. I've never liked spiders!"

The ones he had knocked off were scurrying around their feet. Then they scuttled away, disappearing under green vegetation.

Corey just stood there, shoulders hunched, elbows drawn in to her sides, hands protecting her face. What did it matter what *he* thought? She just didn't care. Didn't care if he called her a coward or a crybaby. Didn't care if he told her she had no business being here. It looked as if she *was* a coward. And obviously she *didn't* belong here.

"Are they a-all off me?" she stammered when he quit slapping at her.

"Yeah. Come on." He jerked her toward him. "We've gotta keep going or we'll never make San Reys before dark."

They kept going, but now she was tucked under the shelter of his arm, where she remained, face turned toward his chest, until the rain stopped and all danger of spiders was past.

chapter
twelve

The rain stopped as suddenly as it had started. Birds began singing. Occasional dappled patterns of blue showed
through the green ceiling above them, and now and then
Corey caught a glimpse of fast-moving clouds. The jungle
itself looked like a storm-ravaged flower garden, the sweet
scent of crushed petals and leaves filling her head.

Ever since the incident with the spiders, when Ash
had reluctantly wrapped an arm around Corey, pulling her
to him, an uneasy, nonverbal truce had fallen between
them. It was partially due to their exhaustion. In the last
hour Ash had seemed to wear down fast. She had sensed it
in his increasingly heavy steps, heard it in his breathing.
And it was hard to stay angry with someone when you
were glued to him, feeling safe, feeling thankful for a
warm body to lean on. But now, now it was time to confront him, find out the truth.

She looked to where he was shuffling through the
leafy debris, scooping up fallen fruit, using his cap for a

basket. He made her think of the Peter Pan boy, the rain-ravaged jungle as his Never-Never Land.

He held his cap out to her. "Lunch?" His soaked hair was plastered to his forehead, coiling down his nape to almost meet the ragged neckband of the sleeveless T-shirt.

She hesitated. The only fruit she recognized was an avocado.

"This is a mango. And this"—he pointed to a large purple fruit—"is called *maraja*. I don't know the English word if there even is one. The skin's bitter, but the inside's not bad."

Corey chose the colorful purple fruit, finding that it had the consistency of a plum, only sweeter and stickier. And much, much better than anything she had eaten in the last twenty-four hours.

After Ash finished his *maraja,* he parked himself under a large tree. Bracing his back against the trunk, he slid down, ending in a squatting position. He opened the pack, pulled out the infamous whiskey bottle of two days ago, and unscrewed the lid. Then he tilted his head back and took a long drink before holding the bottle out to Corey. "Hair of the dog?"

Apparently the truce was over. She shook her head, refusing to rise to the bait.

He simply shrugged and took another swig. Then with a heavy, fatigued movement, he brought the bottle down to dangle it over one knee. "You look like a drowned rat," he observed.

So, they were moving to their prospective corners, getting ready to come out fighting. "You don't look so great yourself."

What a lie. They were having a regular liars' convention here. Confront him, *now,* a voice in her head prodded.

"I want to know the truth," she said with more self-assurance than she felt.

"About what?"

"You know what." She crossed her arms at her waist. "About what happened last night."

"You mean whether or not we got it on?"

She inwardly cringed at his crude choice of words. "Yes."

"You figure it out." He passed a hand over his forehead in a tired gesture, as if his head ached, but she would not allow herself to feel any sympathy for him. Not after what he'd done to her.

"I've already figured it out," she bluffed.

"Oh, yeah? Then what are you buggin' me for?" He closed his eyes and leaned his head against the trunk of the tree.

This was like pulling teeth. "I . . . I just wanted you to admit that we didn't, that we never . . ."

She thought about his scar. About how she knew it traveled well below the waistband of his jeans. Her mind might have forgotten parts of last night, but her fingers would always remember the journey they'd been on. She knew that scar intimately. One-quarter-inch wide, a smooth river running between two muscled surfaces of satiny skin. How could that knowledge be explained if they hadn't, if it didn't happen?

"Let me tell you something." He was staring up at her, and she didn't like the glint in his eyes. It made her think of light reflecting off a gun barrel.

"It's simple, Lily. If I'd—" He paused, seeming to contemplate his next words. "If I'd *made love* to you, you would have remembered. I swear. Even if you'd been comatose."

The smirk was what really set her off. Rage exploded in her. What an egotistical scum! What a lowlife! She had never, never been so furious, so outraged!

He had his head tipped back, ready to take another drink. She lunged at him, bringing him down with a flying tackle, the bottle flying from his hand, splashing whiskey on them both. He landed on his side, Corey planted on his hip. "You bastard!" she cried, pummeling his rock of an arm with two small fists. "You cruel, sadistic bastard!"

Quickly he rolled to his back, catching her hands and stopping the pathetically laughable onslaught. "Let me get this straight. You're ticked off because we *didn't* do anything?"

"You lied to me. Just to be hateful. Just to be cruel!" She tried to wrench her hands free, but he held them in a crushing grip.

"I never lied. You assumed the worst about me, that's all. And I just didn't deny it. If anybody has a reason to be pissed, it's me, not you. And anyway, I don't need an aphrodisiac to get you charged up. And I can prove it."

He took one small fist in each of his hands, then pulled her toward him so that their locked hands touched the ground on either side of his head. Her heart was hammering away at her rib cage.

They were so close that she could see every perfect pore in his perfect face, count every hair in the two-day growth of blue-black mustache and beard. She could have touched with her cheek every wet, spiked eyelash, and could see the starlike lines shooting through the irises of the gray eyes that watched her so teasingly. Ash stared, watching, waiting for her reaction. She was afraid she wasn't going to disappoint him.

"I hate you, Asher Adams," she cried desperately, wanting it to be true, knowing it to be an out-and-out lie.

She was acutely aware of their steaming clothes and their wet, fabric-plastered bodies. Of how she was straddling him, the most intimate part of her contacting solidly with the hard warmth of his abdomen. Her breasts were crushed against his chest, and she could feel the deep bass of his heartbeat as it answered hers.

"I love the way you hate me," he whispered in a sexy voice. Strong fingers moved across her wrists, shifting both her hands to one of his, keeping them firmly anchored above his head, which left his other hand free to roam over her aching, melting body. And roam it did, to finally cup her firm bottom, shifting her so she was settled against the stiff hardness of him, the part of him she had stroked with her hand last night.

That familiar, languid warmth that had been her enemy before was stealing through her whole body, robbing her limbs of strength, her mind of willpower. Through a haze it came to her that what he had bragged about, what had made her so angry, was probably no more than the truth. If they had made love, she most surely would have remembered.

"Come on, Lily—" After arranging her body the way he wanted it, his hand came up to cradle the back of her head. "Hate me some more."

Her desire for him must have shown in her passion-drugged eyes, because a knowing smile tugged at the corners of his mouth before he slowly pulled her head down. Their lips touched, and through the layers of wet clothing she felt his arousal stir against her, and an aching tightness answered in her own body. Then his tongue plunged into her mouth, driving, taunting. He tasted like mellow whiskey, and the sweet fruit they had both eaten. Adam and Eve. Except Ash was doing the tempting.

"God, I want you," came the half-amazed, half-reverent muttering against her mouth. He released her hands to wrap his arms around her, holding her tightly. "So damn much."

Over the roaring in her ears she could hear the bad angel on her shoulder, whispering, telling her to give in to him. Telling her she wanted him as much as, maybe more, than he wanted her. But the next thing she knew she was being pushed away.

At first she just sat there on the ground in dazed confusion, cheeks hot, body going through withdrawal. Then it dawned on her that he'd done it to her again. He'd said he would prove he could get her charged up without any help, and he had. Now, after proving his point, he had shoved her away. What a fool she was. Wouldn't she ever learn?

She glared in his direction. He was lying on his back, one arm flung across his face. And his breathing was strange—short and shallow.

Malaria.

If she hadn't been in such a stupor, she would have recognized it earlier. All the symptoms had been there. His rapidly increasing exhaustion, out of proportion to his earlier energy. His apparent headache. The whiskey.

The whiskey!

Her gaze flew to where the bottle had knocked against the tree, leaving a dark, splattered stain, the contents having spilled completely. She felt sick with guilt, sick for letting her anger rule.

He dropped his arm and looked at her. And now she could see the bruised smudges under his beautiful eyes. See the beaded sweat clinging to his upper lip and forehead. "I'm sorry," he muttered, his eyes falling closed, letting his head drop to the ground. "I didn't do that just to show you how much of an ass I can be."

She knew that now. "The chloroquine?"

He shook his head, eyes remaining closed. "At the reserve."

And no whiskey to lessen the severity of the attack.

Ash started to get up. "You better rest." She put a hand on his shoulder to push him back.

"Can't."

He brushed her away and struggled to his feet. "We've gotta get going, while I can go at all. You might think you're miserable now, but it's hell spending the night in the jungle with no protection." He swayed, then caught himself. "Not only hell, but dangerous. The jungle never sleeps. It'll destroy us if it can. And there are a million ways it can do it."

Fear surged in her. She recalled the prophetic-sounding words of Mike Jones. *Just wait till the malaria's strong in him, an' he goes nuts on you.*

Ash continued to list the jungle's bad points. "If some head-chopping Jivaras don't find us, the bats will."

He must have noticed her stricken expression, because he went on to explain: "Jivaras are about the only bloodthirsty tribe left in the Amazon. And they have this endearing affection for shrunken heads."

She shivered. "And the bats . . . ?"

"A South American bat can drink two pints of blood at a time. Something in their bite deadens your skin, so you don't even know you've donated till the next morning, when you wake up weak and covered with your own blood. *If* you wake up at all."

chapter
thirteen

One step at a time. From experience Ash knew that was the best way to approach this walking business. But when you had two-hundred-pound weights attached to your arms and legs, and those arms and legs were made of mush, it could be hell. Pure hell.

His skin felt as if it were on fire. He reached up and peeled his soaked shirt from his back, then let it drop from his fingers to the ground. He'd had a backpack at one time. But somebody'd taken it from him. That and the pistol.

Bees buzzed in his head. He liked bees. Anything that could defy the laws of aerodynamics was okay in his book. Sometimes he just liked to sit and watch them fly. Watch them hover, then bank. Take off and land. Those little suckers made great three-point landings. Or was that six-leg? Either way, they were enough to make a helicopter pilot sob in envy.

Hammers were pounding in his head. Then an uncontrollable shiver ran through him. He clenched his teeth to keep them from knocking together like a set of ivory castanets. Now he was cold. A guy just couldn't win.

His legs buckled under him and he fell to his knees, then just let his body sag until he was lying flat on his stomach. Nothing like a good crash when you're dead beat. Nothing like just sprawling out flat. He moaned and dug his fingers into the ground as another spasm hit him.

"Ash—"

"Leave me the hell alone."

"You've got to get up."

It was the same voice that had been nagging him for the last thousand—no, make that *three thousand* miles.

The uncontrollable shivering stopped. He opened his eyes to stare at a pair of muddy Nikes. They were on feet that were attached to legs that were attached to Lily. "Nice footgear, Lily," he mumbled. "Glad you left your Jethro Bodines back home on the farm. Betcha wear them when you're plantin' those *straaaight* rows of corn. . . ."

He was conscious of his own voice, meandering on and on. About what? Hell if he knew. Nonsense, probably. He struggled to focus his mind, then just gave up.

He rolled over on his back and opened both eyes. Within his field of vision was blue sky, a nice cobalt blue. Green trees ranging from chartreuse to kelly. And doe-brown eyes. Lily's big eyes. There were parallel worry lines between them. And the pale skin of her face wasn't pale anymore. It was heat-flushed.

Poor Lily. Gotta take care of Lily. Good little girl scout. Good little virgin. Shouldn't be here, wandering around in the woods with the big bad wolf. He just might eat you up. Like to eat you up.

He laughed, startling himself. Here he was, sick and half crazy, and she looked scared to death. Couldn't blame her. On a good day he didn't exactly instill confidence. "Helluva team, ain't we, Lil?" He laughed again, wondering if his laugh always sounded so strange.

Then his mind wandered away, back to the shoes. Small, ridiculous matters suddenly took on enormous importance. Emphasis was placed on insignificant details, ranking them up there with world hunger and nuclear war. Those damn shoes . . .

"You know what kind of shoes are worse than those Bodine jobs? Those clunky black shoes old ladies wear." He locked the fingers of both hands together across his stomach. He could feel the burning heat of his bare skin, and had a vague memory of stripping his shirt from his aching body. When? Maybe a thousand miles ago. . . .

He closed his burning eyes. Right there in front of him, in his mind's eye, were those damn black shoes. He started yacking again, feeling like somebody who had taken truth serum and couldn't make himself shut up. "Those shoes should come with a warning: Quit wearing these damn things, and you will greatly reduce your chances of a broken hip."

He was aware of his own voice, but it was like listening to somebody else. Like his voice had gone on without him. "Where do you think they find those kind of shoes? Who *sells* those damn things? Worse yet, who *makes* 'em?"

"Ash—" There was laughter in the voice.

An ugly suspicion invaded his mind. His eyes flew open and he fixed Corey with an authoritative stare. *"You* don't have any of those black babies, do you?"

"No," she reassured him, laughing.

"Whew."

He let his head drop back, eyes falling shut. "What a relief." A body-racking shiver shuddered through him, and he accepted it, waited for it to pass.

"Ash, you've got to get up."

There she went. Starting to nag him again. "Bet you were a cheerleader, weren't you? Rah-rahing it all over the place."

"We've got to keep going."

"Shaking those damn pompons."

"We've got to get to the reserve by dark. Remember?" The laughter was gone, replaced by worry. "How do you know if we're going in the right direction? How do you know we're not lost?"

"Lost? I can find my way home blindfolded."

No, they weren't lost. Luke was the one who was lost. His brain struggled to focus, but everything was a confused blur. His head hurt. His back and muscles ached. And he was so damn tired. And hot. And cold. And trying to remember something important. Had to remember. Thinking about . . . remembering . . .

Oh, Jesus! Jesus! It hurt! And the blood. Blood everywhere. But he couldn't tell anybody, couldn't let anybody know.

Old Lady Fielding hated his guts, was just waiting to catch him at something.

Shouldn't have ditched school. She'd told him if he got in any more trouble, she'd split them up, send him to another home. And Ash couldn't let that happen. Luke couldn't get along without him. Who would look after Luke?

If only he hadn't swiped Sweeney's bicycle. Well, not swiped, borrowed. He planned on bringing it back just as soon as he sold the soda bottles at the corner market. Who woulda thought a dog the size of a truck would run out in front of him? Right the hell there in the middle of the street? What kind of owner let his dog just roam all over hell?

He'd seen the flash of dog, tried to stop, but it had all happened so fast. The bike crashed into the animal, then Ash was pitching forward over the handlebars in slow motion, complete with tunnel vision. It seemed like he slid across the warm cement for about two hours, glass raining around him, while the dog hightailed it up an alley.

When the slow motion stopped, he looked down at his bleeding palms. Then his knees. Then his side.

Oh, God! It looked as if he'd been sliced open with one long, even slash of Zorro's sword.

At first he didn't feel anything at all. It was as if he were a bystander observing the whole thing. Then the pain hit him, hot and white, like splintering shards of glass. Wave after wave. He was dizzy from it. His head reeled from it.

He couldn't remember getting on the bicycle, but he must have, because all of a sudden he was pedaling back the way he'd come, the front wheel of poor Sweeney's bike wobbling like crazy.

Scared. So damn scared. Scared of being caught, found out. Scared of bleeding to death, gutted like a damn fish, and by a soda bottle. He couldn't tell anybody. No way. If Old Lady Fielding found out, she'd send him away. He'd never see Luke again. Nobody could do that to them. Nobody.

He almost made it to the orphanage. But then the world turned black, and he crashed to the street for the second time.

Ash sat bolt upright and stared into the jungle. Sweat was pouring from him. He was shaking and shaking. But it was his expression that alarmed Corey the most. He looked stricken.

They had been walking for a total of five hours. But had it been five hours in the right direction? The few times when they had come to a place where the dim path seemed to separate, Ash had waved his hand in an almost benediction, then plunged on, insisting he knew the way.

But there had been other times, like now, when he was incoherent and almost raving. Then he would snap out of it and they would continue. But he'd never been this bad. Never been despondent.

She knew malaria could bring on black fits of depression that sometimes carried on long after the victim was physically recovered. And she hated to think of Ash going through such torment.

"No!" His voice rang out stronger than she had heard it in some time. He looked up, focusing unnaturally bright eyes on her. When he spoke, his voice broke and trembled.

"They held this memorial service for Luke. In . . . New York. First I wasn't gonna go. Since . . . I knew he wasn't dead. *Knew* he was still alive. But . . . but it didn't feel right *not* going. Didn't want Luke to think I'd forgotten him—just in case.

"All his Peace Corps buddies were there. Talking about how Luke had been such a damn saint." His voice cracked on the last word. With unseeing eyes he stared at the ground near his feet. Long brown fingers twisted and mangled the white threads of his ripped jeans. Over and over. Twisting, tugging.

As abruptly as he had stopped talking, he started again. "They had these 'In Memory Of' pamphlets. I shoved them on the floor. And I don't know how it happened, but the stand they were on went down too. Along with a green vase full of long yellow flowers." He pounded a clenched fist against his knee. "Glads. Isn't that a *damn* stupid name for funeral flowers?

"I think I even threw a couple chairs on the floor before I left." He raked fingers through his dark hair, then let out a trembling breath. "I don't remember.

"Old Lady Fielding was there. She got what she wanted. Luke and I were split up. For good." He tilted his head back and stared up at the sky and trees above their heads, blinking his eyes.

Corey wanted to go to him, comfort him. At least try to dry the sweat from his rapidly rising and falling chest. But she felt frozen in helplessness as she watched his grief.

"I can still see Old Lady Fielding's face. The disgust on it. The smugness. I knew what she was thinking. That

I'd finally gone off the deep end. And about how I'd always been the wild brother. The rotten one. The bad seed." He took a deep, agonized breath. "The hell of it is, it's the truth. I knew, if life was fair, that I should have been the one to die, not Luke. Not holy, saintly, walkin'-on-the-water Luke." Ash fell silent and deathly still. Then he put his face in his hands.

Through a blur Corey watched his bowed head, saw those broad, strong shoulders begin to shake again, but this time not from fever. A strangled sob escaped him before he seemed able to stop it.

And that's when she moved, knelt down beside him, pulled him to her. He buried his face against her and clung tightly, like a hurt, bereft child.

Ash. Ash, of all people. He was so big, so strong, so tough. She ached for him. She was dying inside for him. She thought about the black shoes, and how he'd made her laugh. And now he was breaking her heart. In the space of five minutes he'd managed to make her run the gamut of her emotions. He did that to her. There was no moderation, no middle-of-the-road for Asher Adams. With him it was all and everything.

His body, hot with the fever that raged through him, trembled against her. Tenderly she combed her fingers through his damp hair, soothing his perspiring temple.

Like a revelation, she saw him, *really* saw him. And maybe understood him just a little, knowing no one could ever understand him completely. True, he had a sarcastic, cruel, and smart-alecky side. But it was there only to protect the gentle side, the side easily hurt.

And with an insight she hadn't known she possessed, Corey saw and understood that in many ways she was stronger than he was. True, he had saved her from the death pit, and saved her from Takari, and saved her from the spiders. Yet she felt that Ash, the macho tough guy, was the one who needed sheltering.

And if Luke were here right now, he would most

likely agree, most likely say that he had watched out for his brother, kept him out of trouble. Just as Ash had protected Luke. They had been each other's balance. And now, without the counterweight, there was no one to keep Ash from falling. No one to keep him from hurting himself.

She rested her cheek against the top of his head and held him until his fever went into remission and the shivering in his limbs subsided.

He drew a ragged breath and looked at her with vague, glassy eyes, still lost in his heartbreaking world of fevered visions and painful memories. She wanted to kiss the tears from his face, kiss away his sorrow.

"You shouldn't be here," he said in a hoarse voice, his eyes clearing somewhat. "It's too dangerous."

"I know."

Dangerous. Dangerous in more ways than one.

"Ah, Lily . . ."

There was regret tinged with sadness in those two words. He reached up and touched her face. His rough fingers moved across her cheek, and for the first time she was aware of the wetness there.

"I'm a real jerk," he whispered to her in a husky voice. "Chromosomes, I guess. Yeah, the ol' jerk chromosome, it'll getcha every time." He sighed, then started to struggle to his feet. "We gotta get going."

Alarmed, Corey tried to hold him back. "We can't leave now." They would become hopelessly lost if he tried to lead them to the reserve in his confused state. "You better wait till you feel better."

"I won't let anything happen to you. Gotta take care of Lily." He stood, pulling her up beside him. "Don't worry. The jungle and me, we're like this." He held up his hand and locked two fingers together.

Then he started walking. When Corey didn't immediately follow, he turned and motioned for her. "Come on. Another hour and we'll be home."

He was down again. Corey collapsed on her knees beside him. Her shoulders ached from where the backpack cut into them. Panic rose in her, and she fought it, tried to not let it take over. But she knew it would be dark in another hour, and it didn't look as if they were going to make it to the reserve.

Ash slapped at the pocket of his shirt—which Corey had talked him into putting back on. "Gotta have a smoke."

"You don't have any, remember?"

"Ah, hell. That's right."

Earlier, he had pulled out a cigarette pack only to find that the cigarettes had coagulated to form one wet, soggy blob.

He struggled to his feet—something Corey had witnessed too many times in the last hour. She knew he shouldn't be exerting himself like this. It was the worst thing a person could do during a malaria attack. It put stress on the heart and kidneys. He could do serious damage to himself.

And yet, to stop, to stay here perhaps all night was unthinkable. If she believed what he said, then to stay could mean dying.

And what if they were just going in circles? What if all this walking had been for nothing? At times Ash had been incoherent, yet had kept going when he seemed to barely know where he was, let alone what direction they should travel in. Rational people got lost in the jungle, so how in the world could Ash lead them to safety?

He was walking on without her. Under the weight of the backpack she struggled to her feet, then hurried to catch up with him.

They hadn't gone far when she heard the faint tolling of a bell off to their left, the sound muffled as it carried through the dense jungle.

A bell! A bell ringing could mean only one thing—people! They must be near the reserve. George Dupree must have returned, found them gone, and was now sounding a bell for them to follow.

"Ash! Listen. A bell! We're going in the wrong direction."

He stopped and she practically barreled into him. The sound came again, beautiful, persistent, haunting. . . .

"It's coming from this way." She took a step in that direction. Ash's hand lashed out, dragging her up against him with surprising strength.

"Don't listen," he said in a weak voice, staring into the jungle with dark-rimmed eyes.

"But we—"

"Don't listen," he repeated in an insistent whisper.

For the last hour he had seemed better, clearer-headed and more coherent, although physically drained. And she had begun to think that the worst of the attack was over. Now he was confused again.

"It's nothing human," he said. "The bellbird. It's the bellbird. If you follow its call, you'll be lost." He swayed slightly, then straightened. "The bellbird's more dangerous than the fer-de-lance snake. Because the fer-de-lance is something *real*, something you can kill. But . . . the bellbird . . ."

He had raved about a lot of things in the last several hours, but this had to be the worst. He was scaring her. Mike Jones's words echoed in her mind, words she didn't want to be reminded of.

Abruptly the tolling ceased. Then, almost immediately, it began again, this time from behind them. Her scalp prickled and a shiver ran through her.

Ash still held her by the arm, and now he looked down at her. "I'm not as out of it as you think."

His eyes were bruised and red-rimmed, but now she could see the lucidity behind them. She felt a tremble course through him, sensed his incredible weakness and fatigue, answering and overriding her own. Filthy and sweating, they must look like a couple of mud wrestlers carelessly hosed down after the match.

He gave her a slow smile, a weary, and funny, and wistful smile. "Yeah, we're a helluva pair. All dressed up and no place to go."

Relief washed over her in a tidal wave. He might be weak and anemic, a condition that would last for at least several days, but his good humor had returned. His endorphins were flowing again. She could take his teasing and his name-calling, but she couldn't take his sadness.

"Give me the pack." He saw her dubious reluctance. "Come on. Give it to me. You've been carrying it for hours. It's my turn."

"My purse and camera are in it."

"That's okay." He stripped the pack from her shoulders and put it on his own back.

"Fifteen more minutes, and we'll be there," he stated, his movements heavy with weariness as he moved in the direction they had been going before Corey heard the bellbird.

Sure, and she believed in Santa Claus, the Easter bunny, and Houdini's promised return from the dead.

But twenty-five minutes later they were stepping into the cleared area around the reserve.

"I don't know how you did it!" she gasped.

"Trade secret of the Flat Earth Society."

"Yeah, sure."

"A bloody mansion," Ash muttered. "It looks like a bloody mansion. The White House. Buckingham Palace."

Corey couldn't have agreed more. In fact, she felt like dropping to her knees and doing some serious ground-kissing.

Like a couple of bedraggled zombies, they waded through a welcoming committee of pants-pecking chickens, and one bleating, butting, milk-dripping goat.

chapter
fourteen

Something wet touched his fingers. Ash came awake to find himself sprawled facedown on the porch glider, Bobbie licking his hand.

"Hey, boy." His voice was a rusty croak. "So. You been keeping an eye on everything? Here's some advice from one male to another," he said in a confiding tone. "Don't let Lily get under your skin." He rubbed the dog's head.

Food. He smelled food. Cooked food. Lily must be practicing her domestic skills. Unless George was back. But George couldn't cook worth a damn, and this smelled like something edible.

Ash was hungry as hell, but he also needed a bath. The metal glider clanged and shifted under him as he dropped his bare feet to the floor and levered himself upright, every muscle screaming for mercy. He just sat there, waiting for his head to clear. While he waited, he became aware of something more than physical discomfort: a nagging at the back of his mind, though he couldn't quite put a finger on its cause. He searched his memory, recalling how he'd staggered up the porch steps the previous night and fallen into the swing. But that was all he remembered. Now, judging from the diffused orange sunlight coming in all three sides of the porch, he must have slept the clock around.

Malaria had a way of burning itself out over a period of years, and he guessed he should be thankful that the days of severe attacks were behind him—days with no beginning or end, days of being too weak to even crawl. But it was still hell.

Ash forced himself to his feet.

It wasn't until he was in the river lathering soap on his chest that he figured out just what was bugging him. Yesterday he'd cried, right in front of Lily. Not only that, she had comforted him, treated him like a damn baby. And he'd liked it. The thought made him squirm.

He rinsed off the soap, then emerged from the river, water running in rivulets from his hair, trailing down his clean, naked body. He picked up the dingy towel he'd left on a tree root and rubbed himself down.

Cried like a baby. And now he had to face her.

Why did he care what she thought? Miss Goody-Two-Shoes probably saw guys crying all the time. Hell, Dudley probably cried in front of her on their dates, whenever they took in a Disney movie. Thinking of Dudley made his jaw hurt.

Out of the blue he had an unsettling recollection. Something he hadn't thought about in years. He had cried after seeing *Old Yeller*. But at least nobody had seen him. He'd prided himself on being the only kid to come out of the theater dry-eyed. He'd even managed a few sarcastic comments about the story, saving his tears for later that night, when he was alone in his bed.

He buttoned and zipped his jeans, then tugged on a T-shirt. It was just plain lucky that Lily would be out of here as soon as George got back, which should be anytime now. If she left immediately, it wouldn't be too soon. He was sick and tired of feeling responsible for her. And his nerves were raw from fighting the primal attraction that raged between them.

Tonight should be a real treat, he told himself sardonically. Just the two of them. Self-control was *not* his middle name. Self-control was something other people practiced.

He had her all figured out. She was the kind of person who wouldn't have sex without commitment. And the word *commitment* wasn't even in his vocabulary.

When he got back to the house, he found Corey in the kitchen in front of the gas stove looking very domestic. She hadn't heard him come in, and he hesitated in the doorway, feeling a flash of shame at facing her after crying in her arms. But it was over and done with, and never having been one to embarrass easily, he pushed the memory to the back of his mind.

He stood there a second, watching her. She'd gone to the river by herself to clean up. Anger and concern shot through him. She shouldn't have gone alone. It was too dangerous.

She must have sensed his presence, because she turned. "Ash!" Her brown eyes flicked over him, taking in the fact that he'd bathed. Her nose was sunburned, making the freckles across it more pronounced. She looked clean and fresh. *Untouched* was the word that popped into his head.

Even though he'd taunted her about being a virgin, he doubted that she could actually be one. Unless Dudley was a steer. But she had an innocent quality that made him feel protective toward her.

"You shouldn't be up. I was going to bring you something to eat." Her expression was open and friendly—something new to him, and he had to wonder at the unlikely chance that maybe she was coming to like him just a little.

His heart jumped, and he felt a stirring in his loins. Why did she have this effect on him? She was sexy, but not centerfold material. She wasn't big-chested, and the rest of her was on the slim side, almost boyish. But he did find her sexy. Even dressed the way she was now, in jeans, and a T-shirt that was too big for her. Even when the only skin showing, from the elbows down, was sunburned and scratched.

"Ash . . . ?" Her face mirrored her concern.

He knew he looked like hell. He hadn't felt like shaving, and after a malaria attack he always had dark circles under his eyes.

He pushed away from the doorframe. "Don't put on that nurse's face. I'm okay. Just a little weak."

"Well, sit down before you fall. I hope you like tuna casserole cooked on top of the stove. It's about all I could find."

"It's got to be better than anything George or I ever came up with. We've had stuff Bobbie wouldn't even touch."

By the time they finished eating, the sun had set.

"You know how to play poker?" Ash asked as he lit the gas lamp that hung over the table. He glanced over his shoulder at her. From the look on her face you'd think he'd just asked if she wanted to get naked and coat their bodies with motor oil. "Forget I said that. For a second there I forgot you come from the Bible belt. How about pitch? You know how to play pitch?"

She shook her head.

"Rummy, then. Everybody knows how to play rummy."

"When I was little I played rummy with my grandmother."

When he was little he had played it for a buck a game.

Opposite poles. She was Kool-Aid; he was Everclear. "Want to play a game?"

She seemed surprised but pleased. "I'd like that." She was smiling at him. He'd never really seen her smile. Not like that.

For some reason it made him think of the time he'd been flying home after delivering some cargo to Santarém. He'd gotten trapped in an electrical storm. Lightning was all around, and his instrument panel went haywire. He didn't know up from down, north from south. In a last desperate attempt to live, he took a guess, then pulled the nose the way he prayed was up. Just when he started to think he'd smash into the ground, the plane broke through the storm ceiling and he was bathed in sunlight. The sensation he'd felt then was disturbingly like what he was feeling right now.

Alarm grew in him. No doubt about it, it would be best for both of them if she got herself out of there—and fast. Ash had been hoping that Mike Jones would bring George back by tomorrow, then take him to his plane. Now he decided if Jones didn't show, he would just walk to his plane, put in the new fuel pump, and fly Corey back to Santarém whether she wanted to go or not.

He went to the desk. After digging in the back of the drawer, he pulled out a deck of white and blue Bicycle cards. Back in that period of his life he now thought of as his vagrant days, he'd spent a lot of hours with a deck of cards. When other kids were running a paper route, or making deliveries for the grocery store, or helping old ladies cross streets, he had been hanging out on corners hustling people with card tricks.

He slipped the cards from the box, and they settled easily into his hands. They were old friends, cool and comfortable, a perfect fit. He liked the snapping and whirring sounds they made when he split and shuffled them, liked the way they gradually warmed and limbered, the way they slowly came to life.

He happened to glance across the table. Corey was staring at his hands in wide-eyed wonder. "I used to do card tricks," he explained half-apologetically.

"My grandmother never shuffled like that."

He laughed. She had a sense of humor. Of course, it wasn't nearly as rough around the edges as his, but she had one. "When I was fourteen, I met this guy named Hogie. No last name, just Hogie. He was a street hustler. One of those con men who hang out on corners doing tricks with three bent cards. He taught me the game. I even hustled for a while. Made Luke mad as hell. But the only people I ever fleeced were small-time drug dealers and neighborhood gang members. It gave me some satisfaction." He looked up from the cards, expecting to see snobby disgust on her face, but she was watching him with that curious, what-makes-him-tick look he was fast becoming familiar with.

The cards flashed, ending up in two small piles. "Seven-card rummy." He slapped the rest of the deck down in the middle of the round wooden table, turning one card faceup. "Deuces and one-eyed jacks wild."

He deftly arranged his cards, then watched with tolerant amusement as Corey carefully put her cards in order, eyebrows drawn together in intense study. When she was ready, she drew, thought about her play for what seemed like two hours, then finally discarded.

She was taking this pretty seriously. Maybe he should let her win. The only reason he'd suggested playing cards in the first place was that he couldn't think of any other way to spend the evening. Any other way but one . . .

"Your turn," she told him.

He drew a seven of clubs. That gave him a run of three. He laid the cards on the table and discarded from the ones remaining in his hand.

Jungle sounds ebbed and flowed around them, sometimes dwindling to complete silence. Then there would be a loud animal call, and the noises would begin all over again, starting out softly, getting louder and louder. Hundreds of bugs drummed against the window screen, drawn to the light above the table.

Suddenly a haunting cry came from the jungle.

Corey's hand stopped, poised to draw a card. "What was that?"

"Howler monkeys."

She picked up the card. "It sounded like a faraway train."

He looked across at her, surprised that she would think so too. "Yeah, it does, doesn't it? The night sounds here—there's nothing like them. They have a way of getting into your blood."

Corey discarded, then sat up straighter, elbows on the table, both hands gripping her cards while she studied them. He was close enough to see that some of the scratches on her arms were deep. "Did you put something on those?"

Without thinking, he reached out and touched her arm, marveling again at the softness. "Infection can set in fast here." Her skin made him think of velvet, or the petals of a flower. He realized what he was doing and pulled his hand away, but not before seeing an answering want in her brown eyes.

He could have her. He knew that. If he pressed her a little, he could have her.

His damn conscience intruded. All his life he had stood up for those weaker than himself. He couldn't remember how many times he'd bloodied his fist on some bully's face. And he more than anyone knew how easy it was to lose your perspective in the jungle. Lose all sense of reality.

"I put some medicine on them this morning." She cleared her hoarse throat. "It's your turn."

Ash reached for the next card. Playing rummy had been a stupid idea. It was only making things worse. Tomorrow he would make sure she was out of here, no matter what. George or no George. Even if he had to drag her.

He drew a one-eyed jack. It would give him a run of hearts. The heck with letting her win; this game had gone on too long already. "I'm out." With one hand he fanned the cards down on the tabletop.

"Shoot! I only needed one more card." She spread her cards out for him to see.

"Why didn't you play your kings?" He tapped them with one finger.

"I like to hang on to my cards until I can put them all down at once."

"But look—" He showed her how she could have played her clubs on his cards. "You could have won if you'd put them down earlier."

She stared up at him, face stubborn. "I *like* to keep them until I can go out," she insisted. "That's how I played with my grandmother. I always thought it was kind of cheating to put them down a few at a time. And it takes the suspense out of the game."

"Okay, okay." He reached for a cigarette and lit it, shaking out the match and tossing it in the tuna-fish-can ashtray. "I don't care. It's only a game. I was just showing you how you could have won."

A huge hard-shelled beetle hit the netting and Ash got up and walked over to look at it. Anything to put some distance between himself and Corey. "This guy must be four inches long," he said, pointing to the shiny green-shelled insect.

There were so many bugs that they were almost a solid cover in places. "It's the full moon. A full moon brings out the bugs like crazy. The whole jungle comes alive with them."

Corey got up and came to stand beside him. He could feel the heat of her body, smell the freshness of her skin.

He looked out past the green netting to the darkness at the edge of the clearing. There was a tenseness in his neck, in his whole body, making him feel like a tightly coiled spring.

"Do you think you'll ever go back to the States?" Corey asked.

Ash thought about the way he'd been before he came here. This place had changed him; the Indians had changed him, made him care even when he hadn't wanted to. If he left, who would translate for them? George had never mastered their language. And Ash suspected that sometime within the next few years George would return to the States. He was getting older, and this kind of life was hard on him.

No, Ash could never go back. This was his home. The Indians needed him. And he needed them.

He took a drag off his cigarette, then exhaled through the screen, watching the cloud of smoke stir up the bugs. "There's nothing in the States I miss. Guess I'm addicted to this soggy hellhole." He gave an abrupt, self-mocking laugh. "I've been back off and on, thinking I needed to get away from the wet heat and the bugs. But I always end up missing the same rotten things I thought I was sick of. It was so damn quiet, I couldn't even sleep."

"Would you like to play another game of cards?" Corey asked.

"No." He walked to the table and stubbed out the cigarette. "Think I'll sack out. Don't forget to douse the light before you go to bed."

Ash left her there, desire crashing through him like a tropical storm. He could have her. He had seen the welcome in her eyes. Why was he tormenting himself? He was no damn hero. No Dudley Do-right. *Take her, Adams. Make love to her.* If he did, would once be enough? Or would it only whet his appetite? Make him crave her all the more?

The bottom line was that he didn't want to hurt her. She had a life to go back to when she left. And he didn't want to think of her going back to her Polly Pure existence wearing a mammoth stain on her conscience.

He knew what he'd do. Get drunk. Stinking drunk.

chapter
fifteen

About an hour later Ash decided he wanted to hear some music. With exaggerated care he placed the whiskey bottle on the porch floor and pushed himself to his feet. He was snapping open the lid to the record player when he remembered he needed electricity.

The moonlight falling in the screened walls provided plenty of light, and somebody had left the generator right in the middle of the floor, so all he had to do was pick it up and carry it outside. The first two tugs of the starter cord resulted in feeble coughs. The third pull and the generator took off, spewing out rust from the muffler as it rumbled to life. Extension cord trailing behind him, Ash stepped back inside and plugged in the old mono record player.

Dog toenails chinked on the wooden floor. Bobbie was standing in the doorway, gray eyebrows drawn together in sleepy puzzlement.

"Just listening to some moldy oldies," Ash told him.

"Any requests?" He shuffled through the albums, the smell of mildew drifting up to him from the mold-encased covers. "Let's see. We've got Grand Funk, Zeppelin—you're a big Zeppelin fan, aren't you? Ah, now here's a classic—Eric Burdon and the Animals. But I feel like some blues. How about Clapton?"

Bobbie was polite enough to wag his stubby tail.

Ash pulled the record from the cover, slid it onto the ancient turntable, and with a hand as steady as a sharp-shooter's placed the needle in the black groove.

The putt-putt of the generator was joined by the chronic *tch, tch, tch* of the scratched record as the needle rode the sunwarped disk like a roller coaster.

Ash settled himself down onto the floor, back against the metal glider, long legs stretched out in front of him, bare feet crossed at the ankles. He took a drink of whiskey while Bobbie came to lie down beside him, heaving a weary dog sigh. Ash reached down to scratch him in his favorite spot—behind his ragged ear.

For a long time Corey lay on her side in bed, head on her arm, staring at the rectangular patch of moonlight on the wooden floor. Sultry night scents surrounded her: damp leaves and earth, night-blooming plants, all combined to invade her head like heavy incense. The insect sounds, the heartbeat of the jungle lulled her. . . .

She didn't know she had fallen asleep until her eyes opened and her befuddled brain became aware of distant music. She rolled onto her back and listened. Eric Clapton. And his voice sounded as if it were coming out of a tin can.

She tossed the sheets back from her bare legs, then slipped on her jeans under her cotton nightgown. Feeling a little like Briar Rose, she stepped out of her room to follow the music through the moonlight-dappled kitchen to the long, narrow porch.

Ash was lying on his back on the floor, bare chest glistening in the muggy heat, top button of his jeans undone. One knee was bent, his other leg was stretched out straight, Bobbie's head resting on his thigh. The whole porch smelled like gasoline.

She pulled her gaze away from Ash's long, lounging length to focus on the gray record player responsible for churning out the tin-can sound. It was like the one Mrs. Streeber, her fifth-grade gym teacher, had used for modern dance.

"Entrez vous,"—Ash made a sweeping gesture with one hand—"for the great stereo effect."

He was drunk. Not sloshy drunk, but drunk all the same.

"You shouldn't be drinking. Not after just getting over a malaria attack." Why was he doing this to himself? He had no common sense. He should be resting.

He braced up his head with one hand. Even his armpit was sexy. Good Lord. How on earth could anybody's hairy armpit be sexy? But Ash's was. If he had been a live model in her nurse's training class, she could have learned the muscle system in a day.

"Whiskey's medicinal. Purely medicinal." He cocked his head to one side and studied her, the dark circles under his eyes looking even darker in the moonlight.

"You know—I'd like to see you get loaded," he decided. "Really loaded."

"No you wouldn't. I've only been drunk once, and it was awful. I've never felt so sick."

"A lightweight, huh?" He scooted to a sitting position, leaning back against the glider. The disturbed Bobbie plodded over and resumed his place with neck stretched across Ash's leg.

"Have a seat."

With one bare foot Ash pushed a cane chair toward

her. "I've been thinking. Can you imagine me living in suburbia? Driving a station wagon to weekly meetings at the Royal Order of the Moose?" He let out a loud hoot.

What had brought all this on? Corey wondered.

"Shackled, that's what I'd be. Hey, they could make me Grand Poo-Ba, or whatever the hell it is. I could ride a moped in parades. Wear one of those caps with the tassels. Pez or fez—"

"Do you have to ridicule everything and everybody?"

"Oh. Pardon me. I suppose Dudley's a Mooser."

Corey moved to the record player and began sifting through the albums. They were all fifteen to twenty years old, and smelled like it. "You're going to have to shut off the generator. The fumes are coming in."

"Can't shut it off yet. 'Layla' happens to be one of my favorite songs. Back when ol' Eric was with Derek and the Dominos. This is the long version, you know. Nothing can touch the long version of 'Layla.' That's one thing I miss about the States," he confided as he rubbed the dog's head. "Good music. I used to go to this joint that played nothing but blues. Had a guy who could make a sax wail like nobody's business."

"Don't you have any current music?" she asked with amusement. There was something so charming, so utterly sweet about his moldy record collection.

"New stuff? Nah. I quit getting new stuff when disco started."

"Disco's been dead a long time."

His hand came out and he lightly wrapped his fingers around her ankle, causing an electrical jolt to run to every nerve ending.

He kept talking, as if he didn't realize he was touching her, as if he did it without thought.

"Remember the group Hellraisers? Saw them at Madison Square Garden." While he talked he drew small circles around her ankle bone with his thumb. The feel of his callused hand against her skin sent shock waves through her. And he was just touching her ankle. Corey's breath stopped as she thought about him touching her in other places. It would most likely send her into cardiac arrest. She pulled her foot away.

"I can still remember what I was doing when I heard that the Hellraisers had split up. I had this Harley . . . had just taken it for a spin to check out the timing. What were you doing when you found out?"

Corey looked blankly down at him. "What are you talking about?"

"You never heard of the Hellraisers?"

She shook her head.

"What am I thinking? You were probably listening to Mozart, or one of those chaps."

"I listen to popular music."

"Let's see. They were mid- to late sixties . . ." He looked as if he were tabulating the years in his head. "You would have just been a kid. Shoot, you wouldn't have even been a girl scout yet. You would have been a Brownie!" He threw back his head and laughed.

"You can't be that much older than I am," she protested.

"Lily, I'm at least a hundred. Here." He pointed to his chest. "And here." He pointed to his head. "While I was stealing hubcaps, you were shopping for patent leather shoes to match your pink ruffled party dress."

She wondered if there had ever been a time when he hadn't been cynical, when he hadn't ridiculed everything. A time when he had been happy . . .

She sat down on the edge of the glider. "Why do you always go out of your way to point out how different we are?"

Ash was looking right at her, one arm dangling over his bent knee. His eyes were clear, sober. Suddenly he didn't look drunk at all. Maybe he never had been. "I just don't want you to forget, that's all," he said. "It's easy to get mixed up when you're in the jungle. I don't want you to forget that you're who you are, and I'm who I am."

"And you think you might corrupt me?"

"That's what's driving me crazy, Lily." His mouth twisted into a lazy, seductive smile. "I'd *love* to corrupt you."

The desire in his smoldering eyes made her catch her breath, caused a sharp thrill to rush through her stomach.

"Think about this. When you get back to the States you'll forget you ever knew me. I'll just be ink on your report. Just the bush pilot who happened to fly you into the Amazon." He glanced down at the dog, petted it. "Hell, I'll bet you won't even mention me in your slide presentation."

Ash gently pushed the dog's head off his leg. "Come on, Bobbie."

Bobbie reluctantly stood up, walked a few feet away, then plopped down again. Ash went over to the record player and shut it off. The only sound was the steady beat of the generator and the clamor of Corey's erratic heart.

"Go to bed, Corey," Ash said quietly. He kept his back to her as he took the record off the turntable.

She got up, but when she reached the doorway she stopped, turned, and looked at Ash's broad, tan shoulders.

He had so much hurt inside him that she ached for him, wished she could wrap her arms around the little boy in him and make everything better. She wished she could wrap her arms around the man in him, comfort the man in him, make love to the man in him.

Somehow her secure, dull world had been knocked out from under her, been blown to bits by a rude bush pilot named Asher Adams. She had felt the pull from the first moment she'd laid eyes on him in the air-taxi building, but she had fought it, put it off as pure physical attraction, even though that wasn't like her—to be attracted to a man in such a way. But then, little by little things had changed.

There had been times when she caught a glimpse of his soul, saw a locked-away pain and sadness calling to her from the depths of his beautiful eyes. And she had felt a brief, fleeting oneness, touched but not captured, remembered in the way the mood of a dream is remembered long after you've awakened.

She clasped her hands together in front of her, arms straight. "Once, when I was little," she said in a quiet voice, "I crawled under an electric fence and my head touched the hot wire. It wouldn't have been so bad, but it had just rained, and I was soaked."

Slowly Ash turned around.

"The shock knocked me down, knocked the air out of me. I remember opening my eyes, and there was this roaring in my head, and it was hard to breathe. A light, bright like the sun, was flashing."

He watched her with still gray eyes.

She took a deep shaky breath. "When you touch me, it's like that. So, you see—" She made a half-apologetic gesture with one hand. "I don't think I'll ever forget you."

She stood there, waiting for his reaction. She wasn't any good at this kind of thing. Would she have to come right out and ask him to touch her, kiss her?

A myriad of emotions struggled across his face as if he fought some inner battle. Then he closed the distance between them and pulled her into his arms.

chapter
sixteen

Ash shifted Corey so she was leaning back in the cradle of
his arms. He looked down at her, moonlight reflecting
in his eyes, turning them a liquid silver. He gently brushed
his knuckles against the side of her face. Then, starting at
her temple, he let her hair sift through his fingers until he
reached its shiny flaxen tips. "Spun from moonlight. Just
like the legend says."

There was an incredible tenderness in his husky voice,
a tenderness she would never have thought possible of
Asher Adams. It made her throat hurt. He combed his
fingers through her hair, cupping the back of her head.

The roaring had returned. She was made spellbound
and breathless by his slow, careful gentleness. Every nerve
ending sang. Every cell craved his touch. *Don't let this
end. Please, don't ever let this end.*

His head came down, slowly closing the small space
that separated their lips, his soft breath caressing the side
of her face, then her parted, waiting mouth. His lips

pressed against hers, and she felt an awakening in her breasts and a tightening in her abdomen. His arm pulled her even closer as she clung to his rock-hard shoulders. She could feel his open hand across her lower back, the firm pressure pulling her against him, his hard angles meeting her soft ones, their bodies touching from chest to knee.

"I want to make love to you," he whispered against her mouth.

A searing flame shot through her. She wanted him. She, who had always feared she might be frigid, wanted Asher Adams. She wanted to know him intimately. She wanted to know the gentleness he hid so well, wanted to be a part of the tumultuous emotions that ravaged through him. She wanted to know how it felt to be made love to by this man, to become a total part of him.

And she was scared to death.

His hand slid down to cup her bottom, pulling her up against him, her hips pressing into his taut thighs. Like sweet, exquisite torture, he licked her lips, moistening them, then he slowly eased his tongue inside her mouth, drawing a shuddering sigh of pleasure from her. He dragged his mouth away and buried his face in her neck.

"I want you so much."

His voice was ragged and she could sense that he fought to keep his passion under control. The idea that she could do this to him thrilled and frightened her at the same time.

"I want to touch you everywhere. Every part of you."

Fear overrode desire, and she stiffened involuntarily.

"Lily." He tilted her face up to his. "Don't be afraid of me."

Don't be afraid! He was towering over her, his broad chest gleaming, face unshaven, looking like a cross between a pirate and a Hell's Angel, and he was telling her not to be afraid?

Suddenly she felt certain that she could only disap-

point him. They were so different. What did she know of
his kind of passion?

"I'm skinny," she blurted out before she could stop
herself, feeling awkward and nervous and afraid of the
unknown. He was so physical, could be so explosive.

A smile tugged at the corners of his sensuous mouth.
"You're sexy as hell."

"I have freckles, in a lot of places."

"I want to find and kiss every one."

The very thought of his mouth moving over the secret
places of her body made her breathless, made her knees
weak. "Sometimes, I used to think that—that I—" She
stopped, too embarrassed to go on.

"Tell me," he coaxed.

"I used to be afraid, think maybe I was—" She
dropped her chin so she wouldn't have to look at him.
"Frigid. I used to think I was frigid."

"Let's conduct a little test." There was a smile in his
voice.

He lightly traced a finger across one nipple. The thin
fabric being rubbed against the pliant tip acted like an
aphrodisiac. A warm heaviness settled over her. Her
breath caught in her throat, and when she looked up at
him, her eyelids felt incredibly heavy.

"Not frigid," he stated. "Definitely not frigid." He
dropped both his hands to her waist. When she could
think again, she continued cataloging her weak points.
"I'm not very . . . worldly."

"Worldly isn't good. Believe me."

He was being so gentle, so patient, so understanding.
Her fear receded.

"Wait here." He let go of her and moved away.

Feeling lost without his arms around her, she watched
in puzzlement as he put another album on the record
player.

He turned around and pulled her into his arms. "Bet
you've never danced in a jungle before."

"No. But I thought . . ."

"What? What did you think?"

A slow lazy smile played around the corners of his mouth, his hands on her back kneading her tense muscles. "That we were going to make love?"

What the heck, pride was such a little thing. She swallowed, then nodded.

He pulled her closer and pressed a firm, hard kiss on her parted lips. "I think we are, Corey McKinney." His voice was rough and very sexy. "I think we are."

"Oh," she breathed.

The music started. And this time she hardly noticed that the record was ancient and scratched and the melody sounded as if it were coming from a tin can.

Mellow, nostalgic, almost-remembered notes meshed magically with the steamy, trance-inducing air, becoming a part of it.

She recognized the plaintive cry of a harmonica, answered by the achingly sweet notes of a violin. It was a song out of time for a place out of time.

She could easily imagine that there was no past, no future. It was just a man, a woman, and the jungle.

Ash swept her around the narrow porch in a slow, exaggerated waltz. The laughing Ash. The man-child. An Ash who wasn't bitter, wasn't haunted by ghosts.

Circling like a river,
Over brightly colored stones,
Breaking up my soul,
and taking part of me home
Leaving the other half,
to tumble all alone,
Love, love, where did you go?

Hundreds of miles from civilization, in the middle of the Amazon jungle, they waltzed to the haunting music, a floating, dreamy song that seemed as much a part of the sultry, humid night as the very air itself.

Both in worn jeans—Ash shirtless, Corey with her old cotton nightgown swirling around her knees, their bare feet skimming the floor—they danced. Her small hand nestled in his large one while his other hand pressed firmly into the small of her back. Occasionally she felt her nipples brush up against his chest, sending a current of electricity through her.

Ash untwined their fingers so he could put both arms around her and pull her closer while the wistful, bittersweet song wrapped itself around them like a cool cotton sheet on a hot night.

When the song ended, Ash slipped away just long enough to shut off the generator, then returned to pull Corey back into his arms. This time the only music was the steady hum of the jungle, the combined erratic beating of their hearts, and their quickening breath.

"I should have shaved." His deep, gravelly voice was husky against her ear. "Your skin is so soft. I don't want to scratch you."

She rubbed her palm against his lean jaw, feeling the sandpaper of his beard, thinking how sexy he was, how he made her blood flow warm and pulsing. "That's okay. I like it." She felt his dimpled smile against her hand.

Boldly she stood on tiptoe and traced her tongue along his lips. The tremor of his muscles passed through her fingertips, and she was awed and thrilled at the same time.

He groaned and pulled her thighs into him, crushing his mouth to hers, squeezing the air from her lungs.

She felt his pulsating hardness straining against his jeans, pressing against her tight abdomen. His hands moved up her sides, slipping her gown higher until both breasts were exposed to his gaze. Damp air brushed her nipples, making them tighten. Then Ash's lips were there, wetting and warming them, his tongue circling, teasing first one tingling nipple till it became stiff and pleasure-swollen, then moving to the other.

He stopped long enough to slip her gown from her, pulling her naked chest against his. Skin against glorious skin.

She looked down to where her breasts were two mounds pressed against the damp hardness of his chest, looking pale and delicate against his brownness.

One of his hands trailed down between her jean-covered legs, and she let out a gasp. She felt as if she were falling, drifting away with the tide. Todd had never touched her this way.

Ash looked down at her, and his expression held curiosity as he continued to stroke her. Her eyes had fallen halfway closed, and she clung to his arms with both hands.

"You've never been touched like this, have you?" he asked in a gentle, slightly shaky voice.

"No," she sighed. "But if you keep it up, the mystery of human spontaneous combustion may be solved."

He laughed.

And Corey thought how very nice it was to feel the deep rumble in his chest. Then he began kissing her again while he unbuttoned her jeans. She heard the sound of the zipper going down. Then his hand skimmed her pleasure-taut stomach, then slipped lower. A finger lifted the elastic band of her nylon panties, allowing his hand to inch inside to stroke the mound of silky hair. She moaned into his open mouth, her legs almost buckling under her.

His callused finger slid lower.

Waves of hot pleasure crashed against her. If he hadn't been holding her up, she would have slid to the floor. His finger circled the small, soft bud, and she couldn't believe that feeling him touch her there could cause such hot, tumultuous sensations in her, and she let out a low moan.

Gradually the heat-swirling world around her cleared, and she became aware that both of his hands were on her waist. She looked up at him with hazy, bemused eyes.

"Corey—" Ash gently pulled her back, his own eyes full of tenderness and a slight puzzlement. "Corey—"

Cloudy eyes fought to focus on him. "Mmm?"

"I know I've been teasing you about being a virgin. But you are, aren't you?"

Her eyes cleared somewhat. "No. No, I'm not." Something flashed across his features and was gone before she could read it. Disappointment? Acceptance? Both? She wasn't sure.

"Then . . ." He seemed baffled. "Then how come you've never been touched like I was just touching you?"

"We just never—I didn't know. We didn't . . ." *Oh, Lord. Save me.* She could feel hot color mounting her cheeks.

Ash laughed and wrapped his arms tightly around her. "That's okay, little one. I get the picture. I just wanted to be sure I didn't hurt you."

"It always hurts a little, doesn't it?" she asked bravely, trustingly.

"Lily, Lily." He swung her half-naked body up into his arms.

"What are we doing?"

"Going to my room. I'm going to teach you that making love is more than tab A going into slot B."

She locked her bare arms around his neck, feeling light and giddy. "You have completely captivated me with your passionate prose." Her lips were wet from his kisses, her eyes drowsy and languorous.

He laughed, and the laugh was pure and clean, like the child in him.

———

He knew it shouldn't have mattered, but he was glad she knew so little about sex. She thought it always hurt! Cripes! Dudley must be quite the Romeo.

Ash put her down on the bed, and the sight of her lying there, her breasts showing creamy and rose-tipped in the moonlight, almost drove him crazy. The air around them seemed to be filled with electricity. Charged impulses skimmed along the surface of his skin.

He sat down beside her. The wide-eyed worry was back in her eyes. Watching her face for reaction, he reached out and touched one nipple. She drew in a breath. Slowly he circled the rosy tip, bringing it erect. He felt her body relax beside him, saw her eyelids flutter, then drift half closed.

The hazy desire in her eyes sent fresh waves of passion crashing through his loins. His gaze traveled over her, and his own breath caught. She was so damn beautiful. Her parted lips seemed to be begging to be kissed, her eyes were dark and liquid and languorous. Frigid? Hardly. Yet there was an air of fragile vulnerability about her that made his heart twist.

"I'd never hurt you." His voice was husky and slightly shaky.

"I know."

His mouth came down on hers, her sweet eagerness sending his pulses racing. When he finally dragged his lips away, she whimpered in protest, clinging to his arms.

He pulled off her jeans, stripping them from her long, beautiful legs. A tremor ran through him.

"You're shaking," she said in an awe-filled voice.

"You're driving me crazy." He could sense the pent-up passion in her that equaled and rivaled his own. He had felt it the first time he had touched her. And now he wondered just what he was unleashing.

He tossed her jeans to the floor, then stood and quickly peeled his own from his damp flesh, her eyes watching him all the while, moving down his body, then back to his face, desire and uncertainty in her face.

Then he was back beside her, letting his hand trail up her smooth calf to her bent knee, to her thigh. Dancer's legs. Firm and shapely, skin so soft.

God, but she was beautiful. This was like a dream.

"Are you real?" he whispered, one hand moving to touch the petal-soft skin of her inner thighs. "Or have I just been alone in the jungle too long?"

Her small hands wrapped around his neck, pulling him down to her so that the soft roundness of her breasts pressed against his chest. "If this isn't real, then we're both having the same dream." Her voice was husky, hinting at the awakening passions that lay just below the surface.

He braced his elbows on either side of her face, so all his weight wasn't on her. Then he slowly brought his head down. He drove his tongue inside her open mouth, and a raw thrill shot through him as her tongue eagerly met his.

Everything was a throbbing orange haze. He knew he was still alive and on earth because he could feel his heart slamming against his rib cage. His erection was straining against the cotton of his shorts, begging for release. But he had to take this slow, do it right.

He leaned a little to the side, so he could slide his hand down. The sweet scent of her naked, perspiring skin drifted up to him, teasing the maddening desire that he was trying so hard to keep in check. If he let loose, he'd be tearing off his clothes and driving himself into her like a jackhammer.

His shaky hand moved to touch her breasts. He rubbed the pliant nipple with his thumb, loving the way she squirmed and moaned under him, loving the feel of her skin under his hands.

"Ash . . ." He could sense her eager, impatient frustration, reveled in it.

"There's no hurry," he said softly. He wanted to savor this. He bent his head and took the tip of her breast in his mouth, sucking and circling it with his hot tongue. She tasted so good.

He felt her fingers dig into his hair, and she arched against him, the fire blazing all around them now.

He moved back long enough to pull off her panties. She lifted her hips, then he was sliding the garment down the rest of the way, kissing a trail behind it. Lying down beside her, he pulled her naked body up against him. He slipped one knee between her legs, pushing them apart. Then his hand moved up her inner thigh, stroking the sweet flesh. He touched the mound of soft hair, combing his fingers through it before moving lower to feel the delicate folds of hot skin.

He would love to kiss her there, taste her, but he knew he couldn't wait. Things were moving too fast.

He parted the dewy folds, stroking, touching. . . .

She let out a moan from deep in her throat and rotated herself against his palm. He slipped a finger inside her softness, a place he thought he'd never be, never touch. God, this was Corey, Lily. He withdrew his finger and began deliberately circling the small bud nestled within the velvet folds of flesh. She writhed beneath him, her hot desire set to flames by his knowledgeable touch.

"Ash." Her voice was a pant, her fingers digging into the flesh of his back. "Do something. You're torturing me—"

"But what sweet torture." He quickly stood and stripped off his shorts, then was back beside her, aware that he trembled.

"I'm sweating," she mumbled in a slurred voice.

"Join the club," he whispered.

She made a sound that he took for a laugh, then her fingers were raking down his back to his hips, digging into his flesh, urgently trying to tug him closer.

He pulled her up against him, thrilling at the feel of her hot wet skin slipping against his.

He stroked between her legs before sliding his finger inside her once more, then two fingers, assuring himself that she was ready for him.

Pressure was building inside him like an active volcano. There was a roaring in his ears. Easy, he reminded himself. This was Lily. Sweet, sweet, Lily. . . .

With a trembling hand he smoothed her wet hair back from her sweating temples, kissing her on the forehead. "If this hurts, tell me. Making love should never hurt. It should only feel"—he had to take a shaking breath before he could go on—"it should only feel good. . . ." He positioned himself over her, trying to keep some of his weight from her.

"Good," she mumbled.

He breathed through a haze of pleasurable sensations. "Sorry I'm not more poetic."

Her small hands splayed across the taut muscles of his buttocks, pulling him down. Feeling her touch him in such a way sent his desire rocketing. He couldn't ever remember so much ache, so much heat.

Her creamy thighs were open for him, and she was pulling him down, her hands urgent. "I won't break," she breathed.

With his fingers he parted the soft folds of her flesh, then slid himself into her. It was like sliding into hot liquid velvet. Slow, so slow. He moved down, deeper and deeper . . . drowning. . . .

Harder, had to be harder, faster. But he held back, forced himself to be gentle, forced himself to stop where he was, buried deep within her.

"Corey." Lights swirled around him, and he forgot what he was going to say. "Ahhh." Her soft shapely legs were wrapped around his naked hips. If only he could die like this.

"Corey?"

He took a shuddering breath. And he'd thought he had no self-control! Jesus. It was taking everything in him to keep from driving into her as hard and fast as he could.

"Are you okay? Am I hurting you?" he said hoarsely.

"No, no."

Her voice sounded far-off and slurred, as if he'd called her back from somewhere.

"God, you feel so good."

He felt as if he were going to burst.

"Like A going into B?" Her voice was like a drifting feather.

"Yeah."

She rolled her hips under him, the sweat-slicked skin of her stomach sliding against his. "This feels wonderful," she said breathlessly. *"You* feel wonderful." He hardly recognized her pleasure-drugged voice.

And then she asked, "Are we done?"

He let out a painful burst of laughter. "We're only halfway there, sweetheart."

"Oh. I'm glad."

He started moving inside her, carefully at first. She was tight, but her silky softness welcomed him, allowing him to stroke deeply within her warmth. He pulled away, almost leaving her. When he slowly brought himself back inside, she arched up, meeting his downward stroke with a driving force of her own that stole the air from his lungs. He pulled back, then plunged again, harder this time, and again she met him, rolling her hips and opening her thighs more to allow him deeper access.

Something exploded in him. He couldn't hold himself back any longer. He drove himself into her—again, and again—the combination of their frictionless, slick skin making their hot bodies slide erotically against each other.

She was making pleasure-soft sounds that drove him mad, that sent flashing heat crashing to every nerve ending. He felt her small body stiffen in his hands, trembling shudders running through her as she desperately clung to him.

Through a mist he plunged into her one more time. Then it seemed like the world was turning to light, a blaze of warmth surrounding him, the likes of which he'd never felt before. Weakness hit him, and he wrapped his arms tightly around her, pulling her closer, crushing her sweetness under him, never wanting to let her go.

Corey felt as if she were swirling through a kaleidoscope of sunlight and warm colors. Flying through clouds, then slowly, slowly drifting back to earth.

Gradually she became aware of Ash's sweat-soaked body pressing heavily into her. His arms were wrapped tightly around her. She could feel the thunder of his heart against her chest, hear his heavy, uneven breathing in her ear while his chest rose and fell against her. She shifted, opening her thighs more, wanting him to stay there forever.

When she could finally talk, she whispered, "What was that?"

"What?" He was out of breath.

"That. What just happened. That feeling I just had. As if I were floating on a magic carpet, drifting . . ."

Silence. Then, "I think that was an orgasm." His breathless voice was laced with amusement.

"Ah," she said in a scholarly tone. "Well, I don't like that word. No, it was more like . . . like an astral flight. Yes," she decided, her voice dropping to a ghost of a whisper, "that's what it was."

She felt him smile against her neck. His hair tickled her face. She loved the way it smelled, like the green jungle.

She became aware of feeling incredibly sleepy, drugged almost.

Before she could protest, he slowly withdrew, then left her, the bed shifting as he got up.

"Ash?"

"Be right back."

Corey's eyes had fallen shut by the time he returned. She just couldn't keep them open any longer.

"I sweat all over you," he said.

A towel was being stroked across her neck, then her breasts and stomach. "Ah, that feels good," she said with a sleepy smile, warmth radiating from every pore. Her body was like lead. Under normal circumstances she would have been self-conscious lying naked while he smoothed the cloth over her, but she felt so lethargic, so heavy. So *good*. "It's my sweat too," she mumbled. She couldn't open her eyes. Her voice was small and slurred.

She felt the bed shift, sensed that he was leaning over her. She felt him smoothing back the hair from her face. "Lily, are you okay?"

"Sleepy," she muttered with a groggy smile. "So sleepy. Sorry."

"Must be a case of astral flight lag." His hand moved down the side of her face in a soft caress. He settled himself next to her, pulling her up against his chest, kissing her brow. "You're so sweet, so incredibly sweet," she heard him whisper. "My Care package." His arms tightened around her.

A damp breeze drifted in the window, skimming the skin that wasn't pressed against Ash. Through a sleepy haze Corey heard the gentle tinkling of the chimes that hung near the front steps. So delicate, like music from a dream. A Stradivarius couldn't have sounded more haunting.

"The chimes . . ." she mumbled against his neck. "Chimes made from gears." It took all of her willpower to keep her thoughts focused, to keep from drifting off again. She had to stay awake to ask him. "Who made them?"

At first he didn't answer, as if he didn't want her to know, as if it embarrassed him. "I did."

She smiled against his salty skin, then turned her face slightly so she could brush a sleepy kiss against his neck. "That's what I thought."

chapter
seventeen

Corey came awake in gradual stages. First she was aware
of a heavy weight across her middle. Then she heard
steady breathing not far from her left ear. Then she realized bare skin was pressing against her bare skin.

Oh, Lord.

She was in Ash's bed, and underneath the white cotton sheet that was tangled around their legs and waists,
they were both naked. And it was morning. No darkness
to hide behind. How could she have done such a thing?

Cautiously she turned her head to the side to look at
Ash. She felt a pang that had nothing to do with remorse
or regret.

He was lying on his stomach, face toward her, asleep.
His hair was tousled, like a scruffy urchin's, and his beard
was even darker than it had been yesterday. He looked
masculine, and sexy, so very sexy. Yes, Asher Adams was a
living, breathing aphrodisiac.

So what was *she* doing in his bed? And worse yet,

what was she supposed to do now? She was a novice at this kind of thing, at waking up naked in a man's bed.

Yet, she didn't feel guilty. Awkward, yes. Unsure of herself, yes. Guilty, no. She, whose views on sex had always bordered on stuffy and old-fashioned, didn't feel one iota of guilt at waking up in Ash's bed. All she could think about was the way his hands had felt on her body, how his skin had tasted, how tender and gentle he had been, how he had made her feel.

She had to get away before he woke up. That's all there was to it. She inched toward the side of the bed. His arm tightened around her and she looked down. Her skin was pale and delicate-looking in contrast to his brown ruggedness.

Born to Raise Hell. Well, he certainly had. The tattoo served as a visual reminder that even though this was her first "morning after," she was sure it wasn't his.

She had to get up, get her clothes. Her clothes!

Frantically she scanned the cluttered room, then recalled that he had stripped her gown from her on the porch, and she hadn't let out a whimper of protest. If he had corrupted her, she had let him, practically begged to be corrupted.

She had to get out of there before he woke up, she told herself again, a fresh wave of panic rising in her. She placed tentative fingers on his wrist, her hand barely wrapping halfway around the strong bones. Carefully she tried to lift his arm from her waist so she could slip away and dress, so she could at least confront him fully clothed.

Ash's breathing abruptly changed. "Going somewhere?" he asked groggily, his voice even more gravelly than usual. But the eyes that opened to stare at her were surprisingly alert.

Quickly she looked away, focusing on the sooty lamp hanging from a hook in the ceiling. "Yes, but your arm—you'll have to let go of me." Heat suffused her face.

Help. She wished she could click her naked heels

together and disappear. *I'm not used to this. I'm no good at this kind of thing.*

He removed his arm from her stomach and rolled to his side so he could watch her, one hand braced under his head. Her hands flashed down, frantically fumbling for the sheet stretched across her waist, tugging, but it was caught under him. He only smiled, not budging. She moved to cover her breasts with her arms, then stopped. She wouldn't allow herself to shrink in front of him. He would probably laugh and ridicule her belated attempt at modesty.

Of course, he didn't appear embarrassed in the least. He was acting as if they woke up this way every day. He'd probably woken up with a lot of women, had lots of practice at being casual.

The thought only made her feel worse, reminding her that what had occurred between them was transient. She had no claim on him; he had none on her.

"I need my clothes," she informed the lamp, trying to keep her voice normal, hoping he wouldn't notice that the last word wobbled slightly.

"Go ahead and get them. Nobody's stopping you."

Meaning she should stand up totally nude and stroll around the room gathering up her jeans and underpants while he stayed in bed and watched.

She drew in a sharp breath as she felt his hand trail from her shoulder to her elbow. For every action there is an equal or greater reaction. The law of motion had taken on a whole new meaning. And she had always thought physics dull.

He touched the soft skin on the outside of her breast, one finger stroking up and down, testing the swell. Hot sensations fluttered down from her chest to her stomach. Silently she cursed herself. Cursed him. Cursed her body that he knew how to play so well.

Then he was looming over her, blocking out her focal point—the oil lamp. He wound an arm around her back, pulling her close, his chest just brushing her rigid, upright nipples. He brought his head closer. . . . She could feel his hard arousal pressing insistently against the soft skin of her inner thigh. Her heart was beating frantically against her rib cage. Hammering, hammering. What was he doing to her? Nice girls didn't do things like this, and enjoy them so immensely.

She held her breath, held her body perfectly still, all thoughts and nerve endings anticipating his next move.

"You look even better in the light." He smiled, his eyes flashing. "I can see all your freckles."

Blood was charging through her veins, singing in her ears. Her thought processes were shutting down, closing up shop. She was floating, floating away. She released her trapped breath.

His mouth, when it finally touched hers, was hot and wet and demanding.

That must have been the final link in the chain of cause and effect. She was gone again. She wrapped her arms around him, moaning, pulling him closer.

A crashing came from outside, followed by loud bleating, but Corey hardly noticed until the lips on hers stilled and the hand cupping her breast paused. Another loud bleat.

He dragged his mouth away. "Damn!" He buried his face in her neck, both arms pulling her close. "Elvira." The word came breathlessly. "Gotta milk Elvira before she tears up the porch."

Elbows on either side of her head, he levered himself up, his smoky eyes still smoldering with desire. Then his expression changed. "Your skin! Your poor skin!" Without warning he jerked the sheet down past her feet.

"Ash!" She made a grab for it, but was too late.

"Your beautiful skin. Oh, Corey," he moaned in obvious remorse, "I'm sorry."

She could feel herself blushing to the roots of her hair

while he inspected her with a critical eye, and a critical hand.

"Why didn't I shave?" he berated himself. "You have whisker burns everywhere! On your neck, your stomach . . ." His hand moved down her flat abdomen to her hips . . . to her thighs. "Your legs."

"That's okay." She gulped. He didn't need to catalogue everything. No man had ever seen her completely naked. Ever. "Ash, please . . ."

He looked up at her face, seeming to finally take in the fact that she was uncomfortable. "I thought you had a year of nurse's training. Thought you were used to seeing a lot of skin. Nurses don't blush."

"I saw other people's skin. They didn't see mine."

"Hey, it's only a body. We all have one, right?" A gleam settled in his silver eyes. "Yours just happens to be especially nice, what can I say?" He bent his head to carefully place a kiss on her navel, his hair brushing softly against her stomach, sending a thrill through her.

His hands were magic—his mouth was magic. He took her breath away. . . .

"You have a sexy belly button. Just sexy as hell." He moved farther down and paused, his arms cradling her thighs. When he looked back up at her across an expanse of her bare skin, there was a devilish light in his eyes.

Why, he was going to kiss her, *there*. Heat flashed through her.

His head went down and he kissed first one bent knee, then the other. "Sexy knees. You have damn sexy knees." He slid back up her body, making a few quick stops along the way, kissing and verbally admiring several of her freckles.

Then he untangled the sheet and pulled it up to her chin, his hands braced on either side of her head. "Better?"

Her throat suddenly felt tight. All she could do was blink.

The goat bleated again, if it could be called a bleat. It was more like a bellow. Hooves kicked impatiently at the porch door.

"Okay, okay!" The bed dipped. "I'm coming."

Ash pulled on his underwear and jeans—completely unself-consciously, she noted wryly—and strode from the bedroom. Half a second later he returned, planted a hard kiss on her astonished mouth, then left again.

Safe in her own room, Corey tugged a shirt over her head, all the while aware of her sexually awakened body. She felt tingly in places she'd never felt tingly before. Every cell, every pore, was alive. Her senses were heightened to a fresh awareness.

She touched her thoroughly kissed lips. They were tender and a little swollen. She could feel places on her body where Ash's face had rubbed. Heat flashed through her as she thought of his mouth moving across the sensitive surface of her skin. Why hadn't it been this way with Todd?

That mocking inner voice was talking to her again, and this time it rang with a truth she wasn't sure she wanted to confront: she and Todd were never meant to be lovers, only friends. That's why his kisses had held no excitement for her, why his touch didn't cause sparks to flicker across her skin.

Asher Adams, what have you done to me?

Merely turned her whole world upside down and inside out. That's all.

Knowing she couldn't very well spend the day hiding in her room, she took a deep bracing breath and walked through the doorway. When she got to the kitchen she could hear Ash's deep voice coming from outside.

He was talking to the animals. She couldn't make out the words, but his tone conveyed patience, kindness.

How could she have ever thought him heartless and cruel when, in fact, just the opposite was true? When he cared about something or somebody, he cared completely. She wondered how it would feel to be included in the aura of his caring. Quickly she caught herself, put a halt to that kind of thinking. It could lead nowhere. She was only a pleasant diversion for him, nothing more. And that knowledge hurt, even though she told herself sternly that it shouldn't.

The second Ash stepped into the kitchen her heart began beating faster. She saw a flash of something in his smoky eyes. Desire? Memories of last night?

He looked fit and healthy, all signs of the malaria gone. He'd taken a bath and shaved. His hair was wet, dripping onto the towel he'd slung around his neck. His chest was bare; clean jeans clung tightly to lean hips. He took her breath away.

A week ago she wouldn't have believed it if somebody told her that she would find herself so physically attracted to a man like Ash. She made a mental list of all his bad points: He was rude, he was a smart aleck, he smoked, he drank, he cussed. The man even had a tattoo. So why did the combination of all those undesirable traits make him so appealing? So incredibly sexy?

She felt a warm glow inside. She thought about his hands touching her, hard calluses sliding over perspiring skin. Quickly, before he could read her thoughts, she averted her gaze, tried to think of anything but Ash.

"Hungry?"

Like a magnet her eyes were drawn back to him. Now that he'd shaved, his well-formed lips contrasted with the smoothness of his skin. She could see the slight, slashing indentations in his cheeks, indentations that turned to dimples whenever he smiled. She loved to see him smile, loved to hear the deep rumble of his laughter.

She conjured up a picture of him as a child. He would have been the class clown, hiding a world of hurt behind name-calling and quick retorts. And he was still hiding, hiding that gentleness, that kindness she had glimpsed and felt more than once.

The warm glow she'd been aware of earlier was still there, only now it was running through her veins like wine.

What are you doing to me, Asher Adams?

"Got some bananas here to help the soggy cereal go down." He put them on the table along with the goat's milk.

Her eyes followed him as he strode to the cupboard and pulled out two bowls and the boxes of cereal. Unconsciously she admired the play of muscles across his back and shoulders.

"White Castle hamburgers." He unloaded everything on the table. "What I wouldn't do for a couple dozen White Castle hamburgers right now. Whenever I go to the States, I hit all the traditional joints. McDonald's, Pizza Hut. You like anchovy pizza?"

"No."

"Anchovy pizza and beer. Lots of beer."

Corey felt a smile tug at the corners of her mouth. So, he was playing his favorite game. The one called let's-forget-about-everything-that-happened-in-the-last-twenty-four-hours. Well, for once she didn't mind playing it with him. She needed time to stabilize, to think, to come up for air.

They ate their cereal. But for the addition of the unusually sweet bananas, she and Ash were playing out the same scenario they'd enacted two days before. Except two days before they had been strangers.

How did one define strangers? Did sharing a thermos of water make you not strangers? Was it gauged by the amount you know about a person? What they knew about you?

Ash slept on his stomach. She knew that. He snored.

He liked vintage rock and roll. What did that make them? Acquaintances? Friends? Lovers?

Corey's mind was a jumble of confusion. She, who had always been so analytical, who always thought things through in a very precise manner, was confused.

The jungle has a way of distorting things, Ash had warned. Was that true? Was that what was happening to her? She certainly didn't feel like the same person she had been just three days before. She'd come here to file a report for her church—a report she had completely put from her mind. Had she put reality aside with it? Lost perspective?

She had to salvage something, get at least one wheel back on track. She gave a small "ahem," then, "What are some of the things you feel you need the most here?" She knew her question would seem to have sprung from nowhere. "I'll put it in my report."

He looked surprised at the sudden revival of her role as interviewer, but didn't hesitate to answer. "There are lots of things we need." His voice was slightly muffled as he swallowed the last spoonful of cereal. "A well, a building to house sick natives. But I'd have to say medicine's number one on the list."

He put down his spoon and tipped his chair, balancing it on two back legs. "There's this new miracle drug called ivermectin. Ever hear of it?"

She shook her head and rested her elbows on the table, chin in her cupped palm.

"It's expensive as all hell, but a real breakthrough in treating river blindness. The Tchikao don't have it yet, but most of the other tribes are infected with it to some degree. I've had mothers bring totally blind kids here, begging us to help."

His clean-shaven face suddenly registered anger, frustration. He shook his shaggy head. "How the hell do you explain politics to natives? How do you tell them that in order for their child to see again, it's gonna take some big bucks and somebody with a lot of influence?"

"You think this drug would make that much difference?"

"It completely cures ninety-five percent of these cases, with no side effects." He lifted his arms and raked back his hair with both hands, then locked his fingers behind his head. "It's so damn frustrating when you know there's a cure out there. And it can be administered easily. Orally, like polio vaccine."

Regardless of what he might say, his hope of finding Luke wasn't the only thing binding him to this wild and dangerous land, Corey realized. No, he was a part of it.

He didn't belong in a world of clocks, of traffic lights and speed limits. No, he was as much a part of the Amazon as the bellbird, as the anaconda.

And it came to her not so much in words, but more like a gentle summer rain: she loved him. She loved Asher Adams. It was the answer, the missing puzzle piece. The reason she'd felt no guilt. Why their lovemaking had seemed so right. Everything made perfect sense now.

The realization stunned her. Shocked her. Left her feeling bereft, lost. What was she going to do?

Ash was a humanitarian. He protected those weaker than himself. And that meant her. That meant that even though he had shown her kindness and consideration, he would have shown the same to anyone.

Love doesn't insist on its own way . . . love bears all things . . . endures all things. He must never know, never find out.

In her thoughts she carved her secret deep in the trunk of a sturdy oak. She, Corey McKinney, loved Asher Adams.

"Corey?"

Ash's voice came to her through a thick fog, and she found herself staring at the dark seam that separated the table into two semicircles. She blinked and dragged her eyes upward, stopping when they locked with Ash's concerned gaze.

Panic! She could feel the sweat on her skin, feel the change in her heartbeat. Did her love show? Could he see it in her face?

She immediately began trying to talk herself out of it, to convince herself that she had made a mistake. Nobody fell in love with somebody in three days. That happened to ditzy girls who wore gobs of makeup and made necklaces out of pop tops. And they usually fell out of love just as fast.

His words came back to her again: *The jungle has a way of distorting things.*

"Corey? Are you okay?"

No! she wanted to shout. *No, I'm not okay. Because I've fallen in love with you.* She pushed her chair back. Her hands and voice trembled. "I . . . I think I'll go take a bath."

He got up too. "I'm coming with you." His voice held concern. "I don't want you going by yourself."

"No!"

He looked taken aback. "Corey."

"No," she repeated, forcing herself to say it calmly so he wouldn't suspect something was wrong.

She had gone through her whole life being so practical. She was the person other people came to for counsel, for help in organizing their mixed-up lives. And she had doled out advice in what she now saw had been an almost patronizing manner, feeling quite safe and secure, knowing her own life lay ahead of her like a straight desert highway.

So why had this happened to her? And why *him?* Why Ash? A man as different from her as the sun is different from the moon.

Nothing made sense anymore. She had to be alone, had to sort things out.

In a half trance she walked to the corner cupboard

and pulled out a towel along with the damp sliver of yellow soap Ash had used earlier. Then she turned, the porch door slamming behind her, leaving him staring after her as she strode toward the river.

Ash knew what he should do. Go get his plane right now. Get rid of her today. That's what he should do. Instead, he waited a few minutes before following her down to the river, stopping near enough to hear if she needed him but not close enough to disturb her.

Emotional confrontations weren't his thing. He avoided them at all cost. But he was going to have to have a talk with Corey. She was flogging herself already. Then another thought hit like a polished-off fifth of tequila. Was she expecting something from him after last night?

That ugly word *commitment* bounced around in his skull. She was engaged, right? That meant he was safe, didn't it?

She had her life mapped out by Emily Post and Walt Disney. Surely she knew what last night had been. But what had it been? Nothing?

Damn! There couldn't be anything further from the truth. He'd never felt anything so strong. She had rocked his soul, if he had one. He'd felt bewildered and overwhelmed by her, by his reaction to her.

And it scared the absolute hell out of him.

He lit a cigarette, absentmindedly pitching the match to the ground. He exhaled slowly.

She'd looked so breakable the first time he'd seen her sitting there in that shack of an air-taxi building. A ray of sunlight in a hovel, like the fragile Amazon lily that grew among the wilds of the jungle.

He'd felt a rage that some idiot had been ignorant enough to allow her to come. On the other hand, he sure as hell hadn't wanted to play babysitter, didn't want the responsibility of making sure she came back alive and un-harmed. He knew the fierceness of the jungle. The jungle took people he cared about, took them and never gave them back.

He heard her coming, and with forefinger to thumb, sent his cigarette spinning away in an arc. Then he stepped out in the open, blocking her path with his arm, hand braced against a tree trunk.

She looked up at him, waiting. Her hair was wet, making it appear caramel brown. It contrasted with her pale face and huge mahogany eyes. Her eyes. Looking into her sad eyes made his chest hurt. "We need to talk—about last night."

"There's nothing to talk about."

Her voice was as calm as the eye of a storm. She ducked under his arm and started walking toward the house. "If you think I'm mad or upset, or that I blame you, I don't." The words were tossed back over her shoulder. Her wet hair had soaked through her blouse, making a wet V down her back.

He came after her, falling in step beside her. "But you *should* blame me."

"Just because your shoulders are broader?" she asked with a half smile. "I know what you're trying to do."

He cut in front, swinging around to face her. "When you get back to the States, I want you to forget this episode of your life ever happened. I want to think of you back in Pleasantville, married to"—something seemed to catch in his throat and he almost choked—"married to what's-his-name. With your nice house and garden and white picket fence; with your two kids and their Kool-Aid smiles, the station wagon, the big front porch."

She stopped; he stopped.

"And a swing?" She smiled. "Will I have a porch swing?"

The sadness was still there, but there was a teasing light in her eyes he couldn't understand.

"Yeah, the goddamn swing. That's the way it should be. The life you should have. And I sure as hell don't want you ruining it by carrying a ton of guilt with you for the next fifty years. Corey, I took advantage of your inexperience. That's the truth. I did things I knew would arouse you. It wasn't your fault."

She buried her face in her hands.

Cripes! Was she crying? What did he know about women and tears? What did he know about comforting someone? Nothing. Not a damn thing. He reached out and tilted her chin up to see her face. "What the hell?"

She was laughing. Laughing so hard that tears were running down her cheeks.

"What the hell?" he repeated. Maybe she was hysterical. If that was the case, then what did he know about *hysterical* women? Not a damn sight more than he knew about crying ones.

"Oh, Ash!" she finally managed to gasp. "I know what you're doing, and it's sweet of you."

Sweet? He'd been called a lot of things in his life, but sweet sure as hell wasn't one of them.

She took a deep breath before continuing. "I want you to know something." She wasn't laughing anymore. "I don't regret last night. And I'm not sorry it happened. Not one bit." She pushed past him and ran for the house.

He stood there staring at the porch door long after it had slammed. Just what the hell was going on here? What the bloody hell?

chapter
eighteen

Corey spent the day finishing off a roll of film and completing several pages of notes. Ash worked on the chicken coop, hammering loudly whenever she happened by.

During supper he quit brooding long enough to inform her that he would be leaving at daybreak to get the plane, and she should have her suitcase packed and ready when he returned.

So when night came—the night that was to be her last at San Reys, her last with Ash—she lay in bed, back propped against a pillow, waiting. He would come, she fervently told herself. He had to. Otherwise she would be forced to swallow her pride and go to him.

She tucked the sheet more securely under her arms, the fabric pulling tightly across her breasts. Under the sheet she was naked. Naked and needing Ash.

More than once today she had almost blurted out her feelings for him. But each time she had caught herself. He had enough problems, enough things to feel guilty for without having something else dropped on him. Better to let him think what was between them was purely physical. And so it was—for him.

Almost as if her inner pleas had conjured him up, she heard the whisper of bare feet upon dusty wood, then the door to her bedroom swung wide. Her breath quickened, her heartbeat picked up. Ash stood there, smoky eyes reflecting the moonlight like a wary wolf's. He crossed his arms over his chest, pectorals bulging and gleaming. He looked sexy and dangerous, and there was a longing in his eyes she'd never seen before.

"I couldn't stay away," he stated quietly. "I want you like hell." He could feel his body heat up, feel the sweat on his skin, feel his heartbeat increase. She looked so damn beautiful in the moonlight. Her eyes were huge, lips parted and still a little swollen from last night. Her pale skin glowed—he could almost taste her.

One of her hands was open, pressing the sheet against her breast in an old-fashioned gesture that for some reason tugged at his heart.

Had she been waiting for him?

His breath quickened. He could see the outline of her taut, uptilted, sweet-tasting nipples through the sheet. How could he be so hungry for her again? But he was. Even more than before, because now he had tasted her skin, touched the secret places of her soft, eager body.

"I want you too," she whispered. "So much—" She let go of the sheet she held to her.

Ash sucked in his breath as he gazed upon her creamy, rose-tipped breasts. There was a stirring ache in his loins. Such a wanting. He'd never felt such a wanting. He unfurled his arms and took a step toward her. "Corey —" His voice was husky and hoarse. He let his eyes feast on her loveliness, prolonging his own agony. She looked so pure with her curly hair and light skin, her eyes like a doe's. An angel. Different from him in every way.

Again he wondered if this was all some fevered dream

brought on by malaria. Good things didn't happen to him. And he didn't expect them to anymore.

"Ash, touch me. Please touch me." Corey could feel the tautness in her body as she waited for his reaction. Why was he just standing there?

Touch me. Touch me. Can't you see I need to feel you next to me? She heard his quick intake of breath, saw the flames of desire leap into his eyes.

In three quick strides he was across the room. The bed dipped with his weight as he pulled her into his arms. He took a shuddering breath, burying his face in her neck.

The masculine smell of his perspiring skin filled her head like a drug. She ran her hands across the taut sinews of his arms, then feathered them over the sturdy struts of his ribs. She could feel the mad thundering of his heart, hear his labored breathing, as if he struggled for control.

"You're making me crazy. I tried to stay away, but I kept thinking about how you felt. What you do to me, how I wanted to taste you, every part of you."

His breathless words sent hot shivers racing down her spine, and she thrilled at his big body pressing against her, her bare breasts crushed to his hard, damp chest. She started to lie back, tried to pull him down beside her, but he held her tightly.

"I want to kiss you." His feverish mouth crushed hers with a ferocious urgency, his arms holding her so tightly she could hardly breathe. He was like a starved man. Then his tongue was plunging deep into her mouth, and she was meeting it with her own, feeling the roughness of it, the softness, the warm wetness.

With his mouth locked to hers, he loosened his hold enough to slide his hand between their two bodies so he could touch her breast. The rough skin of his open palm rubbing the tingling tip created a friction that sent flames shooting through her. She arched, filling his hand with her aching, swollen breast. He leisurely teased both nipples erect, then his fingers skimmed among the soft contours, following a tiny, trickling line of perspiration down, drawing an imaginary line to her belly button.

She was melting.

He tugged the sheet away from her. She could feel the rough material of his jeans under her bent knee, her other leg dangling over the edge of the bed. She moaned into his mouth, then pulled her lips from his to bury her face against his neck, feeling the roughness of his stubbled cheek against her temple.

She was on fire.

His hand moved down to caress and tease the mound of silky hair. The fire in her was now a blue-white flame, her need for him reaching a fever pitch. "Touch me," she gasped, her fingers digging into his hard biceps.

"I am." Breathless laughter was cut off in a gasp. He threaded his long fingers through the springy curls at the apex of her smooth legs, combing, kneading, driving her to a frustrated frenzy.

"Like last night. Touch me like you did last night." Her voice was drifting, carried away by a current of desire.

"I'm going to touch you." He pressed a deep openmouthed kiss against her lips. "Everywhere," he promised hoarsely.

He began trailing wet kisses down her neck, stopping to stroke the rapid pulse in her throat with his tongue. Then his mouth moved downward. She felt his hair brush against her thundering heart as his head followed his hand. He drew the tip of her breast into his mouth, sucking, pulling, licking. She could feel the sheen of perspiration that broke out on her, feel all the hot wet places where his mouth had been, where it was now.

Then he was inching his way down, fingers pressing into her hips as he kissed her navel, kissed her slightly rounded abdomen.

Flames danced behind her eyes, were coiling tighter and tighter inside her. She could feel the hot wet wanting between her parted thighs, then his fingers were there, stroking the folds of her secret places, testing her desire. She groaned and writhed against his hand, eyes clamped shut, head thrown back, breathing shallow.

"Too fast," she heard him whisper. "We're going too fast." Through a warm blur she became aware that his hand had left her body.

"Ash. Please," she begged in frustration. She ran her tongue over her swollen lips, tasting the musky salt of his skin. "I want you, need you—"

"Shhh," he soothed her. Then he was tilting her back, the sheet cool against her hot naked skin. She was aware of his strong fingers framing her hips, aware of his big body crouched at her bent knees. Then, through a haze of passion, she felt his warm breath between her legs, and tensed.

"Ash." She hardly recognized her own voice. "What are you doing?"

"Touching you. I have to touch you with my mouth."

"Ash—"

He shouldn't. He couldn't. She tried to clamp her knees together but succeeded only in pulling him closer to his goal.

"Lily, open for me."

His ragged breathing betrayed his desperate need of her. "If you don't like it I'll stop. I promise." His hair brushed against her lower belly. He slid his fingers down her hips, stroking. Then he brought his hand around to her inner thighs, gently pressing her legs open. "Let me . . ." he said.

As soon as his lips touched her body, flames seared through her and a hazy thrumming began in her brain. The tip of his tongue flicked across the folds of soft skin, then dipped between them. A loud roaring started in her ears, turning her pulsing blood to warm bourbon.

His voice came drifting up to her, across the world of her hot damp skin. "You taste so good." His voice was broken and breathless. "Should I stop? Do you want me to stop?" His fingers were stroking the long, tight tendons of her inner thighs. Then his knuckles brushed down between her legs to the swell of her buttocks and up again.

He was sending her over the edge. She couldn't focus her mind enough to form words. She felt his callused thumbs skimming the soft folds of her flesh, opening them like petals of a flower.

"Tell me . . . to stop . . . and I will. . . ."

"No. Don't . . . don't stop—" Her voice was a broken thread of sound.

He let out a low murmur of satisfaction. Then his hot, open mouth was pressing against the heat of her, loving her slowly, kissing and sucking the overheated flesh while she moaned and twisted beneath him, head thrashing from side to side in mindless ecstasy. His tongue licked and circled the throbbing, pulsing bud. Red hot flames shot through her. She felt a tight spasm between her thighs. She dug the fingers of both hands into his damp hair, squirming and arching her body against his torturing mouth. Her knees clamped against his head. She could feel the stubble of his rough jaw abrading the soft skin of her inner thighs. He cradled her bottom in his large hands, lifting her hips off the mattress, his strong fingers digging into her soft flesh as he levered the coiling heat of her to his hot wet mouth while the tip of his tongue kept up its wicked, wicked, exquisite torture.

She felt herself begin to shake. It started as small tremors that grew and grew like her runaway passion. Tremor after tremor ran through her small frame. Shock wave after shock wave. Lights were flashing behind her eyes.

"Ash. Oh, Ash."

He left her. Through a whirling haze she heard a zipper, the sound of jeans being peeled from sweat-damp skin.

"Ash, hold me, hold me."

Then he was back beside her, pulling her into his

arms. "Corey, sweetheart," he said, his breath warm against the column of her throat. She felt him smooth a stray strand of damp hair back, then he was pressing his mouth against her sweating brow.

He wrapped his arms around her, pulling her up against his muscular chest, their sweating bodies slipping erotically against each other. Then his hardness was easing into her softness, and she let out a pleasurable moan. He pulled himself all the way out, then gently slid back inside, deeper this time. Her hands came up, fingers digging into his firm buttocks, urging him deeper yet as she arched to meet his thrust. Again and again. She clung to him as if she were drowning while she felt another spasm shudder deep within her—a shudder that seemed to start in her body and carry through to his, contracting over his hard arousal. Hazy lights swirled, brightened, dimmed, finally taking them home, together.

Much later Corey lay nestled against his chest, fingers resting on the smooth line of his scar, ear pressed to his heart, taking comfort from its steady rhythm. She couldn't ever remember feeling such peace, such contentment.

The old Corey would be self-conscious right now, embarrassed. But the new Corey wouldn't allow it—not when there was so little time left.

She was not so naive as to think that what had just happened between them was common, that this sense of complete fulfillment was felt by most people. She knew better. What amazed her was her own reaction. She never knew she had such passion in her. Not until Ash.

Even though he had been just as gentle as the first time, Corey had detected an underlying desperation to his lovemaking and wondered if he, too, was aware that time was short and fleeting.

Something drummed against the window screen. A firefly as big as a beetle was clinging to the green netting, its light flickering, casting strange shadows.

"Look at that lightning bug," Corey whispered in hushed amazement.

Ash pressed a kiss on the top of her head. "Natives carry them in cages carved from palm nuts. The first time I ever saw a bunch of natives winding their way through the jungle with their firefly lanterns, I thought I'd tumbled down a rat hole and ended up in Middle Earth. Shades of *The Hobbit*."

The roughness of his hand moved up and down along the soft contours of her ribs and spine, lulling her, making her feel warm and drowsy. "You want to know something really weird? Those little bugs can be tamed. I've seen natives walking around with them on their arms and shoulders, like pets."

The Amazon was enchanting as well as dangerous. Two extremes, no middle of the road. Like Ash.

"It's magical here," she whispered.

"Yeah, it is sometimes," he agreed with a surprising amount of feeling, and she fleetingly wondered if they were talking about the same things.

"Wish my plane was running." He rubbed his chin across the top of her head. "I'd show you magic. There's nothing so beautiful as flying over the Amazon River at night when the moon's full. The tributaries shine like threads of liquid gold. It's just humbling as all hell."

She rolled to her stomach and looked up at him, her mouth only inches from his chest. This was the first time he'd ever admitted that there were things about the Amazon he liked, that it was more to him than just a buggy hellhole, or the land that had robbed him of his brother. "You fly at night? Isn't that dangerous?"

"It's worth it. There's nothing like being up there in the sky, the world under you. And then there's always the remote chance of seeing *Pororoca*."

"*Pororoca?*"

"It means 'wall of water.' It's an Amazon legend. A gigantic tidal wave. It comes in with the floodtide. The first person who ever told of it was the skipper of Columbus's *Niña*. The crew saw it when they crossed the equator. I guess it scared the holy hell out of them. Made them good and religious real fast."

"But you've never seen it?"

"No. Actually"—his voice dropped—"there isn't any proof it even exists. It could just be a legend like the lost cities of gold—Eldorado. Still, sometimes when the moon is full and the tides are high, I take the plane up and look. Just for the hell of it."

She forced herself to breathe slowly and carefully, afraid a sob might accidentally escape her. How many other reasons were there for loving him? How many reasons that she would never know of?

He chases the moon. . . .

Her life would never be the same because of this man. It was going to take her a very long time to get over him. Very probably a lifetime. Maybe an eternity.

She would never marry Todd. She would bake cookies for other people's children instead of her own because she would never have any of her own. No, she wouldn't be sharing that big front porch with anybody.

But at least she would have this night, a treasured keepsake to clutch to her heart, to be wrapped in lavender, folded and tucked away with her other memories like a delicately embroidered handkerchief, each stitch taken in love.

In years to come, on warm summer nights when the air was heavy and a chorus of crickets sang out, when the dew lay heavy on newly mown grass, she would be transported back. She would be here again, with Ash.

She ran loving fingers over his scar. She wanted to know all she could about him. "How did you get this?"

He lifted his head from the pillow so he could look at her, a teasing light in his eyes. "Would you believe, a duel?"

"Come on."

"How 'bout a bike wreck?"

"Only if you're talking bike as in motorbike."

"Nope. Bicycle. Like the kind with two wheels, one gear, pedal brakes."

"You're kidding."

"It's the truth. I swear."

"And I figured you got it in some barroom brawl."

"Never been in a barroom brawl."

"Liar," she whispered.

"Well, none that I can recall."

"That's more like it." She pressed her lips against his scar, right where it started, below his left breastbone. She heard his breath catch, could feel the muscles tense in his stomach under her palm.

"What are you doing?"

"Kissing you."

He had the most beautiful skin. Men shouldn't have such satiny smooth skin. "Just kissing you."

She kissed a little lower, and his muscles tightened more. "Want me to stop?" she asked, aware that she echoed his earlier words to her.

"No," he gasped out. "By all means, continue."

"Do you brush your teeth before or after breakfast?" Ash asked later.

"Both."

He groaned. "Should have known. And I'll bet you floss twice a day. What kind of car do you drive? Wait, let me guess. A Volkswagen."

"No, a Toyota."

"Is there a difference?"

Corey's heavy lashes feathered down against the smooth skin of his chest. She loved the way he smelled, loved the way he felt.

"I used to have this fifty-seven Chevy," he reflected

while his hand gently kneaded the back of her neck, his finger drawing small circles that made her feel pleasantly drowsy. "It was blue, metallic blue. Dual exhaust, turbo blowers, the works. Just gaudy as all hell." He let out a sigh. "It was something. Sold it to make a down payment on a little Cessna, and I didn't even know how to fly yet."

"You bought a plane that you couldn't fly?"

He laughed. "Yeah. Wiped her out a year later. Crashed in this guy's bean field. You should have seen his face. He thought I was the crop duster he'd hired, till I plowed a furrow down the middle of his beans with the belly of my poor little Cessna."

He talked about it like somebody else might mention stubbing their toe. She wished he wasn't so reckless. It scared her.

He was quiet for a moment, then asked, "Do you live with—" The fingers at the back of her neck stopped their rotating motion and became stiff and tense. "Do you live with what's-his-name?"

"No. I had my own apartment for a while. But now I live with my parents in the house I grew up in."

She felt his hand relax. "Have any brothers or sisters?"

"No. I'm an only child."

"You always had to have your own way?"

"Always," she said with a smile.

"You used to lie down on the floor, kick, and hold your breath till your face turned blue?"

"That was me." She laughed.

"Now who's a liar? I'd bet my right arm that you never had a tantrum in your life."

He rolled over so she was lying on her back under him. "Let's see. Bet you were a cheerleader, right?"

Her body was tingling again, coming alive to the length of him pressed against her from knees to chest. "Just like you had to be the class clown."

"A lucky guess. How 'bout prom queen?"

"How did you know?"

"President of the French Club?"

She hesitated, before saying sheepishly, "Vice-president of the Spanish Club."

"Hey, I'm on a roll. Bet you wore braces."

"Mmm."

A teasing light danced in his eyes. "Bet you were just cute as a button."

Cute as a button. His words weren't something Asher Adams would normally say. No, they would seem more appropriate coming from a proud grandparent. They touched her, made her throat hurt.

Suddenly his head swooped down and he pressed a hard kiss against her wistful mouth, then drew back to look down at her, elbows braced on either side of her head. The teasing light in his eyes was gone, replaced now by something she couldn't read; she only knew that she was once again glimpsing the dark corners of his mind, and she worried about him, wondering what could have triggered the sudden mood change.

She blinked, and when she looked again, he was smiling in that sexy way of his, the way that told her he planned to kiss her very thoroughly. Maybe the moonlight had fooled her, cast shadows on his face and in his eyes that weren't really there at all.

Then he was kissing her, making her forget everything but the feel of his body against hers.

Ash lay on his side, head resting in his open hand, elbow braced against the bed, watching Corey as she slept. She was on her stomach, face toward him, one hand curled delicately on the pillow. Her skin was slightly flushed, her lips red and full from his kisses, eyelashes dusting her cheeks. He could hardly hear her breathing, it was that light, that soft.

The sense of foreboding he'd felt before was heavy in him again. He was aware of a pain deep inside, weighing against his chest and lungs, and it scared the hell out of him to discover that he hurt as much right now as the day he'd gotten the message that Luke was missing.

That's when it hit him like the deep-felt shudder of a sonic boom: She was going to break his goddamn heart.

Shocked, he rolled to his back and stared up at the wood-slatted ceiling. *Why me? And why her? Why her of all women?* He'd never even been hung up on anybody before. Back in his teens he'd gotten a kick out of flashing wolfish grins at nice girls, good girls, just to watch them blush and scurry away. Then there were the horny girls. They propositioned him, making *him* blush, teaching him very thorough lessons in the field of supply and demand. He quickly learned to leave the "good" girls alone—they were more trouble than they were worth. And he'd always stuck to it, until Corey.

He would have laughed if it didn't hurt so much. Here he was, with a soul so black a bat couldn't pick it up on radar, and Corey. So pure, so lily-white. She could never love somebody like him. And he wished that thought didn't hurt so damn much.

He had no idea how long he lay there, heart racing, naked body coated with a sheen of nervous perspiration. Scared. He didn't know when he'd been so scared.

He had to get out. Get away before he did something crazy, like beg her to stay.

It would be dawn soon. If he ran part of the way, he could reach his plane in three or four hours. In another three or four he could have Corey on a flight to the States, to Pleasantville, where she belonged.

He had to fight down the urge to kiss her before he left. He couldn't risk her waking up. If she looked at him with those eyes of hers, he'd be lost. He'd find some excuse for staying, for waiting another day, then maybe another. . . . No, he had to go now, while he could go at all. Because, he thought with bitter mockery, self-control was not his middle name.

Carefully he slipped from the bed and left the room. He stuffed some things in his backpack, told Bobbie to "stay," and headed through the thick haze of the early dawn and dripping jungle, accompanied by a desolate pain that had lodged itself in his chest and throat.

She was breaking his goddamn heart.

chapter
nineteen

Before Corey opened her eyes, she knew Ash was gone. It was a feeling, an absence—like a concert hall after the music is over and the people have all left.

Which meant she would be leaving soon too. In less than twenty-four hours she would be home.

She stared up at the wood-beamed ceiling. For once in her life she had acted with no thought of tomorrow, no thought of the possible consequences of her actions. She had only wanted to touch and be touched. By Ash.

Had she made the right choice? Or had the heavy Amazon air clouded her judgment? There were so many variables. How could she know what was right when life was not simple, not a roadmap with routes clearly marked. Sometimes you just don't know if it's the right path until you take it. And even then you can't always be sure.

Bang, bang.

Elvira's small, dainty hooves impatiently battered at

the porch door. With a sigh Corey threw back the sheet and reached for her clothes.

"Do you realize what a rude old goat you are?" Corey asked through the screen, one hand gripping the wooden framework of the door. Elvira looked up through blasé eyes with strange rectangular pupils, bleated, then kicked again.

"Of course you do. After all, you were taught by the master," Corey said with a wry-tinged sadness.

Corey milked the goat, fed Bobbie and the chickens, then went down to the river to take a bath.

Two hours later she tossed her suitcase on the bed and started packing. Ash had told her to be ready, and she would be ready . . . with emotions tucked safely away.

She was snapping the last lock of the suitcase when she heard a plane overhead. She took a quick glance around the small cluttered room, slung her camera and bag over her shoulder, picked up the suitcase, and went out to wait for the landing plane before her bravado weakened.

As she waited, the midday sun beat through the back of her shirt. She could feel its heat on her hair. She shaded her eyes with her hand and watched as the plane landed and the oil-burning engine sputtered to a stop, shimmering heat waves rising from its metal fuselage.

She gripped the handle of the suitcase tighter as the airplane door was flung wide. Then Ash was in the opening, looking surprised to see her standing there.

She had intended to remain aloof, but found herself uncontrollably drawn to him, as she had always been, ever since that very first day in the air-taxi building when he'd taken off his dark sunglasses and she'd seen his eyes, felt herself looking into the depths of his tired soul. Drawn like a magnet to steel—or in her case, like a frail moth to a wing-singeing flame.

Watching him now, with his frayed sleeveless khaki shirt faded to almost white, his shaggy mane of hair that needed cutting, knowing of his perfections and imperfections, love for him rushed through her, strong and sharp and painful.

"You're packed." There were frown lines between his eyes as if he were puzzled or just in a bad mood, she couldn't decide which.

She dropped the heavy suitcase to the ground. "You said to be ready when you got back." Her voice was steady, the insignificant shrug that followed hopefully conveying just the right amount of nonchalance. She hadn't known she was such a good actress.

"I know I did, but—"

He jumped to the ground and strode toward her, the frown lines deepening. When he reached her, he stopped and slapped at his tattered shirt pocket, long brown fingers making a quick search for the cigarette pack.

Corey watched as he lit a cigarette and tossed the match to the ground, watched as he drew the smoke deeply into his lungs. There was a nervousness about his actions that was unlike him.

"You shouldn't smoke." The words came out before she could stop them, before she was aware of thinking them at all.

He expelled a cloud in one long breath, as if her comment had taken him by surprise. The smoke just hung there in the heavy, steamy air, then finally dissipated. "Why the hell not?"

Was it possible that they were the same two people who had made love only hours before? Now they seemed hardly more than strangers. She crossed her arms over her chest. "It's bad for you."

"Oh, *really?*" He laughed, but the sound didn't contain much humor. "I like to do bad things. In fact, if I quit the things that are bad for me, there'd be nothing left."

"Why are you always doing that?"

"What?"

"Trying to act so hardened, so tough?" She knew his reason. Defense. But she wondered what he would say.

"Is that what you think?" His eyes narrowed against the smoke as he took another long drag, then flicked the unfinished cigarette away in a spiraling arch. "Do you think that under all this"—he spread his arms wide— "there dwells the heart and soul of some rutabaga, some really swell guy? A Dudley Do-right?"

"I know there's more to you than you let on, than you want people to think. I've seen you with the natives. They trust you. I know you care, know you can be kind." Her voice dropped as she thought about how gentle he had been with her, the incredible tenderness he had shown. Her throat tightened. She couldn't keep her expression or her voice passive anymore. "I know you can be gentle."

An answering light grew in his eyes, along with something else she couldn't identify. She only knew that he wanted her too.

How she wished he would pull her into his arms as he had last night, when he first came to her room. She needed to feel that barely controlled desperation—see if she had only imagined it. But when she needed to feel his mouth on hers one last time, he was acting as if they were no more than passing acquaintances.

Ash took a step toward her before stopping himself. He loved her. That was very clear to him. The sun rose, the sun set. He loved Corey McKinney. The thought didn't surprise him. Surprise wasn't the word for the heaviness he felt inside. Surprise didn't make your chest hurt.

Once again he thought of her on that big front porch. Cat on her lap. Baby sleeping inside the house. A lazy world of Sunday afternoon ice cream socials, maybe even a few white gloves in the crowd. It was probably idealistic —now, that was funny, coming from one of the world's biggest cynics—but that's how he thought of her, where she belonged.

She had to go back. And he would have to watch her leave. And it would be easier for them both if she hated him. And Ash was a master with words. As a kid he had quickly learned that the English language was much more effective than a few sticks and stones.

He looked down at Corey, at her expectant expression. He knew she was waiting for some response from him, or at least some slight reference to last night. An odd, sad smile lifted one corner of his mouth. He knew he had to make this convincing. He'd warned her off gently once before, but it hadn't worked. She'd seen through him. He had to make sure she didn't see through him this time.

"You're a hell of a woman, Lily. For a novice, not to mention a goody-two-shoes, you turned out to be one of the best lays I ever had."

He saw her mind struggle, not wanting to comprehend. He saw the shocked acceptance finally melt to hurt and anger, and still he drove her to hate him even more.

"Dudley should be real impressed. Just think of all the new tricks you'll be able to show him. I especially liked—"

Her arm came up and she landed a flat-handed blow across his face. It should have stung, but he barely felt it. "You bastard."

He couldn't move. He just stood watching her, distantly aware of the warm imprint her fingers had left on the side of his face.

He'd hurt her. Something he had never wanted to do. From the first moment he'd seen her, his instincts had been to protect. He'd thought she looked too frail to go into the jungle, he was afraid she would get hurt. But it had never crossed his mind that he would be the one to hurt her.

The despair he felt was old. And very, very familiar. It seemed he'd spent a lifetime trying to let go of the people he loved.

Her small, injured voice, a voice trying hard to be

strong, came across to him, dealing him a much harder blow than her hand ever could. "How I hate you, Asher Adams."

As a penance he made himself watch the tears that welled in her eyes, then rolled down her pale cheeks.

"I know," he finally answered woodenly.

Jesus. He never thought it would come to this knife-in-the-belly kind of thing. "That's what I've been trying to tell you all along. You *should* hate me. I'm just surprised your mother never warned you about guys like me."

Slowly he bent to pick up her suitcase, then turned and headed for the plane. *She'll be okay,* he assured himself. *She'll be okay as soon as she's home with her own people.*

But would *he?*

What she had said was true: When he cared about somebody, he cared completely, and never stopped. Because that's the way he was.

He tossed the suitcase into the cargo hold. One thing for sure, he didn't want to turn around and look at her again. He'd faced death many times and never flinched, but he couldn't stand to see the hurt on her face, knowing he'd inflicted it, knowing he was the cause.

"Damn!" He slammed his fist into the metal wall of the plane, not feeling the skin scrape from his knuckles. How was he going to stand the three-hour flight to Santarém?

Suddenly the sound of a motor came to him. A plane. Mike Jones. Nobody else was so jerky with a throttle. So, George was back, he thought dully. About two days too late. . . .

As soon as the plane stopped, George Dupree came barreling out the thrust-open door, a squat, balding, gray-haired dynamo.

"Kiss. my feet if you feel the inclination," he announced, arms outspread, grubby tan T-shirt pulled tightly over a round stomach. "Buy me a drink, I deserve it! The grant's been approved!" He swaggered toward them. When he got to Ash, he grabbed him by his upper arms and gave him an impatient shake. "The grant, remember? What we've been busting our buns for over the last three years." Then, as if talking to a slow child, he repeated, "The foundation's approved the grant—we've got our Eldorado!"

Ash tried to focus his attention on his friend, tried to clear the numbness from his mind. "That's great, George."

George didn't seem to notice Ash's lack of enthusiasm. He let go of his arm to pound him soundly on the back. "You should have been there to hear my presentation. I was rolling along on this adrenaline high, eloquence bursting from every pore. My words brought tears to some of those crusty old bastards' eyes. After listening to me they couldn't help but pass a unanimous vote. It was yea all the way."

Ash pulled himself together, trying to dredge up a lukewarm response to the news they'd waited years to hear. "Did it ever enter that bald head of yours that they may have passed it to get rid of you?" he joked.

George took off his horn-rimmed glasses to wipe them on his T-shirt. "They were getting pretty sick of me always hanging around there."

Corey had been standing to the side, and now George settled his glasses back on his nose and gave her a good looking-over. "Hey, now. Aren't the natives getting prettier all the time?"

"Back off, you old lecher. This is Corey McKinney, the social worker you invited here, remember?"

"Good Lord!" George said with embarrassment. "You poor girl! I'm so sorry! Especially for leaving you stranded here with this"—he motioned toward Ash—"uncouth vagrant."

"George." Ash tried to get his friend's attention, hoping he would shut up, but George was too busy giving Corey the third degree.

"I hope he didn't make your life too miserable. He has all the charm and finesse of a rabid dog."

That didn't get the smile George had obviously expected.

"The grant," Corey asked. "You said something about a grant?"

Ash had never considered himself a coward, but he didn't want to be around when George explained to Corey that she had come to the Amazon for nothing. With the help of the Brazilian Indian Foundation, they would now have all the money they needed. "Got to find some matches," Ash muttered.

He could feel two pairs of eyes watching him as he strode to the house.

Five minutes later George came in the kitchen. "So, sounds like you were your old, charming, asinine self while I was gone," he commented drily, shoving Ash's crossed feet off the tabletop.

Ash took a deep drag from his cigarette and propped his tennis-shoed feet back where they'd been. "Don't give me one of your lectures."

"I know you were against a social worker coming here. But hell, did you have to be rough on her? She's hardly more than a kid. Couldn't you keep your sarcastic tongue still for a day or two?"

"Apparently not." Ash leaned forward enough to crush out his cigarette. "The votes are all in and it's unanimous—I'm an ass, okay?"

"Whatever you did, it sure made an impression on her. She couldn't get out of here fast enough."

George's words didn't really sink in until Ash heard the sound of an engine choking, followed by the turning of a propeller.

"Son of a—" Ash's feet dropped to the floor and he almost knocked George down in his lunge for the door, practically ripping it from its hinges as he raced outside.

Jones's plane was standing at the end of the runway, the engine cranking the propeller to a high-pitched whine. Then the plane began to roll.

Son of a bitch.

Ash ran for the aircraft, reaching it before it could pick up speed. He jumped on the wing, the draft from the propeller plastering his hair to his head. His first impression after wrestling the passenger door open was that of Corey shrinking away from him.

"You crazy bastard!" Mike Jones shouted over the roaring of the engine. "What the hell do you think you're doing?"

The cockpit reeked of Jones—of his cheap whiskey and stale, acrid sweat. There was no way in hell Ash would let Corey leave with a lowlife like him.

Mike tried to jam the throttle forward, but Ash lashed out, knocking his hand aside. Then he flicked the switch and the propeller wound down to silence, the plane coming to a standstill.

Ash's eyes bored into Corey's. "Get off the plane."

"No!"

"There's no way I'm letting you fly with a piss-poor pilot like Jones."

"You don't care about me. I'm just an excuse for you both to fight."

Frustration and anger mounted in him. "I don't want you to get hurt."

She laughed bitterly, and he thought about how short

a time it had taken to put that bitterness there. "Hurt? You've more than taken care of that, let me assure you. Now, leave me alone!"

God, but she was stubborn! He reached down and jerked her seat belt open.

Her small hands tried to push his away, tugging at the nylon belt, trying to pull it back together.

"Corey—" He'd drag her out of there if he had to.

Her hands stilled. She tilted her head back to look up at him. "I'm not going with you," she said in a taut, distant voice. In her eyes he could see her hurt, her confusion, see the beginning of tears.

What a mess he'd made of everything. "Corey, I—"

His words broke off as Mike Jones's heavy body came hurtling against him, knocking the air from his lungs as he pitched sideways. Corey screamed. Ash flung out his hands, managing to grip the metal doorframe to keep himself from tumbling out the open door.

"You heard her, Adams," Mike snarled. "Get the hell off my plane!" He braced his hands against the ceiling and aimed a booted foot at Ash's stomach.

Ash agilely dodged the wildly swinging foot and grabbed Mike's leg, sending him sprawling backward.

"You always did fight like a damn sissy," Ash said in a breathless voice after pulling himself inside.

Mike scrambled to his feet, levered a fist, and swung. Ash blocked, then hit Mike with a right hook, knocking him back in the pilot's seat.

Mike's hand flew to his face. "I'm bleeding!" he roared, staring in horror at the blood on his hand. "You've given me a bloody nose!"

"Go to hell," Ash said wearily, dismissing him with a flick of the hand.

He turned to look down at Corey. Both her feet were on the seat, knees drawn up to her chin, eyes huge and shadowed. He reached for her. "Come on."

She hesitated. He felt her distrust and confusion. He could just imagine what was going through her head, wondering which maniac to go with. Hell of a choice. "Let's go. I'll take you back," he coaxed, more gently this time.

She glanced at Mike, then put her trembling hand in Ash's and he pulled her to her feet.

"Corey, I'm sorry."

He wanted to wrap his arms around her, wanted to make her feel better, make himself feel better, but it was too late for that.

"Adams!"

Something in Mike's voice made Ash turn.

Mike was sitting upright in his seat, blood mixed with the sweat and hate on his face. In his hand was a .22 Magnum revolver, the five-inch steel-blue barrel pointing at Ash's chest. Ash heard Corey's quick, indrawn breath and shoved her behind him.

"What the hell do you think you're doing, Jones? That could go off!"

"No shit." Mike pulled back the hammer, the click echoing loudly within the metal walls of the aircraft.

Ash's mind raced. He could rush him. There was a good chance the gun wasn't even loaded. But he couldn't risk it. Not with Corey in the plane.

"Corey. Get out of here," he said in a low, insistent voice.

"Stay where you are!" Mike commanded. "You wanted to go with me, now you're going with me. Get off the plane, Adams." His voice was full of raw malice.

"It's okay, Ash," Corey said shakily. "I'll fly with him. Please, just do what he says."

She was behind him, right in front of the door. All she had to do was step outside. Then he'd wring Mike's neck.

"Corey, just get the hell out of here," Ash said, beginning to feel slightly exasperated. "Step out the door. Go on."

He heard Corey move, but didn't turn to look.

Ash heaved a heavy sigh. "Put the gun away, Jones. Come on. This is just stupid as hell. You're all talk. Sure, you'd like to put a bullet through my head. But don't you think I know you're too much of a chicken shit to risk facing a firing squad?"

Deep-rooted hatred flared in Mike's eyes. "I'm not worried about a firing squad," he spat out. "This is the Amazon—it doesn't count. You should know that." He licked his lips, then wiped the back of his hand across his mouth. "A person can dust whoever they want here. If you come up missing, they blame it on the jungle. No questions asked. Just like Luke." He let out a loud, disgusted snort. "Or I guess I should say, Saint Luke."

Ash stiffened. He knew better than to let Mike get to him through Luke. But it was hard. And Mike knew it and reveled in it, played it for all it was worth. "Leave Luke out of this."

Mike laughed. "All these years . . . you been lookin' for a dead guy. Cracks me up. Just cracks me up."

"You don't know what you're talking about, so shut your stupid mouth."

"You know, Luke was always nice to me." A strange gleam mingled with the hatred in Mike's bloodshot eyes. "Like somebody's nice to a stray mutt. It's okay to feed it, just so it don't come too close. No telling where it's been. That's how Luke treated me." His expression grew cunning. "Maybe I know Luke's dead for a fact. Maybe I know he's dead . . . because maybe I killed him."

"You better tell me you're lying." Ash's hands clenched into tight fists.

"Don't worry. I did him a favor. Can't be a saint till you're dead."

"I'll kill you." The fact that Mike was still pointing the gun at him meant nothing. With a furious roar Ash lunged.

"Ash! No!" Corey screamed.

Ash felt himself being knocked sideways, a small body slamming against him even before the sound of the pistol report stopped ricocheting off the sheet-metal walls.

Corey. Sweet Jesus.

chapter twenty

Corey's world was an explosion of pain. There was no room for anything else. She clenched her eyes shut as fire ripped through her shoulder, the pain bringing her to her knees, making her muscles contract until she lay curled on her side.

Through a haze she heard Ash call her name in a strange, anguished voice, then heard his roar of rage. Another deafening gunshot exploded in the small compartment, followed by grunts and sounds of flesh striking flesh.

"Christ almighty, Adams," Mike stammered, his voice full of terror. "I never meant . . . Y-you shouldn't have come at me like that." His next words were practically a scream. "Don't shoot me!"

This was a nightmare. A horrible, horrible nightmare.

"Ash!" Corey cried in horror. "Oh, God!" A strangled sob escaped her. "Don't kill him!"

"Don't shoot me, Adams!"

"Ash!" Corey sobbed.

She heard rasping lungs struggling for air.

"If I ever see your face again," Ash threatened in a voice cold as death, "I'll kill you." The last three words were a vehement promise.

Time became elastic.

"Corey . . . ?"

She heard Ash's voice. But so different now. Cautious, gentle.

Scared.

She didn't want to open her eyes. Somehow, she felt if she kept them closed, then maybe the last few hours would go away.

"Corey. Let me see." She felt his hands on her wet, sticky arms. She forced her eyes open. Ash was kneeling in front of her. There were grim lines at the corners of his mouth, and she saw that his face reflected her own shock, her own disbelief.

She bent her head to numbly stare at her blood-drenched blouse. The only gunshot wound she'd ever seen had been part of a slide presentation on trauma situations. *Bring the bleeding under control and watch for signs of hemorrhaging. . . .*

Her mind refused to take in what was happening, refused to comprehend that the warm stickiness running down her side and soaking into the waistband of her jeans was blood.

Things like this don't happen in real life to real people, she thought dully.

She looked back up at Ash. "I've been shot," she stammered, her voice rising, then dropping. "I . . . I've never been shot before."

The lines in his face deepened. "Don't worry."

"It hurts."

In his eyes she saw her own pain and distress.

Panic clutched at her, wrapping icy tendrils around her heart. "I'm scared," she sobbed.

"Shhh . . . Everything's going to be okay, Corey," he said soothingly. "I'm gonna take you to Santarém in my plane. It's faster. Okay?"

She blinked in acquiescence and let out a long, shuddering sigh. It would be okay. Ash was here.

Slowly he lifted her into his arms, pressing a kiss against her clammy forehead. Then he carefully stooped through the doorway and off the wing. The movement sent renewed currents of pain tearing through her tortured flesh. Why couldn't she just pass out, she wondered weakly, breathlessly.

There was a slam, and George came running toward them. "I heard shots. Good Lord!"

"Go warm my plane," Ash ordered.

"You'll have to take off," George shouted over his shoulder as he hurried past. "You know this strip's too short for me!"

While Ash settled her in the cargo area, Corey was distantly aware of the sounds coming from the front of the plane: switches being flipped, then the engine fighting to turn the heavy propeller. The engine finally won the struggle and the heavy prop began to whir and pop, the plane vibrating under her.

"Give the engine five minutes while I get Corey stabilized," Ash shouted up to George. Metal scraped metal as Ash dragged the medical case closer, then flicked it open.

The pain wasn't quite as bad now that she was lying down. She stared up at Ash's face. He shouldn't look so serious, so worried. Then her eyes were drawn to his shirt, the shirt that had been almost white but was now sticking to his chest because of all the blood. "I'm sorry," she whispered in an unsteady voice, suddenly feeling like bursting into tears. "Sorry I'm causing so much trouble. Sorry I got blood"—she paused—"all over your shirt."

"God, Corey."

His voice sounded shaky to her ears, but maybe it was due to the vibrating airplane. "You took a bullet for me, for chrissake!" Paper rustled. "How do you think that makes me feel?"

She didn't know. *How does it make you feel? Guilty? Beholden? Afraid of having to pledge your life to mine until the debt can be repaid?*

He unbuttoned her blouse, deep furrows between his brows, white brackets around his mouth.

His eyes came up, momentarily locking with hers. She recognized stark pain. He felt guilty.

"Have you ever been shot?" she suddenly heard herself whisper on a shallow breath.

"Lots of times." His answer came distractedly, his attention focused on her shoulder.

She knew his body. He didn't have any scars left by bullets. "Liar." The single word came out a gasp as she felt him place a thick gauze pad against the oozing wound.

"I'm sorry. I'm going to have to put pressure on this. It'll hurt."

In her mind she saw the bullet trapped within torn tissue and shattered bone. *Do not attempt to remove the foreign object.*

Ash pressed against her shoulder. Corey's breath caught and she clamped her lips together so she wouldn't cry out.

"God, I'm sorry, Corey—" Ash's face was chalky, and his voice sounded strange.

Earlier, he'd hurt her with his terrible words. She should be angry, but she wasn't.

"You know what one of the first things I noticed about you was?" Corey whispered after the pain had dulled to a hot, aching throb. "Not counting your beautiful eyes?"

"What?"

"That you were a liar."

A wry, self-mocking smile touched one side of his mouth, but he kept his eyes focused on her shoulder.

"Tell me the truth this time." Her voice dropped even lower. "My freckles"—she could feel a faint warmth rising in her cheeks—"you really didn't mind them?"

His eyes flashed to hers. "No, Corey." The sincerity in his voice came across like a blow. "I didn't mind." He smoothed her hair back from her face, then looked to the front of the plane.

"We're ready, George. Get back here and I'll take off."

"Keep up a firm pressure," Ash told George once they'd traded places.

Corey looked up at Ash's friend. She liked George. He was the kind of person who made you feel at ease.

"I'm sorry," she said haltingly. "Ash told me blood makes you queasy."

"Total fallacy. And this is just a tiny scratch. A tiny scratch."

Another liar. It must be contagious. "And you take off like a gooney bird, Ash told me that too."

"Now, that's the truth, but don't worry. The air is my element."

She tried to smile, but it was just too much of an effort.

Switches flicked in the cockpit area, then Ash pushed the throttle forward and the plane rapidly picked up speed. In her mind she could see his strong, sure hands on the controls. The craft lifted from the ground and Corey felt a heavy tugging in her shoulder. A moan escaped her lips before she could stop it.

After they were on course, Ash and George exchanged places again.

"The bleeding's not slowing like it should," George said in an undertone.

Ash removed the saturated pad and quickly replaced it with a fresh one. Then his fingers were moving past her collarbone, searching for the artery.

Ash had been so cool and efficient the day he'd operated on Para. Now there was a sheen of perspiration on his upper lip, and she could feel his fingertips trembling against her hot, sticky skin.

How much blood had she lost? Her head was feeling light; lethargy was creeping over her. It was a long way to Santarém. "I wonder . . . I wonder if I'm going to die."

"No!"

She hadn't realized she'd spoken out loud.

There was anger in Ash's face, but somehow she knew it was there only to mask the fear that had momentarily flashed across his features before he could hide it. "It's only a shoulder wound. All we have to do is stop the bleeding. Just lie still. Everything's going to be okay."

"Tell me about the wall of water." Now her tongue was feeling thick, as if she'd had too many glasses of wine.

"Pororoca?" he asked, surprised.

"I love to hear your stories about the Amazon," she told him groggily. "I think my favorite is the one about the wall of water."

Haltingly Ash's words came to her through a slowly increasing haze, deep and comforting. She caught only parts of what he was saying, but the content wasn't really important. She just wanted to hear his voice.

Mercifully the pain had now faded to a hot numbness. But it was becoming harder and harder to concentrate, and she had to fight an overpowering urge to keep her eyes from falling closed. She yawned. Sleep pulled her, coaxed her. It's rude to sleep when somebody's talking to you. But she just couldn't help herself. Too tired to talk. Too tired to even listen. Her heavy eyelids drooped closed.

Disjointed thoughts came and went, flickers of ideas, of dreams. Voices intruded, fading in and fading out.

"Have you got this plane cranked all the way up?" Ash's voice demanded.

"We're doing top airspeed now. If we go any faster,

this rag just might come apart. How's everything back there? Has the bleeding stopped?"

No answer. Then, "No. It's slowed. Some." Another pause.

"Why her? Why her?" There was an edge of panic in Ash's usually bland voice.

Asher Adams never panicked. Corey forced her eyes open and he let out a long breath.

"Corey, how are you feeling?" His voice was strange, gruff. She was distantly aware of his hand smoothing her hair. Over and over.

"Kind of floating . . . Tired. . . ."

She'd been thinking of flowers and her Aunt Genevieve, somebody she hadn't thought about in years. Flowers and Aunt Genevieve just went together. Most people planted vegetable gardens, but up until she died, Aunt Genevieve had planted flower gardens. Huge ones. Todd said she was crazy, but then, Todd was a realist, so he didn't understand.

"Aunt Genevieve . . . always plants her tulip bulbs . . . on the south side of the house. That way, they come up . . . early in the spring."

She watched a myriad of emotions flit across Ash's face, finally settling on what Corey vaguely perceived to be alarm.

"They can be frost-killed . . . if the weather takes a sudden turn. Guess that's the price . . . you have to pay for early tulips."

Her thoughts just naturally flowed from tulips to jasmines.

"One night, when I was little, Aunt Genevieve took me out to watch the night-blooming jasmines. We waited hours and hours. I was wearing my new nightgown—the one with . . . the pink roses. It got wet from the dew, and . . . grass stains on it. The grass was cold . . . on my feet, and I was getting . . . so sleepy. . . ."

She shivered, feeling those tendrils of cold creeping through her, pulling her down, but at least the pain had stopped.

"They say . . . when people are freezing to death, they quit feeling the cold. I wonder . . . if that's true." Her eyelids fluttered closed again. "Just like the little match girl. That story always made me . . . sad. And it's supposed to be a Christmas story. A child's story. I would never . . . read it to my child at Christmas."

Corey was aware of being covered with something heavy, but it didn't help the chill that had seeped into her bones. Like the little match girl's matches, it only gave the illusion of warmth.

"Corey. *Corey.*"

Ash. So damn insistent. What a stubborn, stubborn man.

"Lily."

This time she heard the fear in his deep, rusty voice. Now, wasn't that strange? She didn't think there was anything or anybody Ash was afraid of.

She forced her heavy lids open, and when she looked up at him, she was surprised to see that his eyes were shining.

But then, that wasn't really so strange. After all, his eyes always had reminded her of stars.

One fell on her cheek.

She must be dreaming.

Stars were falling from Ash's eyes.

She had a whimsical thought that she would like to collect his stars. Keep them in a glass jar on the windowsill. That way they would always be there to guide him home, no matter how dark the night.

She suddenly realized that they weren't stars at all, they were tears. How very, very strange. Macho guys like Ash don't cry.

Then she remembered seeing him cry once before, and she had comforted him. When?

Her brow furrowed as she forced herself to concentrate. Luke. When he had told her about Luke. Ash had cried for Luke because he loved Luke. And now he was crying for her.

There was something in Ash's face, something she'd seen before but never recognized.

Why, he loved her. *Asher Adams loved her.* And she was hurting him. She didn't want to hurt him. He'd had enough of hurt. A world of hurt.

Don't love me. She swallowed because of the pain in her throat. *Please. Don't love me.*

Her eyes drifted shut, and a warm, comforting blackness wrapped itself around her. . . .

Ash touched Corey's bloodless cheek with trembling fingers. She was cold and clammy. Quickly he felt the pulse in her wrist. Weak and rapid.

Shock. Sweet Jesus, she'd gone into shock.

He put her cold arm back under the sleeping bag, tucking the soft flannel side around her.

Lily, Lily.

This was his fault. His emotions had always gotten him into trouble. He had never learned to control them. Never cared about controlling them until now.

He hadn't believed the gun was loaded. You should never assume that a gun isn't loaded.

It should have been me. It should have been me. . . .

She'll get through this, he swore to himself. If he had to make a pact with the devil, she'd get through this.

Ash plopped down in the vinyl waiting-room chair and took a long drag from the cigarette he couldn't remember lighting. His lungs had that raw feeling they got whenever he chain-smoked, and his eyes had that gritty feeling they got whenever he'd stayed up all night.

He stabbed the half-finished cigarette into the sand-filled container next to his chair. "Just how the hell long does it take to get a bullet out of somebody?"

George looked up from his magazine. "Relax. You know more about that kind of thing than I do—so you should realize she'll be okay. She lost some blood, but they'll put it back."

Ash jumped to his feet and raked his fingers through his hair, then crammed his hands into the front pockets of his jeans. "I can't understand what's taking so damn long," he muttered.

He was the first to hear the whisper of Dr. Perterka's paper-covered shoes in the hall. The dark-skinned surgeon tugged the green surgical cap from his head, thick curly hair springing up in every direction.

"She's going to be fine," he said in heavily accented singsong English.

"Thank God," Ash croaked.

"There was much blood loss—three or four pints. And there were pieces of cloth pushed deeply into tissue and muscle."

A cold sweat broke out on Ash's skin.

"To remove the bullet we had to make a four-inch incision."

Ash had a vivid mental image of the scalpel slicing into Corey's white skin, skin he had tasted under his lips —had it been only hours ago? It seemed like years.

"She was very lucky, very lucky. If the bullet hadn't lodged in the scapula, she would have had a very big hole in her back. Bullets make a little hole going in, a big hole coming out. She most likely would have lost her arm and shoulder. Probably would have died. Very lucky, indeed. Oh, I almost forgot." The doctor held out his hand. "A twenty-two short. Very lucky. If it had been a different caliber . . . say, a twenty-two long, or a Magnum . . ."

Ash could no longer hear what the doctor was saying. There was a huge roaring in his head. Then, for the first time in his thirty-five years, Asher Johnathan Adams lost consciousness without the aid of alcohol.

chapter
twenty-one

George kept hold of Corey's elbow while she stepped from the cab. It had been a week since her accident. Her recall of that day was sketchy, but she didn't mind. It was just too soon to think about it. Too frightening. She had almost gotten Ash killed.

Ash hadn't even come to see her while she was in the hospital, and she could only suppose that he would heave a huge sigh of relief as soon as she stepped off South American soil. He had been right all along. She'd turned out to be every bit as much trouble as he'd predicted, even more. Well, she was leaving now, going home.

George leaned in the cab window, paid the driver, then picked up Corey's suitcase from the curb. "Sorry Ash couldn't bring you to the airport," he told her for the second time. "Something came up."

George was one of the most inept liars Corey had ever come across. Ash's absence probably seemed rude, especially since she'd "taken a bullet for him," as Ash had put it. But it would never have happened if she hadn't gotten in Jones's plane. "It's okay," she assured George. "You don't have to make excuses for him. I understand."

He held open the thick wood and glass door, a blast of cool air ruffling the gray tufts that surrounded his shiny bald spot. "I feel lousy about this whole thing. Just lousy." He indicated her arm that was held immobile by a heavy canvas sling.

"Don't worry about me. Dr. Perterka says I'll be fine with a little physical therapy."

Her flight was almost ready to board. Corey's heels clicked across the lime-green tile as she walked to the ticket counter. After getting her seat assignment and checking her luggage, she held out her hand to George. "Thank you." He gripped it with one hand and patted it with the other.

George's bushy eyebrows furrowed above his black-rimmed glasses. "Ash should have come to see you off. But don't think too badly of him. His mind doesn't function like yours and mine. Never learned to walk when the sign said walk."

"I know."

"Doesn't play by the rules."

"No. Maybe that's the way to be. I just wish . . ." Her words trailed off. She almost said she wished Luke were still alive, wished Ash would find him. "I hope everything works out for you both," she said instead. "And I'm glad you got the grant."

"The money is important, but it means nothing without Ash. No other person can relate to the Indians the way he can. He might not believe it, but the project would fail without him."

"I believe it. I saw him with the natives."

Her flight was called.

Corey looked over her shoulder, toward the long rampway. "I better go."

"You have the pain pills Dr. Perterka gave you?"

She nodded.

"You sure somebody's picking you up in Chicago?"

"Yes, thank you."

"I'm sorry. About everything. It was my fault for inviting you here."

"Don't be sorry. I'm not." Her smile was sad and wistful. She felt old. A hundred years old. "Look at it this way—it was probably the greatest adventure of my life."

"Something to tell your grandkids?"

"Yes, my grandkids."

Tears gathered behind her eyes and she blinked and turned away so George wouldn't see them. She cried so easily now. Dr. Perterka said it would pass, that it was due to the trauma.

She started to walk away but found she couldn't leave, not yet. She turned back.

"George?" She knew Ash wouldn't eat right. Knew he would drink too much. Smoke too much. Not get enough sleep. "You'll watch out for him? He's so reckless."

With all the calm acceptance of the weary parent of an ungovernable child, George shook his head. "He's mellow compared to the way he used to be. From what I hear, he was really wild as a kid. Luke said it drove him crazy worrying about him."

She could picture Ash at ten. Wearing a scruffy black T-shirt, jeans, and grimy tennis shoes.

She had to ask, "Do you think there's any chance Luke is still alive?"

George took off his glasses and cleaned them on the hem of his shirt. Corey had been around him enough to know that he did this whenever he contemplated something. "Luke had a magic about him, an untouchable holiness, and it's real hard to think of that kind of person as dead. But I can't see how he could have survived one day in the jungle, let alone three years. Luke wasn't the outdoor type. He wasn't at home in the jungle like Ash is."

George put on his glasses. "No, I guess deep down I believe Luke's dead."

Corey wished it didn't have to be that way, but she was afraid George was right. "Would you give Ash a message for me? Would you tell him—"

She thought of him sauntering through the jungle as if he owned it; thought of the teasing laughter in his gray eyes; thought of him dancing with her, moonlight streaming in the windows, their bare feet skimming the wooden floor.

Tell him that I loved the little boy in him, and that I loved the man in him. Tell him I loved his sad side, and his laughing side.

George waited.

Corey swallowed painfully. This was so hard for her. She felt like she might shatter into a million pieces.

"Tell him . . . just tell him I said goodbye."

"I'll do that."

She turned and walked down the narrow, colorless rampway.

It was dark by the time Corey's plane reached Chicago. She stared out the window, deciding there was nothing more depressing than the winter darkness that settles prematurely over a midwestern landscape.

The pilot announced that the Chicago area skies were clear, then wryly added that the temperature was a balmy five above zero.

Corey slipped her good arm into the sleeve of her wool jacket, draping the other sleeve over her injured shoulder. She murmured a quick apology when she accidentally bumped the person next to her. She hadn't even been aware of him, and now she was dimly surprised to see a middle-aged man getting up from his seat.

Walking down the rampway, she could feel the bone-chilling cold seeping through the thin, accordion walls. Even when she stepped into the warmth of the airport she felt cold. Would she ever be warm again?

Yesterday she'd left a message on Todd's answering machine. Had he received it? She'd almost called her parents, then decided against it.

Grace McKinney's love was almost fanatical in its intensity. And right now Corey didn't feel she had the energy to cope with that kind of intensity. Plus, she planned to keep her accident a secret, and she needed time to stabilize before facing her family.

"Corey!"

She looked through the sea of people and spotted Todd's styled hair and clean-shaven face as he cut through the throng with self-assurance. Women stared at him as he passed, and Corey felt surprised that he drew their attention. She had never really thought about his looks, but now she could see he was handsome in a conventional, Ivy-League sort of way. A lot of people would probably think Todd better-looking than Ash, but in Corey's mind that would be like comparing a house cat to a lion. As she watched Todd approach, she felt as if his features were almost too perfect—mannequin perfect, as if he'd just stepped out of the pages of a men's clothing catalogue.

"I'm so glad you're back." Arms gathered her to his chest, her cheek brushing the lapel of his herringbone topcoat. He smelled like expensive aftershave, the disinfectant used in hospitals, and breath mints. Bending, he pressed cool lips against hers, then held her slightly away. "What happened to you?"

She tugged her jacket closer together at the neck. "It's nothing, really."

"Nothing?" He drew her to the side so the people behind them could pass. "Your arm's in a sling." Disapproval poured from his dark-lashed blue eyes.

Before the trip Todd and her mother had put their heads together and decided that Corey shouldn't go to

Brazil, that she was too delicate for such a thing. And she shouldn't concern herself with foreigners, especially not savages. Now Todd would gloat over having been right.

Fatigue washed over her. "It's nothing. I pulled a muscle, that's all." Her shoulder throbbed with pain, seeming to mock her lie. Wryly she thought that she had at least learned a craft while she was gone: the fine art of lying.

"Well, give me your luggage stubs," Todd said, taking charge, dismissing her injury as trivial. She noted his pale, neatly trimmed fingernails as he removed the stub from her hand, then he was guiding her through the crowd.

He would make somebody a nice husband, she thought distantly.

"I have so much to tell you. Dr. Pearson thinks he can get me on at St. Michael's in Boston. There's a lot of money there. They do quite a few face-lifts and liposuctions. This yours?" He indicated a tidy leather suitcase coming around the treadmill.

"No." She pointed. "The black one." She had a nicer valise at home, but she liked this one. It had been her grandfather's.

"You could do with a new set of luggage." He hefted the bag from the treadmill. "Guess I know what to get you next Christmas."

"Mmm."

"I thought we'd go into downtown Chicago and eat since we're this close."

"Todd. I'm tired."

"Oh. Well. Okay. Another time. I know a great new place."

"Did you call my folks? Do they know I'm coming?"

"Not yet. I thought you might want to stop at my place for a while first. It's been over two weeks since I've seen you."

Meaning, *let's have sex.* "Todd . . . I'm tired. I want to go home."

He didn't press it. "I said you shouldn't have gone to South America. And your mother's been sick with worry. Calls me almost every day."

"Mea culpa, mea culpa."

"What?"

"Nothing." Ash had definitely rubbed off on her. First the lying, now she was getting cynical.

The outer door opened automatically and a blast of frigid winter air hit Corey in the face, taking her breath away.

"Your mother kept worrying that you'd have some horrible accident." Todd laughed. "Get cooked and eaten by natives, I guess. And here you are, safe and sound, if we don't count a pulled muscle."

"Yes. Safe and sound."

He opened the trunk to his tidy BMW and put her tattered suitcase in the carpeted trunk.

"Did I tell you Pearson thinks I can make as much as six figures my first year?" He slammed the trunk shut. "Josh Myers doesn't make that much, and he's been at Mayo five years."

"I thought you were going to practice in Pleasant Grove." Her words were slurred through half-frozen lips. "You said Pleasant Grove needed a good anesthesiologist."

"It does. But how can I pass up an opportunity like this?"

He held open the passenger door. She ducked her head and got in. Sitting on the leather seat was like sitting on a block of ice. Everything in the car smelled new and clean and impersonal.

Todd slid into the driver's seat, tugging the tail of his heavy topcoat out from under him. Methodically he unsnapped his leather key-ring holder, found the correct key, separated it from the others, then snapped the holder shut again while the cold seeped deeper and deeper into Corey's bones.

The pain in her arm was getting progressively worse. It had become so intense that she was finding it harder and harder to concentrate on what Todd was saying. Longingly she thought of the pain pills in her purse, wishing she had taken one before getting off the plane. She couldn't get them out now, in front of Todd. If he found out about her accident, he would never let it rest. He would tell her mother, who would coddle her to death and make Corey feel guiltier than she already did.

He finally got the engine going. Then came a methodical check of mirrors and lights. "You won't mind living in Boston, will you?" he asked, adjusting the air vents. "I know what a homebody you are, but you'll get used to it. Especially if we have a nice big house. Something with enough room to entertain other doctors and their wives."

She dully supposed that a lot of women would kill for the kind of life he was describing. But thinking about it only made her feel hollow, empty. What was important to him wasn't important to her.

Tell him now. "Todd, about us . . ."

He was intent on swinging the car onto the freeway, the headlights illuminating the interstate sign.

"About our getting married." She hesitated, wondering what he would say, wondering if there would be an ugly scene. She didn't want that. Didn't know if she could take it. Not now, when she felt drained of all strength.

"Do you want to wait longer? Is that it?"

She couldn't be tactful. The pain in her shoulder had become almost stupefying, aching trails of fire shooting all the way into her neck and down to her elbow. "Maybe I want to wait forever. We shouldn't get married just because other people expect it of us."

He glanced over at her, then back to the road. "I told you that trip would wear you out."

His voice was so damn condescending.

"You don't have the energy for that kind of thing.

Remember the summer you worked the night shift at St. Mary's? You came down with mono."

"Todd. I'm not coming down with anything."

He reached over and patted her on the knee. "You might not be getting sick, but you're exhausted. You'll be okay after you get some rest."

This was useless. Mentally she was in no shape for this kind of battle, not when she was dying inside. Later. She would discuss it with him later.

She bit her lip and stared out the window, at the stars. Ursa Major. There was Ursa Major—the Great Bear. It had never looked like a bear to her. But they say stars had changed. It might have looked like a bear at one time. There was the Big Dipper. She followed the front of the cup, the pointer stars, until she found the North Star.

Todd was making adjustments to the radio, changing it until he came to a classical station. "It's amazing how a good long sleep can put somebody back together again."

"Do you ever go to those astronomy meetings anymore?" she asked, remembering how intense he had been about stars and the universe at one time. How he had taught her the names of so many of the constellations. It was a good memory. A childhood memory. Just as Todd had been a very real part of her childhood. But now she had changed; and he had changed.

"I haven't gone to any meetings for years. Kid stuff."

"Yes." She thought of a man who chased the moon.

She continued to stare up at the North Star, feeling as if she were trying to cling to something that was already lost to her.

Then she wondered how a person went about putting herself back together once her soul had been shattered.

Three hours later, when they reached her parents' home, Todd did the talking, and for once Corey was glad.

"She's worn out," he explained to Grace McKinney.

"Poor thing! I'll fix her something to eat, then she can go right to bed."

"No, Mom." Eating was Grace McKinney's solution to every problem in life. Corey had never understood how her mother managed to stay so petite. "I'm too tired to eat."

"Oh, my Lord!"

The sling had been spotted. Corey's mother stared at it, eyes wide with horror, her small, weathered hand pressed to her mouth. "Oh, my Lord!" She bustled around, helping Corey off with her jacket. "I knew something terrible was going to happen to you. You broke your arm! Your left arm. The same one you broke when you were bucked off that horse I didn't want you to get."

"Pony."

"It's only a pulled muscle, Mrs. McKinney," Todd assured her with his recently acquired doctor's air.

"She's dead on her feet," broke in a low, gruff voice.

Her dad was standing in the kitchen doorway, stocky and rugged-looking with his burly red-blond beard turning to gray, the cuffed waffle-weave of long underwear covering his forearms below rolled-up sleeves. Safe. He looked safe and comfortable. Relief washed over her. "Daddy."

Corey was enveloped in a careful bear hug, her father's flannel shirt smelling reassuringly familiar, like wool and wood smoke and outdoors. He let go long enough to look at her with keen dark eyes, eyes that read more from her expression than she would have liked.

"Go up to bed," he told her calmly. "There'll be plenty of time to talk in the morning."

She nodded, then in a haze of fatigue managed to make it up the carpeted stairs to her room, Grace McKinney following close behind.

She flicked on the light. Her room looked exactly the same as it had the day she'd left. But that shouldn't seem so strange. She hadn't been gone a lifetime. Only two weeks. Two weeks.

The four-poster was still covered with the bright patchwork quilt Grandma McKinney had made. The braid rug still lay tidily across the waxed pinewood floor. The dollhouse her father made for her sixth birthday, full of miniature furniture that she and her mother had collected, stood against one wall. Many quiet hours had been spent cutting tiny fabric pieces, tiny bits of wallpaper. It came to Corey that there was much love in the room.

She turned to look at Grace McKinney. They were almost the same size and height, but that's where their similarities ended. Her mother was dark-haired, showing more gray all the time, skin brown from working outdoors alongside her father. There were smile lines at the corners of her eyes and mouth.

Corey thought about Ash never having anybody to care about him, never having anybody to make Kool-Aid for him, or read him bedtime stories, comfort him on dark, shadowy nights, kiss his hurts and make them better.

She reached out and hugged her mother.

"Thanks, Mom. Thanks for worrying about me. It's good to be home."

Grace McKinney smiled her mother's smile. "You go ahead and get ready for bed. I'll bring you up some hot chocolate."

"That would be nice."

After her mother left, Corey moved to the window seat and sat down. She stared through the paned glass to the darkness outside. A lonely light at the corn crib reflected off the icy lane. Another light shone in the lot where the sheep were kept at lambing time. Snow, where it had been blown by chill winds, lay in huge drifts along barbed-wire fences. Bare tree branches cast long, naked shadows.

She should take a pain pill before her mother returned, but it seemed such an effort. Instead, with one finger she reached up and slowly traced the delicate pattern of crystal ice that had formed on the glass. So cold. Cold and frozen.

From a distance came the eerie cries of coyotes. The sound was full of sadness and despair. She had always thought they sounded too much like people—like abandoned, suffering souls. The crying stopped and the crisp silence of winter descended, wrapping itself around her like a funeral shroud.

But someplace, someplace very special, she knew the call of the howler monkey echoed through dew-laden leaves, sounding like a faraway train, and bugs were singing their night songs. Someplace very special, life went on without her. . . .

Corey sat staring at the blank screen. She should probably turn on the television, but it didn't seem worth the effort. Pulling the heavy quilt tighter around her, she sank deeper into her mother's overstuffed couch.

She had returned to work two weeks before, and still couldn't get in gear. The problem was that her heart wasn't in it. She just didn't care about her job anymore. Part of it was the fact that she had changed and now found it very difficult to sympathize with many of her cases. The last welfare application she'd filled out had been for a woman who chain-smoked and needed a bath. Corey knew very little of the money would filter down to the woman's children, and it made her feel frustrated and useless.

Corey sighed and shifted her aching arm. She had quit wearing the sling, mainly to stop the questions, but her shoulder was stiff and sore. At least Todd had quit mentioning marriage. She didn't know if he'd finally taken her refusal seriously or not. It seemed more likely that he was just waiting for her to get back to "normal." He still came by almost every day, but Corey felt he did so out of habit. It was hard to stop something you'd been doing most of your life.

She forced herself to get up from the couch, flicked on the TV, then settled back down to stare at the screen.

News. Corey hated watching the news. It was too depressing. So why had she bothered turning the set on at all?

She was almost asleep when the lead-in for the upcoming story caught her attention. Something about somebody being his brother's keeper. . . .

A mild flicker of interest kept her waiting through a commercial full of dancing hamburgers and giggling teenagers, then her favorite jeans ad. One of the men in it had dark, tousled hair, needed a shave, and had a sexy smile. He made her think of Ash.

The news came back on.

"In my twenty years as newscaster," the distinguished anchorman said, "it has been my job to relate more bad news than good. So tonight I am pleased to bring you a story that is more amazing than fiction, that smacks of romance and adventure, danger and heroism. Some of you, many of you, will remember a man who not too many years ago touched our lives for far too brief a time. Well, gather 'round, and I'll tell you the story of one Lucas Quincy Adams. . . ."

Corey froze. It couldn't be. Oh, God. It couldn't be. She held her breath, not daring to breathe, not daring to move.

Orphaned as a child, Lucas Adams grew up surrounded by poverty. By age ten he and his younger brother, Asher, were streetwise hoodlums. Growing up with such a disadvantaged perspective on the world didn't launch Lucas Adams into a life of crime. Quite the opposite. By age twenty-five Luke had established several soup kitchens in New York

*City and across the country. By age thirty-five he
expanded his arena of altruism to include South
America, specifically the Amazon jungle.*

The newscaster looked ahead, indicating that the camera
should roll with the prerecorded story.

An aerial view of a wide, winding river filled the
screen. The river was hemmed in by a mass of green trees
so solid it looked as if you could walk across their tops.

*It's hard to imagine a land so vast and unexplored
that a two-hundred-mile-long river was only recently discovered in the Amazon region, and that
was due to satellite pictures. Into this inconceiv-
able vastness Lucas Adams vanished over three
years ago.*

Corey's breath lay suspended; she didn't dare to hope,
didn't dare to think. . . .

Today Lucas Adams came home.

"Oh, God!"

The shocked whisper issued from Corey's constricted
throat. Her hands were clenched so tightly that her fingernails dug into her palms. Her eyes were awash with tears,
and she blinked, willing herself not to cry. She could cry
later.

The picture on the screen changed, showing two men
emerging from an airport rampway.

"Ash!"

The camera wasn't close, but she recognized him. A
sob escaped her and she clamped a hand over her mouth,
keeping her eyes fastened on the set.

*After living with a tribe of primitive Amazon Indi-
ans for over three years, a tired but happy Lucas*

Adams stepped off a plane at Kennedy International Airport.

The camera closed in on a gaunt-faced man with graying blond hair. Luke. Ash's Luke. Looking much older than he should.

When asked what he thought about being compared to Dr. Livingstone, this was Lucas Adams's reply: "Dr. Livingstone was never really lost."

Luke smiled, and the smile was sad and sweet; Ash's smile without the bitterness.

"I was."

Her vision blurred and Corey quickly wiped the back of her hand across her eyes. She couldn't miss any of this.

Luke looked out with soulful eyes, eyes that seemed to carry the weight of the world. A Jesus face. In this man was unconditional love of all things. He had done, and would do, great things. Just like Ash.

Ash was towering behind his brother, looking so . . . so Ash. As if he'd just crawled out of bed. As if he could use a shave and a change of clothes.

"I'm just awfully lucky to have such a stubborn little brother."

Luke's voice was as smooth as Ash's was gravelly.

Lucas Adams was found by his brother, Asher, who never gave up hope of finding him.

He'd done it, really done it.

Without taking her eyes from the screen, Corey felt

across the top of the end table for the tissue box. She pulled out a tissue and wiped her eyes.

The camera closed in on Ash. He was thinner. Television was supposed to add pounds, not take them away. And tired. He looked tired. But happy.

He was asked how it felt to have proven the rest of the world wrong. "Great. It feels great."

His jaw clamped shut, and it looked as if no more information was going to be pried from him.

Why, he's nervous, Corey realized. She'd never seen him nervous. It was fascinating.

Asher Adams is being called a hero. But his reaction to that label was less than enthusiastic.

Ash's nervousness seemed to fall away, and that familiar, self-mocking smile played at the corners of his mouth.

"That's a bunch of—"

The last word was blipped out.

"And there you have it," the newscaster commented drily.

He turned over a sheet of paper and eyed the camera. "A quote for the history books."

Lucas Adams told us he's seen enough of the jungle and has no immediate plans to return. On the other hand, when we asked Asher Adams the same question, he said he would go back as soon as his brother was settled, saying the Amazon was his home.

And so this night at least, our newscast ends on an upbeat note. Lucas Adams is alive, and

Asher Adams proved that he was indeed his brother's keeper. Have a good weekend.

For a long time Corey stared at the screen with unseeing eyes. Stunned. Dazed. And proud. So very proud.

Maybe life could be a Walt Disney movie. Maybe it did help if you clapped for Tinkerbell, if you truly believed.

chapter
twenty-two

Ash swung the car into the left lane and stomped down on the accelerator. The little four-cylinder choked, almost died, then shot forward.

Rental cars were a bitch.

He glanced over at the '57 Chevy he was passing. Bright winter sunlight reflected off its gray fenders and sparkling chrome. The occupants were a couple of old-sters out for a Sunday jaunt. Just tooling around, taking in the scenery.

He must be getting close to Lily's hometown.

What the hell was he going to say to her?

He pulled back into the right lane. He could feel himself beginning to sweat. Here it was, a notch below freezing, and he was sweating. It was the damn clothes. He hated the restrictions of bulky winter clothes. Why would anybody want to live in a place where they had to put on twenty pounds of dead weight just to step out the damn door? He unzipped his leather flight jacket and rolled down the window a couple of inches, letting in the chill air.

Actually, he didn't mind the jacket all that much. It was a World War II Flying Tigers job he'd won in a poker game some years back. He liked the way it felt, soft and worn, and the way it smelled—like aged leather, with a hint of mildew.

Would she even be home?

He'd always wanted to be a Flying Tiger. But he'd been born about thirty years too late.

The radio kept fading in and out, so he fiddled with the dial, hit a couple western stations, then a top 40, finally coming to an all-request rock. He settled back to listen to some vintage Neil Young while trying to get his nerves to stop jumping.

When he spotted the quaint little sign announcing the edge of Pleasant Grove, Illinois, he braked and swung the car off the road onto the graveled shoulder.

This was stupid. Just stupid as all hell.

He grabbed the flattened pack of cigarettes off the dash, lit one, and tossed the match out the window. He inhaled, exhaled, then came to a decision.

Tires squealed as he whipped the car into a tight U-turn. He went approximately three miles before he pulled off the road again.

He was just going to see her, assure himself that she was okay, for chrissake. He owed her that much. He wouldn't mention that in order to find out how she was, he'd caught a plane from New York to Chicago, then rented this excuse of a car.

Denial. He supposed that's what he was doing, denying his feelings for her. But denial was a form of protection. Truth was, he didn't know why he'd come. He only knew the pull had been too strong to ignore.

Well, he sure as hell hadn't gone to all this trouble to chicken out like some wimp. He swung the car back around.

This time, when he reached the edge of town, he pulled into a gas station to ask directions.

Stepping inside the old rundown station was like stepping into a slice of rural America. And Ash got the distinct feeling he didn't wear the Midwest well. Not well at all. It fit him like a rented tux.

Behind the linoleum-surfaced counter was a tall, lanky kid of about sixteen wearing a seed-corn cap and denim jacket.

"I'm looking for the McKinney farm," Ash told him. "Know where it is?"

The kid shrugged. "South of here somewhere. Slim could probably tell you." He pointed his half-finished Coke bottle at the old men sitting at a card table in front of the pot-belly stove. The one in bib overalls looked up from his cards.

"If you're wanting to see any livestock, forget it. I can tell you right now that Les McKinney don't talk business on Sundays."

"It's not business."

Now all three of the men were staring at him, not even attempting to hide their curiosity.

Let them wonder.

The man in faded overalls spoke again. "Just go up the hard road out here till you see the sign marks the beginning of Jackson County, then take a left. It's about a mile. Can't miss it."

"Thanks."

Before leaving, Ash bought a pack of cigarettes. As he walked past the rusty gas pumps to the car, he was sure at least three pairs of eyes were on his back.

The farm was easy to find, just like Slim said. Ash stopped the car by a barn-shaped mailbox, then turned up the gravel drive.

This was stupid as all hell. Just stupid as all hell. He shut off the engine and climbed out of the tiny car, slam ming the door behind him. For a moment he just stared at the white two-story house.

There it was—the big front porch. And the swing, it was there too, attached to the porch ceiling to protect it from winter weather. Yep, he was standing smack-dab in the middle of a Norman Rockwell.

He raked his fingers through his hair, thinking that maybe he should have gotten a haircut. When had he last had one? He couldn't remember. He shrugged his shoulders. It wasn't as if he were picking up a date for the prom. It only felt that way. Stuffing his hands deep into the pockets of his jacket, he strode up the walk to the house and knocked on the door.

The door wasn't answered by Corey, or by her mother, or by her father. There was some guy standing there. He was wearing a green tie and a yellow pullover sweater, tweed pants. And, oh, Christ, he was wearing loafers—with tassels. Ash had probably interrupted his reading of *Gentleman's Quarterly*.

What was really irritating as hell was the way this guy was looking at him, as if he were some scurvy lowlife who had crawled out from under a rock to mooch a meal.

Then it hit him: Dudley. This guy had to be Dudley. He wasn't nerdy like he'd expected. He wasn't zit-faced and ugly either. Ash grudgingly supposed he was nice-looking in a bland, boring sort of way. But that wasn't what rubbed him wrong. No, it wasn't his squeaky-clean looks, it was his attitude problem. Dudley was a snob.

Ash had known and hated guys like him before. It seemed to be a phase some doctors went through when they finished their internships. Cocky. Thought they were a couple of notches above everybody else on the planet. Most of them grew out of it, but some never did.

A feeling of disappointment washed over him, and he realized that deep down he'd been hoping to find that Lily had given Dudley the skids.

Ash took his hands out of his pockets and settled one

high on the white woodwork of the doorframe, leaning closer. "Corey home?" he asked with false pleasantness.

Dudley's eyes narrowed as he made an inventory of Ash's shaggy hair, leather jacket, and old jeans. "She doesn't handle casework from her home. You'll have to call the county office tomorrow."

He tried to shut the door, but Ash quickly wedged his shoulder against it. It was all he could do to keep from grabbing Dudley by his eighty-dollar tie. "I'd love an excuse to knock the shit out of you," he said.

Ash had the satisfaction of seeing Dudley blanch and draw back.

"Todd, who is it?"

Lily's voice. Ash smiled at the man in front of him.

"Todd . . . ?"

Her voice was closer this time. Then the door opened wide, and there she was.

"Ash!"

Disbelief was in her face and voice. *"Ash."*

He let his hand drop away from the doorframe, forgetting all about Dudley. "Hi, Lily," he said quietly.

She pushed past the dumbfounded Todd and reached for Ash, picking up one of his hands, gripping it tightly while her gaze traveled over him once, then again before she spoke.

"You found Luke. You fought the mighty Amazon jungle, and won. I'm so terribly glad. So terribly proud." She swallowed. "I wish I could have been there—" Her voice broke, and for a second Ash was afraid she was going to cry, but she took a deep breath, then smiled up at him, her eyes watery. "You don't know how happy I am for you."

Ash schooled his features, trying not to let his shock show. But looking at her wrung the heart he never thought he had. Scared him. She was even thinner than the last time he'd seen her. Her bruised eyes looked huge in her pallid face, and there was something about them, something in them that hadn't been there before, and he didn't like it. A strange kind of acceptance maybe.

He'd had George put her on a plane as soon as she was well enough to travel, believing she would get better faster in her own element, around her own people. But she was just as pale as she had been right after surgery, before coming out from under the anesthetic.

Ash wanted to pull her into his arms, hold her, talk to her, find out why she looked like a lost waif, why her eyes reminded him of some poster child's. But he couldn't forget Romeo standing right behind her. He was tempted to tell him to beat it, to go back to reading his market report, but then, with a strange sense of loss, he remembered that this guy was her fiancé, and Ash himself was the outsider.

The hands still clinging to his were like ice. "You better go inside," he told her quietly. He glanced at Todd, at the person who should be holding her. "And I better leave."

"Leave? You can't leave. You just got here." Two bright spots of color appeared in her cheeks. She tugged at his hand like a child, urging him to come inside with her.

But still he hung back. "Corey, I don't think this is a good idea. I shouldn't have come."

"I'm so glad you came. Come in the house. I want Mom and Dad to meet you. *Please.*"

Her eyes pleaded with him, and her voice held an underlying note of desperation. And he, more than anyone, was no stranger to desperation.

He followed her inside.

What are you doing here, Asher Adams?

Corey couldn't believe Ash was sitting at the round oak table in her parents' kitchen, wedged between Todd and her father, eating her mother's chocolate cake, looking endearingly out of place.

He must care more than she had thought. He must care at least a little.

Her logical self pushed away that small spark of hope. He had come only to make sure she was okay. After all, the bullet intended for him had hit her.

There had been a brief moment of panic when he'd asked how her shoulder was, but she had quickly assured him it was fine and the subject was dropped.

"This cake's great," Todd told Grace McKinney in his best Eddie Haskell voice.

Todd hated chocolate of any kind, but he'd certainly fooled Grace McKinney all these years. Yet he could never see that the joke was on him, because she always served him chocolate cake.

"Thank you, Todd." Grace sat down between Corey and Les McKinney. "I know how you both are about chocolate."

From across the table Ash regarded Corey steadily. "How are you about chocolate?"

"I . . . ah—" She glanced down at her plate, then back up at him, a wry smile on her face. "I guess I like it a little too much."

As Ash looked on, Todd patted her hand in a possessive gesture. Corey pulled it away.

"Corey's a chocoholic," Les McKinney said with a deep, rumbling laugh.

Her father had immediately taken to Ash. On the other hand, it was no surprise to find that Ash and Todd got along like oil and water. And Grace McKinney kept staring at Ash with what Corey took to be a cross between fear and fascination. She couldn't blame her. Corey was sure she'd looked at him with the same expression more than once herself.

Even though Ash had shaved recently, and his sweatshirt—with faded black T-shirt ribbing showing around the neck—was clean, that wild, barely suppressed recklessness that always lurked in him could be sensed, felt, even in such a tranquil setting. And it surprised her.

She thought Ash would be different now that he'd found Luke. More mellow. But mellow was probably the wrong word to use in referring to Ash, since much of that raw kinetic energy was simply his nature, yet she had hoped he would have found some measure of peace. But he was still the tightly coiled spring he had always been.

"Remember the time we were little," Todd began.

Corey heaved an inward sigh. This was the third "remember when" story he had told so far.

"Remember how you used to hide chocolate everywhere? What about the time you had me hide some for you in my schoolbag? And it melted all over my homework?" Todd laughed—a rare sound coming from him nowadays. When he laughed like that, he seemed like the old Todd.

Corey smiled and nodded. It *had* been funny. "Mrs. Jamison didn't believe you until you slapped the dripping papers on her desk. Then she made you stand in front of the class and eat them!"

Maybe that was why Todd hated chocolate so much. The thought made Corey laugh out loud.

"Those were fun times," Todd said, his laughter dying to a chuckle.

Corey had hoped she and Todd had finally come to an understanding, but apparently he hadn't been listening to a thing she'd said. Right now he was quite obviously staking his claim to her, wanting Ash to believe she was his property.

"I understand you're an anesthesiologist." Ash spoke with the mockingly pleasant tone he'd been using whenever he talked to Todd.

"That's right," Todd answered grudgingly.

"I used to know an anesthesiologist." Ash's eyes were reflective as he let his gaze drift from Todd to the white-curtained window above the sink. It seemed as if he were gathering his thoughts so he could present his tale properly.

"Ash—" Corey's voice was part plea, part warning. How could she possibly forget the crude anesthesiologist story he'd regaled her with on her first day in the Amazon? She'd always wondered how that story had ended.

Ash's eyes, when they shifted from the window to focus on her, were as wide and innocent as a child's. He gave her a reassuring smile that did little to reassure her before turning back to the sulking Todd.

"Forget it." Ash waved his hand, dismissing the crude story while Corey let out a relieved breath. "You probably don't like to talk shop when you're away from the hospital. So, tell me, what do you two do for entertainment around here?"

Todd compressed his lips. "My schedule is very tight," he said coldly. "I don't have much spare time. And Corey hasn't really gotten back her strength since that foolish trip to the Amazon." The last was spoken as if the very word *Amazon* dirtied his mouth.

Ash didn't so much as bat an eye. And that was very strange, very strange indeed, considering his temper. Corey had the uncomfortable suspicion that he was biding his time.

"So you don't do anything together?"

"You both went to that dinner theater just last week," Grace McKinney supplied.

"Ahh . . ." There was a satisfied quality to Ash's voice, like the trapper who sees that his prey is about to step into a most carefully placed snare.

"Dinner theater, huh?" Ash draped an arm over the chair back, and it struck Corey how very much at ease he looked, yet she knew it was an act. She could sense the tension in him, detect the almost undetectable glint in his eye. Ash was getting ready to enjoy himself at Todd's expense. Todd shouldn't have said that about the Amazon.

"You know, I went to a dinner theater once." Ash's voice was nothing but a sinfully smooth smoke screen.

Corey was used to the outrageous things Ash said, and she doubted if he could really shock her anymore. But Todd might be in for a surprise, not to mention her unsuspecting parents, her poor, naive mother.

"I guess it could be called a dinner theater. There was this center ring, so you could watch the women mud wrestlers while you ate."

The kitchen suddenly became so quiet that the only sound to be heard was the clock ticking above the sink.

"They didn't have a stitch on—unless you counted the mud. But, hey, they knew some interesting holds. Needless to say, the front-row seats were always filled."

To her right Corey could sense her mother's shock, like a tangible wall. A strangled snort came from the direction of her father, but she didn't dare look up.

Hysterical laughter bubbled in her, the kind that comes when you're in a library, or standing face-to-face with strangers in an elevator. Corey bit her lip and focused intently on her cake. The frosting was a quarter of an inch thick with little circular swirls. Her mother had a special tool for that.

She had to move, do something. Her fork clattered against her plate as she sliced into the cake.

Ash kept at it. "Ever take in one of those kind of shows, Todd?"

"Very amusing," Todd sneered.

Todd's very obvious *un*amusement seemed to spur Ash on. "Aw, come on, Todd. Surely you've at least taken in a skin flick sometime in your life."

Todd heaved a stoic sigh, the kind one might use around a hyperactive child. "No."

"Well, if you don't go out much, then what do you and Corey do? Stay home and play bingo?"

Corey choked on the chocolate cake. Grace McKinney immediately began slapping her between the shoulder blades, unknowingly increasing her daughter's distress by jostling her barely healed injury. Eyes blinded by tears, Corey groped for the milk. Her fingertips made contact with the cool glass, and through a blur she saw that Ash had guided it to her hand. She glared at him over the napkin she held pressed to her face. The corners of his mouth turned up, but the smile didn't reach the steely gray of his eyes, and Corey wondered what she could have done to have incurred his wrath.

"Never pound someone on the back unless the food is lodged in their windpipe and they can't breathe," Todd informed Grace McKinney.

"Oh. Are you okay, honey?" She quit her pounding and leaned down to look at Corey's face.

Corey took a swallow of milk and wiped her mouth. "I'm okay, fine," she gasped.

Then she sprang to her feet and began swiping at the cake crumbs with her crumpled napkin. "I'm sorry." She could feel the heat in her face. Her blood was churning, thundering through her veins.

"Bingo?" Todd was still trying to figure out what Ash was talking about.

"Yeah, Corey and I played bingo a couple times while she was in the Amazon. She really got a buzz out of it."

Corey swung around and faced the kitchen sink, her hands clenched into tight fists.

A *buzz* out of it! She'd kill him! She'd strangle him!

She turned the water on full blast and stuck the dish-rag underneath, water splashing her sweater. With an angry motion she turned it off. She hadn't been this mad since . . . since South America!

A buzz out of it!

Everybody had to know what Ash was talking about. It was so obvious.

"I never knew you liked bingo," Grace McKinney said with the slow, hurt tone that always made Corey feel guilty.

Corey wrung out the dishrag, imagining it was Ash's neck. "I'm not crazy about it," she muttered. "It's okay."

"I have a bingo game stuck away somewhere," Grace said. "Why don't we play?"

Todd let out a muffled groan.

Corey swung around. "No! Really, Mom. I don't think so."

"Why not?" Ash was regarding her steadily, gray eyes reflecting the light. "Are you tired of it? Been playing too much since you've been back?" His eyes never left her face.

Why was he doing this to her? She didn't understand, but suddenly it was important that he know the truth. "No." She looked at the twisted dishrag in her hands, then back to Ash. "No. Not even once."

Corey's dad had been watching with great interest. Now he looked from Ash to his daughter, then back to Ash. He slapped his hands together. "Let's play a game." He smiled, suddenly looking almost as satisfied as Ash.

While Grace McKinney passed around the bingo cards, it was all Corey could do to keep from openly laughing at Todd's expression. Horrified would be putting it mildly. She was sure bingo was much too simpleminded a game for him to participate in, but she also knew he wouldn't leave, not as long as Ash was still around. The whole situation was taking on the absurdity of an *I Love Lucy* show.

"I don't know what happened to the markers," announced Les McKinney as he came in from the back porch with an ear of corn. "We'll have to make do with corn." With his thumb he shelled out individual mounds next to everyone's card. "We save some whole ears to feed the squirrels through the winter."

Next to her Todd squirmed and sighed heavily.

"I'll call the numbers." Ash picked up the shaker box. "Mark your free space." He shook a wooden disk into his palm, then called out the first number.

Ten minutes later Mrs. McKinney had won one game, Ash three.

Corey's mother seemed to be getting over her fear of Ash, having actually laughed at some of his jokes—which he'd thankfully kept clean.

"Bingo!" Ash shouted after they'd barely started another game.

"Bingo? How could you?" Corey demanded. "You only called six numbers."

Ash slid his card over to her, tapping it with a long brown forefinger. "See for yourself."

He was right.

"Straight across. *Horizontal,*" he added with exaggerated pride.

"Oh, brother." She couldn't help but laugh as she pushed the card across the table to him.

He smiled at her and leaned back in his chair to reach into the neck of his sweatshirt for a pack of cigarettes. Then he slapped at his pockets until he found a crumpled book of matches.

"What?" The innocent yet ornery expression she loved was in his face.

She hadn't realized she'd been openly staring. Because she couldn't think of anything else, she said, "You're going to smoke one of those awful things?"

Lazily, he lit his cigarette, shook out the match, then let his gaze drift up to meet hers again. "I always smoke after a game of bingo."

chapter
twenty-three

It felt strange to laugh. Corey hadn't laughed, really laughed, in a long time. Then it came to her: *Ash had brought the color back.*

She had always known that there was nothing moderate about her feelings when it came to Ash. He had a way of making her laugh all her laughter, cry all her tears.

She was like Dorothy opening the farmhouse door, seeing the bright, colorful world out there, just waiting.

While the bingo game continued, Corey sat at the table, slightly dazed, trying to absorb it all. Now she knew she'd only fooled herself into thinking she was getting along okay, fooled herself into thinking her life was moving steadily forward, when it had been doing nothing but standing still. The last two weeks might as well have been spent in limbo.

Joy, embarrassment, anger. Since Ash's arrival she'd felt the emotions that had been lying dormant in her. Now there was one more thing she was feeling: fear. She was afraid for herself because she knew Ash would be leaving just as abruptly as he'd come, and, like Dorothy, she would return to her black and white world.

With a forefinger she rearranged her allotment of corn kernels into a geometric pattern. It wasn't fair. Wasn't love supposed to be kind, be gentle? Then why the sharp edges? It shouldn't hurt like this. Yet she knew it would be so different if that love were reciprocated. It would still hurt, yes. But it would hurt in a different way. A good way.

"Honey, you're not paying attention," her mother said. "You missed the last two numbers."

"Oh . . . sorry."

The interruption gave Todd the opportunity to push his card to the center of the table. "I hate to break this up, but I'm going to have to leave," he announced, looking at his watch. "I have to be at the hospital in an hour."

"Too bad," Ash murmured.

Todd ignored him, focusing instead on Corey. "Walk me to the door?"

She was watching the almost graceful movement of Ash's long, sensitive fingers as he collected the wooden bingo numbers and tamped them into the box.

"Corey."

Reluctantly her eyes drifted from Ash's hands up to Todd's face. He was annoyed. His words finally clicked. "Oh, I'll see you out."

They barely made it out of earshot of the kitchen when Todd started in. "You know, I had almost come to accept the fact that you didn't want to marry me anymore," he said in frustration. "That kind of thing happens, I understand. But now I have to tell you I'm completely baffled."

"Todd. Not here, not now." She reached for the door handle.

"It's because of him, isn't it?" He jerked his head

toward the kitchen. "He's the reason you don't want to marry me, isn't that right?"

Corey could hear the deep rumble of male voices carrying from the kitchen, followed by her father and Ash's combined laughter. "Todd, it's not that simple. I've changed. I'm not the same person I used to be."

"Are you blind? He's a loser. Surely you can see that."

"He's not a loser. You don't know him like I do."

"Apparently not," Todd said sarcastically.

She didn't want this to get ugly. Not with Todd. "What if I told you I love him?"

"Then I'd have to say you're confused. Corey"—he put his hands lightly on her upper arms and looked down at her, his clear blue eyes serious—"come to your senses. Nobody falls in love in that short a time. It just doesn't happen."

He didn't know, that's all. "I never thought so either. But I found out differently." Maybe someday Todd would find out differently too.

"Corey." With a heavy sigh he lifted his hands from her. "I didn't want to have to tell you this, but your friend in there—he cheats at bingo. Think about it. What kind of person cheats at bingo?"

He settled both hands on his hips, waiting for her reaction. She had the absurd notion that he expected her to gasp and clutch her throat in some dramatic Victorian gesture of horror.

She tried hard not to smile, tried to keep a sober expression. "He was cheating?" she asked slowly.

"I saw him. I really should have won that last game, but he palmed the call number."

"Did he?" She couldn't suppress her smile any longer. How typically Ash.

Todd couldn't seem to see the humor in it. When had he started taking himself so seriously? Or had he always been that way and she was only just now noticing?

It was strange. . . . If she'd never gone to the Amazon, never met Ash, she would most likely have been perfectly content with Todd. She wouldn't have understood those fleeting flashes of emptiness that come upon a person from time to time. Now she knew what they were: the yearning for what could have been, for the road never taken.

"Goodbye, Todd." She opened the door and waited for him to leave.

"Corey, I just can't believe this."

"Todd, please don't make it any harder than it is. I never wanted to hurt you, believe me."

She thought about the years they'd spent together, all the binding memories they shared. "I'm doing the right thing," she told him, her voice catching, then dropping to a hoarse whisper, "for both of us."

He started to say something, most likely argue, but stopped himself. His blue eyes were intent. At that instant she could see him mature a little as he seemed to try to understand her. He pressed his lips together and nodded, then stepped through the doorway and onto the wide front porch. She was closing the door when he suddenly yelled through the two-inch crack. "What am I going to tell people?"

"Just tell them we changed our minds, that's all." *That's all.* What terribly inadequate words.

The door clicked shut with finality. Corey leaned her head against the cool wood and closed her eyes, trying not to think of the boxes and boxes of curled photographs upstairs—of a blond-haired little girl and her inseparable playmate, a pretty, blue-eyed boy.

Maybe someday when Todd met and married a person who was right for him, who loved him and adored him, who thought he was the smartest, most handsome doctor in the world, maybe then they could talk, reminisce over their childhood memories.

It hurt to let go of the past, it really did. . . .

"So, when's the big occasion?"

Ash.

She straightened away from the door and her eyes locked on him. He was carrying his jacket.

Her heart thudded in sudden terror, his question hardly registering. All she knew was that he was leaving. She was just standing there at the door, letting the men in her life walk away.

She wouldn't beg him to stay longer, beg him to take her back with him.

When she was old, when she was so cold inside that she had to wear a heavy sweater on the hottest summer day, children would talk about her behind their hands, giggling nervously to hide their fear of the old maid.

And she would think: *This is what you did to me, Asher Adams.* Just by being who you are.

"Todd said you were cheating at bingo—that's how you won so many games."

"Did he now?"

"Yes. He saw you palm a number."

"I must be out of practice." Not even the merest flicker of embarrassment touched his rugged face.

"You're leaving." It was a statement, not a question. She hadn't had a chance to ask about Luke, ask about George and Bobbie.

"I'll be expecting a thorough account of my visit to be printed up in the county paper." He shrugged into his worn leather jacket, and the softly mingled smells of mildew and airplane drifted to her, bringing with them an overwhelming feeling of homesickness.

"There were a couple old geezers at the gas station," he went on, "who are dying to find out who the hell I am, and what I came here for."

Ash had stopped at Sisna's station? The thought made her smile. "What should the paper say?" Even though she knew what his answer would be, she had to ask. "Why *did* you come?"

"To inquire as to the health of a certain Corey McKinney."

"And you found her healed and back to normal."

"Yeah." The agreement came with some hesitance. "And a good time was had by all."

"A good time was had by all." It wasn't fair for him to have come, she decided almost angrily. To touch the corners of her world with his shadows. Now it would be worse than before, because she would remember him here. And numbness was preferable to pain.

Tell him goodbye and let him go. That's what he's waiting for. Just let him go. She was trying to form the words, when her father came up behind them.

"Why don't you take Ash out and show him the orphan lambs?" he asked innocently. Too innocently for her father. In his weather-worn hands he carried the two bottles they used for feeding the lambs.

Yes, touch another part of our lives before you walk away. Leave another shadow somewhere.

She remembered the time Ash had challenged her, asking if she'd ever milked a goat. "Ever bottle-feed a lamb?" she asked.

"No." He eyed the black-nippled pop bottles with suspicion. "Can't say I have."

Les McKinney thrust the warmed bottles into Ash's hands. "You two go ahead." He looked at some point beyond them. "Mother and I are going into town to the Bible-reading class at the church."

That was the most ridiculous thing Corey had ever heard. Reverend Michael had been trying to get her father to come to his adult Bible class for years and years—without any luck.

"And I suppose you'll take Mom dancing afterward?" Another thing her father detested, said it made him look like a fool.

"We might," he said thoughtfully. "We might at that."

chapter
twenty-four

The heat lamp made the small barn stall warm and cozy, causing mingled smells of straw and wool and hay to drift toward the rafters. The sweet scent of alfalfa was an elusive reminder of summers gone by, a whispered promise of summers to come.

Corey looked from the sheep she was feeding to Ash. The intentness on his face as he bottle-fed the baby lamb caused her chest to tighten. A yearning filled her, a deep, melancholy yearning for what could never be, for what they would never share, never have.

He was rough, he was gentle. She liked to think that she was one of the few who had been touched by his gentle side.

That would make him laugh, to know she thought of him in such a way. But it was true. Ash had a beautiful soul.

It struck her again, how out of place he looked. He didn't belong here. It wasn't so much that he didn't belong on a farm. He didn't belong in a gray world where everything was dead. He didn't belong in a place where the cold crept deep into your bones, stealing every bit of warmth it could find, dragging your energy away and never giving it back.

No, Ash belonged where it was hot and steamy, where things flourished, where it was green, *alive*.

He must have felt her gaze on him, because he looked up. "What?" he asked defensively. "Am I doing something wrong?"

"No." She smiled. "It's just that you look a little out of your element, that's all."

"I've been on a farm before."

"Oh?" Corey asked suspiciously.

Outside, car doors slammed, a motor started, tires crunched over ice and gravel. Her parents were leaving for church.

The lamb tugged out the last drop of milk, then started butting at Ash's knees, searching for more. "Took a field trip to a farm once. I'll have to admit"—Ash rubbed the lamb's woolly head—"this place would probably be a helluva lot more appealing in the summer."

"You don't like cold weather?"

"Let's just say I don't believe in living someplace where you can't pass out on your front steps without having to worry about freezing to death."

"Wise sentiment."

They were small-talking. Certainly not the kind of small talk that went on at the corner store, but small talk all the same. And now the lambs had been fed, and there was nothing to keep Ash from leaving.

They stepped out of the pen, away from the warmth of the heat lamp. Ash handed Corey his empty milk bottle, then lifted the heavy oak gate to draw the cross bar. "They don't know, do they?"

She could see his breath in the chill air.

"You never told your parents or Todd the truth about

your shoulder." He looped an elbow over the top beam of the gate and looked down at her. "Why not?"

She made an aimless, half-apologetic gesture with one hand. "You've met my mother. She would have been hysterical. Let's face it. She'd still be hysterical."

A look of frustration flitted across his features before he shoved his hands deep into the pockets of his jacket and tilted his head to stare up at the rafters. "You should have told somebody. I thought you'd be taken care of when you came home."

He stood there quietly for a moment, lost in thought. Then he blew out a long, steamy breath and slowly headed toward the sliding barn door. Through the square opening Corey could see that darkness had fallen.

This is it. He's leaving.

He stopped in front of the red International tractor, running a hand over the heavy tread of the massive tire.

"Ever drive a tractor?" she asked, coming up behind him.

He glanced down at her, then up at the cab. "No. I always thought it looked like something I'd get a charge out of. Kinda like flying. Only you're all alone on the ground instead of the sky."

"It's peaceful. A lot of hours to think." She wouldn't be looking forward to it this year. She would be trying not to think. "Daddy started me out when I was thirteen. Not on this. We had a John Deere back then. He just turned me loose in a big open field."

She knew she was chattering, rambling, but the longer they talked, the longer he would stay. "Mom had a fit. By the next year I was discing and cultivating. Two more years and I'd graduated to planting."

"What do you like best?"

"Cultivating, I guess."

The curious child in Ash had become active. He reached up and opened the door to the cab, climbing up the ladder and stepping inside. He tested the seat with a couple bounces, then reached above his head. "FM stereo." He flicked the switch, but nothing happened.

"Dad takes out the battery in the winter."

He flicked it off, then ran fingers over the array of levers next to his leg. "Yeah, I think I'd like this."

Corey stood on the ground, watching him sitting there, his hands gripping the steering wheel. In the dim light cast from the solitary bulb dangling from the barn ceiling, he looked so young. Like a teenager. Too young to be a hero. Too young to have done all he'd done, lived the kind of life he'd lived.

"I never heard how you found Luke."

"Come on up and I'll tell you all about it," he invited.

She leaned the bottles against the huge tire, then grasped the cold metal side rails of the ladder and climbed inside.

There was only one seat, so Corey sat on the gearbox to Ash's left, making her higher than he was, her right knee almost touching his waist.

"You had a lot to do with my finding Luke," he told her.

"Me?" She didn't understand. "I wasn't even there."

"Let me show you something." He shifted so he could dig around in the front pocket of his jeans. "Hold out your hand."

In her open palm he placed a smooth red pocketknife, warm from his body. His fingers brushed the chilled tips of hers.

"Your hands are freezing." He took both her hands in one of his, then reached up and touched his knuckles to her cool cheek.

"Come here." He pulled her down beside him, their bodies pressing together from hip to knee. "Why didn't you say something? Why didn't you tell me you were cold?"

"I'm always cold." She didn't tell him she harbored a fear of never being warm again.

"Put your hands inside my coat. Better yet—" He took the knife from her, then pressed her hands between the hard heat of his inner thighs.

He shifted, leaning to one side, putting the knife back into his pocket, not seeming to have noticed how his nearness was affecting her. And not seeming to be affected by her nearness.

It took extreme effort for her to draw her thoughts back to the conversation. "The knife—it looks like the one you gave Takari." Her senses were full of Ash: the way he smelled, the way he felt. She had never thought she'd be this close to him again.

"It is. I went back to the Tchikao reservation to check on Para, see how her leg was doing." His coat was unzipped, and he pulled her against his chest, cocooning her inside the warmth of his jacket. It didn't go all the way around her, but she didn't care. The bittersweet scent of old leather evoked a million memories, all of them good, all of Ash.

"While I was there, I tried to get my knife back from Takari, make a trade, but he told me he didn't have it anymore."

Ash rested his chin on top of her head, as if it were natural for him to do so, as if he weren't even aware of it. Through her jacket she could feel his hand stroking her back.

"He told me he'd traded it to somebody else. That's when he brought out this damn parrot. The parrot could talk—English. When I asked Takari who he'd gotten it from, he said from a man with hair the color of the sun." For once there was no irony in Ash's voice, no cynicism.

"Luke," Corey whispered and blinked rapidly, her throat tight. She wouldn't cry. She'd cried in front of him too many times.

"Yeah. It was Luke," he said quietly.

She heard the smile in his voice, could have sworn she

felt his lips brush the top of her head, but she probably only imagined it.

"He was living with this nomadic tribe. They'd been through only two days earlier. All I had to do was track them. Just think, if I hadn't traded Takari the knife for you, I might not have found Luke."

"It's so strange how things happen. How one single event can change a person's life." In this case three people's lives.

She slid one of her hands inside the warmth of his jacket, her fingers feathering across his rib cage. She felt him stiffen, heard his quick intake of breath. He wasn't as immune to her as he pretended.

She burrowed closer, pressing a cheek against the soft cotton of his sweatshirt, hearing the bass rumble of his heartbeat. Heat ran through her veins, warming her from her fingertips to her toes. "Did you bring Bobbie to the States with you?"

"No. I decided to leave him at San Reys with George," Ash said breathlessly.

"The cold probably wouldn't be good for him."

"No." The hand on her back stopped its soothing motion. His chest was no longer rising and falling; he was holding his breath. Silently waiting.

She reached up and lightly touched his face, trailing a finger along the stubble of his jawline. His hand came up and stopped her, strong fingers wrapping around her small wrist. "What are you doing?"

"Touching you," she whispered. "I love—" She almost blurted out her secret. "I love to touch you."

"Lily."

It seemed impossible that she had been intimate with this man, that she had been touched by him in ways she'd never been touched by anyone else. To be with him like this, so close, seemed new, and frightening, and wonderful.

"I think you've forgotten something."

"What?" She didn't want to have to think. She was tired of thinking. Just feeling was nice.

"The two-car garage. The kids who'll be taking piano lessons. Dudley." That all too familiar sarcasm was back in his voice.

She didn't feel it was a good idea to tell him she wasn't marrying Todd. She didn't want him to think she was playing for sympathy, didn't want him to feel guilty, in case he might think their breakup was his fault.

"Yeah, you'll be wearing a tidy string of pearls and going to PTA meetings. Have shoes to match all your dresses."

"Is that what you think I want?"

"That's the way it should be."

Then it occurred to her that maybe Ash was jealous of Todd. And if he was jealous, that meant he cared about her.

It wasn't like her to be bold, but if there was a chance for them, she couldn't let it slip away, couldn't let him walk out of her life without even trying to stop him. She was desperate. At this point she could even pretend that she didn't care if he would never love her in return. She knew only that she had to be with him.

"Take me with you."

"What?" Her words galvanized him into action. He held her away from him so he could see her face.

"Take me with you when you go back to the Amazon."

"What the hell are you talking about?"

She reached up and slowly traced the tip of one finger across his bottom lip. She had to tell him. She couldn't keep it to herself any longer. "I love you," she said simply.

At first he merely looked stunned, and she wondered if she'd made a dreadful mistake. Then his expression changed, was replaced by one of suspicion, then finally comprehension.

"I get it. This is some kind of joke, right? You're

trying to get back at me for the bingo thing. Well, for what it's worth, I feel kinda bad about that. It was a cheap shot."

This was ridiculous. It had never crossed her mind that he wouldn't believe her. But then, there hadn't been much love in his life. He probably didn't recognize it when he saw it.

"I'm not joking. I wouldn't joke about something like this."

"No?" Still as suspicious as ever.

"No."

"What about Dudley? I thought the two of you had your whole future set in concrete. Thought you'd spend a quiet, apple-pie life together."

"That's just it. I never realized how gray my world was until I met you," she told him quietly.

His brows drew together. She sensed that he was holding his breath, could detect a flicker of desperation in the star-patterned eyes probing hers. She leaned closer, so her mouth was just inches from his.

He let out a tormented groan and pulled her to him, his fingers digging into her arms.

She stiffened as pain shot through the tender flesh of her newly healed shoulder.

He sprang away. "God, Corey, I'm sorry." There was agony in his voice, pain in his eyes.

"It's okay!"

"No, it's not okay. How in the hell could I have forgotten your shoulder?" He stared into the distance, as if the weathered barn wall could give him some answer. His expression was strange, unreadable, a little lost.

How the hell could he have forgotten the worst day of his life? How could he have forgotten something that had been in his thoughts ever since it happened? And now the nightmare replayed itself with heart-stopping clarity. He could see the blood, *her* blood, all over his hands, feel its sticky warmth, knowing it should have been him, not her.

He'd never been so scared in his whole damn life. Never wanted to be that scared again.

"I have to go," he announced abruptly.

"Go? But—"

"Look. I'm sorry. I shouldn't have come. It was a mistake."

She was staring at him as if she couldn't believe this was happening.

He seemed destined to carry the image of her stricken face to the grave with him. He'd also carry the memory of having to helplessly watch her suffer, afraid she would bleed to death in his arms, and that image gave him the strength he needed. "You have to understand," he told her. "What was between us, it was just sex, okay? That's all. I was never playing for keeps, and I didn't figure you were either."

This was hurting like hell, like nothing had ever hurt before. But he couldn't let her come, couldn't risk putting her in that kind of danger ever again. Next time she might die, and he knew he couldn't handle that. No way in hell he could handle that. It was better this way. He would be able to think of her here, safe in her little rural setting.

Before the pain in her face could make him change his mind, he opened the door and jumped to the ground.

He stopped, wondering if he should try to explain, reassure her in some way, but there just weren't any words that could make any of this right.

He felt the weight of her sadness behind him. He couldn't help himself, he turned and looked up at her. Why couldn't she just hate him? It would be easier that way.

It was almost as if she read his mind, as if they were on the same wavelength. "I hate you, Asher Adams." Her words weren't spoken harshly, they were spoken with sorrow.

"Yeah," he answered quietly. "I hate you too. I guess I've always hated you. Ever since that time I saw you sitting in the air-taxi building." They were both lying; and they both knew it.

He turned and walked away, out the barn door and into the chill midwestern night.

At first Corey just stared fixedly through the windshield of the tractor. Then she turned her head.

She could see Ash walking up the rutted lane toward his car. He walked slowly, hands in his pockets, winter wind tugging his hair. Then the picture blurred.

She couldn't stand this. She didn't have the strength. It was killing her. She tried to blink the tears away, but it was like trying to stop the rain, stop a storm, stop time itself.

How could she let him leave her here like this?

But she was not a grabbing, take-charge kind of person. She had always stood on the fringes of life, waiting for things to happen, for life to come to her. It wasn't her way to be forward, wasn't her way to go where she wasn't wanted.

With trembling fingers she wiped at her damp cheeks and looked through the glass of the cab. Ash was halfway to his car.

All her tomorrows loomed ahead of her, like dark, empty souls.

He reached the car. She knew watching him leave only added to her pain, but she couldn't help herself. She climbed down from the tractor, making it to the doorway of the barn in time to see the red glow of the taillights fade into the lonely night.

"Maybe I'll follow you, Asher Adams," she whispered in a tight voice. "Maybe I'll follow you." But she knew she wouldn't.

She felt the roughness of the weathered barn wood under her fingers and gripped it tighter, trying to think of what she should do. Not tomorrow, but now, this minute.

It was too hard. All she could seem to do was cry, huge gulping sobs that tore at her raw throat. How long would it hurt? How long before the blessed numbness returned?

She had no idea how much later it was when she heard a car slow to turn down the lane, saw twin headlight beams bounce across the stubbled corn field.

She stepped to the side of the door. Right now she couldn't face her mother's probing questions, her father's quiet sympathy.

She would look at the lambs, that's what she'd do. It felt somewhat comforting to be able to make such a small decision.

She found the lambs curled up under the heat lamp, asleep. She thought about how the mother had died when they were born. It seemed sheep didn't have a very strong will to survive.

"Lily."

Quickly she wiped her eyes and turned.

Ash stood in the doorway, the night sky stark and huge behind him like some great tapestry, the stars woven with silver threads.

"You came back."

"I got as far as the gas station, but I kept thinking about . . ." He made a frustrated gesture with one hand. "Aw, dammit, Lily." His words came out a belligerent, angry rush. "Truth is, I hate like hell to think of you spending the rest of your life being anesthetized by Mr. Morphine."

Just what did he mean by that? What on earth was he trying to tell her?

She had an idea. Not a very new idea. Women had been using it for years. Centuries. "Did you mean it when you said I was one of the best lays you ever had?" she asked daringly.

He couldn't have looked more stunned if she'd punched him in the stomach. "I'm sorry about that," he managed to choke out.

"But did you mean it?" she asked, proud of the fact that her voice stayed so steady, that she didn't even blink.

"Yeah." He looked dazed, even slightly confused. "Yeah, I meant it." His expression changed. Suddenly she could see the little boy in him standing there in all his insecurity.

"Did *you* mean it?" His voice had become a vulnerable, croaky whisper that tore at her heart. "Did you mean it when you said you loved me?"

Her newfound strength was shaken. She gripped the wooden ceiling brace, clinging to it for support. Here she'd been prepared to offer him sex with no ties, and he turned it all around, confused her by talking about love.

I'll die if you leave me again, she wanted to tell him but knew it would sound terribly melodramatic. He might even laugh.

And if she said yes, it was true, she did love him—what then? How would he react? Would it scare the Peter Pan boy—the part of him that wouldn't want any responsibilities? Would it be better to take a page from his book and lie like hell? Say she just enjoyed him in her bed?

Who could say what went on inside his head, his heart? It would take a lifetime to figure out who he was, maybe longer. She only knew that she wanted to have that lifetime.

What should she do? This was the most important moment of her life, and she didn't know what to do, what to say to convince him that it was right for them to be together.

A strange, dreamlike memory came to her. Ash was bending over her, his eyes like stars. Only they weren't stars at all. She pulled in an amazed breath, the frigid air stinging her lungs.

They were tears. . . .

A slow smile touched her lips while a sweet, sweet ache—a good ache—warmed her soul.

What a fraud you are, Asher Adams, a master at setting up smoke screens.

She let go of the beam she'd been clinging to so desperately. "I *did* mean it. I *do* love you."

He stood there looking at her, gray eyes wary. "I'm no Dudley Do-right."

"I know."

"I can be a real bastard without even trying."

"That's no secret."

"I'm a smart-ass."

"You're not telling me anything I don't already know."

"What I'm saying is, I'm no noble do-gooder. Don't expect anything like that from me." His voice held a note of pure panic.

He would never know his worth, never believe that in his own way he was the very hero he so vehemently denied being.

"I wouldn't expect anything different of you," she assured him, smiling at the immediate relief that washed over his features. It wasn't really a lie. She didn't expect the sun to come up every day; it just did.

"This is scaring the hell out of me. If anything happened to you—"

"Ash, I'm not expecting you to marry me. I know you're not that kind. I just want to be with you."

He gave her a slow smile and shook his head. "Always trying to corrupt me, aren't you?"

He closed the distance between them, enfolding her in his arms, careful of her shoulder. He rocked her against him, stroking her hair, kissing it, kissing her eyes, her mouth, making her feel a warmth she hadn't felt in a long, long time, had feared she'd never feel again.

"I love you, Lily," he said thickly, his voice muffled against her hair. "The Amazon's just not the same without you. There's nobody to dance with in the moonlight."

She smiled. Poetry. Asher Adams had poetry in him.

He brought a hand to her face, then slowly, starting at her temple, he threaded his long, sensitive fingers through her hair until he reached the ends. "Still spun from moonbeams."

Mesmerized, she watched as his head came down, the soft mist from his breath caressing her cheek, her parted lips. Her eyes fluttered closed and she let out a sigh as his mouth pressed hers. She felt a tingling in her stomach. Then the tingling sifted lower and her diaphragm tightened. His mouth left hers, then he was trailing wet kisses down the side of her neck.

He let out a low groan. "Winter clothes are a bitch," he mumbled, the soft wetness of his lips against her earlobe. "I can't find you under all this stuff."

But both of his hands found their way under her coat with no trouble at all. His palms cupped her bottom, pulling her compactly against him. "That's better."

A heavy ache settled between her legs. She tilted her head and let out a low sigh. "I remember this feeling," she murmured, clinging to him so she wouldn't fall.

"No kidding," he agreed with a breathless laugh. "No damn kidding. The question is, did you like it?"

"Very much." She buried her face against the warmth of his neck, breathing in the scent of him. She wasn't homesick anymore.

chapter
twenty-five

They were going home, back to San Reys.

The bush plane hit a pocket of hot, steamy air, lifted, then dropped. A month ago Corey would have clung to the edges of her seat for dear life. Now she only stifled a yawn, the heat in the cockpit making her deliciously drowsy.

Her eyes were drawn to Ash, as they had so often been the past four days—since the night in her parents' barn. He was wearing a T-shirt, the soft cotton stretched across his chest and biceps, the New York Yankees baseball cap was slanted away from his face, his capable hands rested on the controls.

She let out a sigh of contentment. A month ago she could never have imagined feeling this way. She hadn't known love between a man and a woman could be so strong.

Two days ago they had been married by Reverend

Michael, the only witnesses being her parents and Luke, who had flown in from New York.

Corey smiled, recalling how, after the ceremony, Ash had totally flustered Grace McKinney by giving her a bear hug and kissing her on the cheek. He'd even called her "Mom," promising to bring Corey back at planting time so she could teach him to drive the tractor.

She and Ash had spent the last forty-eight hours secluded in a hotel in Santarém. There were times when, lying together in a tangle of sheets, the ceiling fan cooling their damp bodies, Corey would glimpse a haunting fear mixed with love lurking in the farthest depths of Ash's eyes. Then her breath would falter, and her chest would ache. Fear for the person you love is the strongest kind of fear. She knew that very well.

She also knew no words could ever convince him he'd done the right thing by bringing her to the Amazon with him, but she had faith that he would eventually discover that truth himself. Until then she would continue to smooth the lines of worry from his brow and kiss him until he hauled her into his arms and overwhelmed her with his gentle and passionate love.

Forcing her eyes away from him, she looked out the window.

Ash had told her he preferred to navigate by the river, so they were following the wide, twisting grandeur of the Amazon. The sun had just gone down and the moon was rising, its fullness seeming to drip right from the waters, bathing everything in an orange glow. A swirling mist clung to the places where the thick canopy of treetops dipped to form their elevated valleys.

"You like tree houses?" Ash suddenly asked.

"Tree houses? I don't know. When I was little, Marvin Frasier had one but he wouldn't let any girls in it."

"I started this Swiss Family Robinson job a couple years ago. Three floors, an observation deck. You can see way the hell to the Akarai Mountains."

He builds tree houses in the sky.

"Still have most of the walls and ceiling to do. I'll have to order windows from Santarém."

Corey wondered if she would ever discover all the reasons there were for loving him. Once she'd taken a photography course where an assignment had been to focus a tripod-steadied camera on a barn and snap a picture every hour from dawn to dusk. When the negatives were developed, Corey had been surprised at the variance in the pictures. In some frames, deep shadows completely hid the upper barn windows, seeming to change the shape of the barn itself. In others, she could see every knothole and every grain in the weathered board.

That's how it was with Ash. Just when she thought she saw him clearly, the light changed, brightened, revealing more of him to her.

He misread her silence. "You're scared of heights, right? That's okay. I understand."

She shook her head, giving him a tremulous smile.

"Then you like the idea?"

"I love it."

The plane hit an air pocket and dropped. Ash gripped the controls tighter.

"Son of a—" He nudged her arm and pointed.

"What?"

"There. Over there—"

She peered intently through the bug-splattered windshield, eyes searching the lushness below them. She could sense Ash's suppressed excitement as he guided the plane toward a strange strip of white that stretched across the river from shore to shore.

As they closed in, a gasp escaped her. The spectacle before them was biblical in its majesty. The strip of white was actually a giant wall of water at least ten stories tall—churning upstream, against the current, ripping out massive, towering trees as if they were shallow-rooted weeds, sending them crashing into the foaming water.

"Pororoca!" Ash shouted to her above the combined roar of the water and plane engine as they shot over and past the huge tidal wave. He full-throttled, putting the plane in a tight bank, the force pushing Corey against her seat.

In the short time it took for them to come back around, *Pororoca* had vanished. The only evidence left was the muddy, foaming water and toppled trees.

They sat in a mutually shocked silence while the plane's motor kept up its steady hum, mud-red water rushing beneath them.

Finally Ash lifted his cap and resettled it, slanting it back on his dark hair. "Wow," he breathed. "Nice touch. Real nice touch. Kind of a surprise homecoming display."

It wasn't until then that Corey even thought about her camera. "I didn't get a picture," she whispered to herself in a rush of guilt.

To her, *Pororoca* had been a fascinating legend like the Lost City of Atlantis. She hadn't really believed in it. But Ash had waited years for this day. She felt like crying.

"It's okay," he told her quietly.

"No. No, it isn't. Nobody will ever believe us."

"So what? You know it's real, and I know it's real." He reached over, wrapping warm fingers around her wrist. Then he brought her hand to his mouth, slowly pressing his lips against her fingertips.

The simple bittersweet act brought tears to her eyes and soothed her soul.

"Just you, and me, and the Amazon." He smiled at her, slashing indentations showing below each cheekbone.

Relief washed over her, knowing he was talking about more than just today, knowing he had come to terms with himself. She could see the light reflecting from his eyes, see that the shadows haunting their gray depths were gone. Ash, unlike most people, was a believer. And it seemed that whatever he believed in had a way of coming true.

"Wanna hop in back and check out my record collection?" he asked. "I'll just put this bird on autopilot."

She laughed through her forgotten tears.

"Got Norman Bates singing a catchy medley of show tunes."

"You're crazy."

"How about my tattoo? Like to hop in back and check out my tattoo?"

"I'd love to."

"You would?" he asked in surprise. "My scar. Would you like to see it? Touch it, maybe?"

"I'd love to do that too."

She couldn't miss the flame of desire that leapt into his eyes before he looked to the front. "We better talk about something else before I lose control here, forget I'm supposed to be flying this thing."

"I like it when you lose control."

She heard his breath catch. Then, "You do?"

"Mmm. Very much."

She glanced below them and saw a stretch of bare ground—a *playa*. A perfect place to land. "We don't have to be at the reserve tonight, do we? After all, George isn't expecting us."

He followed the direction of her gaze, a slow, knowing smile touching the corners of his mouth. "What did you have in mind?" he asked in a lazy, sexy voice.

"Oh, about an eight-hour layover."

In less than a heartbeat he had the nose of the plane pointing downward. "And here I always thought layover meant a break in travel." His expression was a combination of bland innocence and love. The pure, unconditional love of a child; the intense, white-hot love of a man.

It felt good to be warm again.

About the Author

THERESA WEIR lives with her husband and two children on a working apple farm in Illinois, not far from the Mississippi River.

Her book *Amazon Lily* was selected by the *Romance Reader's Handbook* as an All-Time Recommended Read, and won her the *Romantic Times* Best New Adventure Writer award. Theresa has loved to write ever since high school, when she entertained her friends (if not the administration) with stories generated from the typing class IBM.

Don't miss Theresa Weir's searing new novel
LONG NIGHT MOON
coming from Bantam Books in Spring 1995

"A fresh and electrifying voice in
romantic fiction."
—*Romantic Times*